North of Supernova

North of Supernova

LINDSEY LEAVITT

GODWINBOOKS

HENRY HOLT AND COMPANY
NEW YORK

Henry Holt and Company, *Publishers since 1866*
Henry Holt® is a registered trademark of Macmillan Publishing Group, LLC
120 Broadway, New York, NY 10271 • mackids.com

Our books may be purchased in bulk for promotional, educational, or business use.
Please contact your local bookseller or the Macmillan Corporate and Premium Sales
Department at (800) 221-7945 ext. 5442 or by email at
MacmillanSpecialMarkets@macmillan.com.

Library of Congress Cataloging-in-Publication Data

Names: Leavitt, Lindsey, author.
Title: North of supernova / by Lindsey Leavitt.
Description: First. | New York : Godwin Books, 2023. | Audience:
    Ages 10–14. | Audience: Grades 7–9. | Summary: Twelve-year-old Stella
    North (Virgo) is shaken up by her father's surprise engagement; she takes
    fate into her own hands with astrology, tarot, and crystals, and even
    Magic 8 balls.
Identifiers: LCCN 2022047057 | ISBN 9781250858498 (hardcover)
Subjects: CYAC: Stepfamilies—Fiction. | Friendship—Fiction. |
    Astrology—Fiction. | Tarot—Fiction.
Classification: LCC PZ7.L46553 No 2023 | DDC [Fic]—dc23
LC record available at https://lccn.loc.gov/2022047057

First edition, 2023
Book design by L. Whitt
Printed in the United States of America by Lakeside Book Company,
Harrisonburg, Virginia

ISBN 978-1-250-85849-8
1 3 5 7 9 10 8 6 4 2

TO MY BLENDED LIMES:

LOGAN, EMILIA, JAMES, TALIN, MACKAY,
RYLEE, LINDSEY, TAYLOR, AND MILES—

FOR FINDING FAMILY IN EACH OTHER.

USUALLY.

Chapter 1

It's hard to pinpoint the exact moment a journey starts. Not everyone steps onto a yellow brick road like Dorothy or flies away on a ship like Peter Pan. Instead, it's regular old days that somehow skid away from regular without any planning or warning. At least that's what happened to me.

My destiny begins in a sticky booth at a Tacoma, Washington, Panda Express. Well, I guess if we're getting technical, my destiny started when I was born. Or maybe *before* I was born, like when my parents met or . . . the dawn of time? Look, I don't know the exact moment, but I can recognize a turning point when I see one. And Thursday is a doozy.

"You know this food isn't good for you, right?" my aunt Maggie says. "The sugar content is too high."

I bite into my orange chicken, which I make sure doesn't touch my noodles. Dad never takes me out to eat. If he gets home in time for dinner, he cooks an omelet or sloppy joes. When he's not home, which is often, I make cheese and crackers for my ten-year-old brother, Ridge. Maybe grilled tuna sandwiches if I'm feeling fancy. This week with Aunt Maggie cooking for us while Dad is in Las Vegas for business has been the culinary highlight of my life. Tonight she let me choose the restaurant, even if she made a face when I picked Panda Express.

"Thanks for taking me," I say. "Are you going to eat your fortune cookie?"

"I'm off white flour." She tosses it across the table. "Knock yourself out."

So here's where the destiny stuff starts. My first fortune says, "Smile like you mean it." Of course I throw that nonsense away. But my next fortune says, "You will soon receive monumental news of a personal nature." I'll hang this one on my mirror with other favorite quotes and sayings. Because I have been waiting for monumental news all day.

I check my phone again. Still no evite.

"If you sit there staring at your inbox, the email won't come," Aunt Maggie says. "That's science."

"Science would look at the probability of the email coming at this time of night based on Talia's schedule. Or it would look at Talia's parents' work schedule, if they're the ones sending the evite, or their household internet speed—"

Aunt Maggie holds up a hand. "I get it."

I don't think she does. Get it.

Two booths over, a group of teen girls burst into snorts and giggles. One girl's hair frames her face as she snaps open a fortune cookie. Whatever it says must be important because they go silent as they pass the fortune around, considering. Then this other girl, who wears a ring on each finger, flicks a noodle, which lands on her friend's cheek. More laughter.

They're all glowy hair and glory eyes. No one has their phone out. They have no idea I'm watching them. Nothing else is happening in their world besides that moment. They could be in Tacoma or Tucson and still they'd be surrounded by light.

And that light, that *belonging*, is what I've been waiting for all day, all year, my whole life. I've had some friends here or there, kids I sit by at lunch or in art class. But nothing strong enough to seal off the galaxy. Which is why getting an invite to Talia Huang's twelve-year-old birthday party is such a big deal. It's a cake-decorating party at a bakery so she can only invite five girls. I usually get invited to the whole-class-can-come parties, but not the VIP lists.

I might be close now, finally, with sixth grade ending next week. Talia sits by me at lunch and she even mentioned her birthday the other day. She didn't come right out and say she was inviting me, but . . . why else would she mention it? Plus, we've started walking home from the bus together. She texted me a funny meme the other day (and I spent fifty minutes coming up with a cool reply). Being friends with Talia—birthday-invite kind of friends—would ease me into a friend group for the rest of middle school. High school! College roommates! Bridesmaids!

Unless . . . I'm number six on her list of friends. Then I wouldn't make the cut. Or maybe she told me about the party because she wants me to work at it? I unclench my fists, which tend to ball up whenever I think about not-so-great possibilities. Ones that might happen but probably won't. My old therapist, Dr. Matt, called it "negative thought patterns." He also taught me breathing exercises, but I always worry I'm not doing them right, so I keep holding my breath, which starts more negative patterns, and . . . anyway. I'm fine.

"Stella?" Aunt Maggie nudges my foot. "You there?"

I smile an automatic smile to make *her* feel better, but not so much me.

"I'm going to say this," she says. "Your worth isn't defined by an invite, okay? If you go, you go. And if you don't, well . . . you're wonderful just how you are, okay? I deal with this in my business, where women put so much happiness on social success, and that's not where joy comes from."

Okay, Aunt Maggie. This is a lady who is "off white flour" and probably sleeps with full makeup. Who totally devoted the last ten years of her life to building a major corporate website for small female-owned businesses. She wears pantyhose. *Pantyhose.* Aunt Maggie can say she's loosey-goosey all she wants, but she still makes me sit on a blanket to keep her car seat clean.

The girls stand. I take inventory of their hair, clothes, nails, shoes and file it all away in this mental space of things-I-need-to-improve-about-myself. Maybe I can start with my hair, which isn't brown or blond, isn't curly or straight. It just *is*, like my clothes, which all get the job done, but that's not the point of fashion, is it? Should I start wearing rings on all my fingers too? Get a signature jacket? Cut swoopy bangs?

"You ready to go?" I get up too, not wanting to lose their light. "The internet here is garbage."

"Yes." Aunt Maggie pauses like she's going to say more, then nods. "Let's get home. There's something I need to show you."

The sky is a kaleidoscope of oranges and purples with a clear view of Mount Rainier. Aunt Maggie plays her music on the car ride home, the alternative rock that Mom loves. They used to go to concerts together in Seattle. They were often mistaken for twins—same toothy smile, same wild brassy hair. Mom still has her nineties band T-shirts. Or I'm guessing she does. She moved out last year and it's been four months since I've seen her T-shirt collection or even, you know, my mom.

Aunt Maggie's energy is nervous, which makes me nervous by association. I name the trees as we drive—douglas fir, maple, oak, more douglas fir. Meanwhile, Aunt Maggie keeps clearing her throat like she's going to announce something. One time she chokes on her spit and starts coughing.

We pull up to the house, which surprisingly has Dad's car in the driveway. Aunt Maggie scrunches up her nose. "It's the first, right? He told me he'd be back on the second."

"You probably got the dates mixed up. Dad wouldn't."

Ridge runs out to our car and pounds on the window. His brown floppy hair is matted from gaming headphones. Dad monitors our screen time, but he doesn't check our usage when he's out of town. Ridge probably played more of his favorite video game, *Cosmo Kingdom*, this week than he has in months.

I push open the door. "Oh my gosh, what?"

"Dad's home."

I point to his car. "Obviously. No more video games for you tonight."

"No, listen. Dad's here." Ridge grabs my shoulder. "And he's not alone."

Chapter 2

Aunt Maggie offers to talk to Dad because he's . . .

 1. Home early.
 2. With a guest.

"We're good." I lean into her car window.

Even her mouth looks buttoned up. "Okay, but I have something I need to give you."

"It can wait, right?"

"Hmm." She picks imaginary lint off her sweater. Her seat belt is still on. "I guess it can for the night. I'll come by tomorrow. We have to—"

"Tomorrow, for sure!" I need a break from her dramatic throat clearing. Besides, I don't know what we're walking into here. I figure the fewer people involved, the better.

Ridge and I open the front door quietly, like we might disturb the weirdness that has clearly entered the house. Dad pokes his head into the living room. He's holding my emotional support pug, Pog. Pog barks and barks. Dad lets go and Pog skitters across the floor into my arms.

"Come to the kitchen," Dad says. "There's someone I want you to meet."

"It's a lady," Ridge whispers.

I stare at my black phone screen. All I want to do is put on my Christmas pajamas and sit with Pog in my panic room, refreshing my email over and over and over and over until Talia's evite arrives. Okay, it's not *technically* a panic room, because those have security and stuff. This is a storage closet Dad let me take over after Mom moved out. My panic room has an old TV, a weighted blanket, snacks, and decent Wi-Fi. Some people get freaked out by small spaces, but I crave them. Elevators—great. Open fields—yikes.

I carry Pog into the kitchen. Dad's leaning against the counter, tie loose, swigging a carbonated water. He's travel-weary, handsome. One time, at school pickup, I heard a school mom compare Dad to a marble Renaissance sculpture. I don't know if it's because we're white or because those sculptures have a lot of muscles, but either way it's a weird thing to say and a weirder thing to hear.

There's an olive-skinned woman with straight black hair standing close to him. She's in a business suit, even though there isn't any business happening in our kitchen at nine o'clock on a Thursday. Her body is turned toward Dad's in this open, I-know-this-person way.

"Stella! Ridge! Hello!" the woman says. "Oh, your dog is so darling."

I wrap my arms tighter around Pog, saying nothing.

"Kids, meet Whitney Lionetti," Dad says. "We reconnected in Vegas. Funny story actually."

"It really is!" Whitney grins.

"Do you want to tell it?" Dad asks.

"Where do I start?" she asks. "First, I recently got a promotion at my hotel administration job at Caesars Palace."

She says the name of this place like we would know the name of this place but why would we and who is she and things already feel *off*.

"And I'm down there to interview for a short-term project," Dad says. "Can't remember the last time I went to Vegas. So I'm checking in and I hear someone ask if they can help me."

"And I don't even work the desk!" Whitney says. "They had me training in different service positions."

Pog yips for me to put him down. I don't blame him.

"And I know this voice," Dad says. "My college girlfriend. We met sophomore year. In chemistry study group."

"Chemistry," she muses. "I thought I'd go into the sciences, wound up in hospitality. And then you—an engineer? Big switch from a music major."

"You were a music major?" I ask.

"Your dad was always playing the guitar," Whitney says. "He was such a Deadhead."

The Grateful Dead is a band from the sixties or seventies. A Deadhead is a hard-core fan.

"Hey, even boring engineers can love the Dead," Dad says. "You know, Stella's named after the song 'Stella Blue.'"

Dad doesn't mention that my mom chose my name—first and middle. That my parents met at a Grateful Dead concert. That she used to sing me "Stella Blue" before bed.

"So cute!" Whitney says, but I don't think she cares. Being named after a song is a detail about me. She's here to talk about herself. "Anyway, back to the *moment*. So I turn around and it was like time stopped. Or time never existed. Because standing right in front of me is Micah North. Just as handsome as ever."

Ridge takes a step backward, like he's about to run out of the room. How did we get trapped in such a boring story? I nod like I'm listening but keep glancing at my phone.

Usually, I'm more anxious about meeting strangers, but I'm too hyper-focused on receiving the birthday party invite. I tug on my ear, which is a signal Dad and I came up with when the situation is more than I can handle. He doesn't notice. He's lost his handle on just about anything but this snoozer story.

"So I say, 'Of course you can help me, Whitney!'" Dad laughs. "Your face when you recognized me."

"I was shocked!" Whitney says. "I've run into plenty of people vacationing in Vegas. But the chances of seeing you? There? Now?"

I turn to Ridge, not bothering to lower my voice. "What is going on here?"

"Dad is finishing sentences with a stranger," Ridge says.

"—and then I said, 'I'll bet twenty dollars you won't go to lunch with me,'" Dad says.

"Which is hilarious, because there's a roulette table across the room from us," Whitney says.

"And I lose! But actually, it's a win." Dad beams. "We go to lunch, then dinner, then breakfast."

"All the meals." Whitney clutches Dad's arm. "It was like twenty years never happened."

"Right back where we left off."

"Dad?" A low, steady alarm rings in my head. "Cool story, but . . . what's the point?"

Dad throws his arm around Whitney. I've never seen him

touch another woman besides Mom, and it's been a few years since I saw that. He lives in a box of personal space, even with Ridge and me.

"The point is . . . the expression is wrong." Dad's smile has gone so far up that it's looped back on itself. It's a circle now, a circle of unexplained joy. "What happens in Vegas doesn't stay there."

Bing! My phone pings with an email. I hold out a finger to Dad as if to say his random how-we-*re*met story will have to wait.

And . . . it's there! The Email!

I'm there.

Stella! I hope you can make my party. Can't wait for us to hang out more this summer! XO—Talia

I click on the evite—mint and peach with a cake illustration.

FROSTING AND FRIENDSHIP! YOU'RE INVITED TO TALIA HUANG'S TWELFTH BIRTHDAY PARTY. JUNE 10TH, 2 PM AT CREATIVE CAKE DESIGNS.

That moment catapults me into a Panda Express booth with Talia and all her friends. We split fortune cookies, throw noodles at each other. Then we're at the beach and we're at a concert and we're lounging on the floor of my living room, bored but not really. We have everything in common but we're all unique. In a good way. And no one remembers the sad things kids used to whisper about my family. I'm beyond that version of me.

I look right at Dad, preparing myself to share the huge news, but he's gazing at Whitney, who is holding out her hand. There's a turquoise ring. I don't get why she's showing me this ring. I don't get why Dad is hugging her, like actually *hugging* her. I don't get why she's in my kitchen.

Am I supposed to kiss the ring? Is there some tradition I forgot? "Yes . . . it's a nice ring. Uh, Dad, I got invited to this birthday party, which is *massive* news—"

"News? Stella!" Dad says. "Don't you have anything to say?"

"To what?" I ask.

"This isn't happening," Ridge says.

And then I get it. Finally.

You will soon receive monumental news of a personal nature. And that's the moment when my fortune comes true in a totally different way than I could have ever imagined.

"We're engaged!" Whitney says.

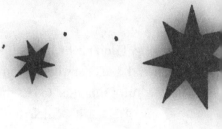

Chapter 3

My life went from nothing to everything overnight. Whitney stayed until Saturday, then went home to prepare for our arrival. Because they still think they're engaged (so weird).

That was over a week ago, and now I guess we're getting on a flight for Vegas. Tomorrow. School just ended and I haven't packed a suitcase because Talia's party demanded my full attention. And it's a major pack because we're staying with Whitney, *a total stranger*, for two weeks (so, so weird).

"What time is the party over?" Dad asks me as we sit in his car outside Talia's modern wood home.

"Five. Actually, it could go longer."

Dad drums his fingers on the steering wheel in an even rhythm. "Okay, call me. You can walk home or I can pick you up."

"Great." I do not move. Perched on my lap is Talia's present, wrapped in a blue-and-yellow bag with double the tissue paper so it looks fancier. I got her a clay bead kit. I heard once you should buy a gift you'd want yourself. But now I'm worried it might be babyish. Everything I'm doing might be babyish?

"You got this," Dad says. Sometimes I think he can read my brain. Or read my actions.

"Okay." I smear on lip gloss in my favorite rhythmic pattern—one long swipe, two fast ones, then another long one.

"Focus on your breathing." Dad kisses the top of my head. There is no one around to see, which is a relief. But I also don't hate when he's like this. Aware and understanding. Because social situations are rough, especially when I don't know all the details before I walk in. Like are they mad I'm ten minutes late and am I dressed right and who will I talk to once I walk inside and do I take off my shoes and will anyone know who I am?

"Text me if you need to," Dad adds.

"I will." I'm a statue. A statue with everything she's ever wanted just a few steps away. "Okay, I'm leaving."

Dad leans over me to open my door. "Now unbuckle your seat belt. Almost there."

I move in a swift motion—seat belt off, legs out of car, body moving moving moving toward Talia's front door. I left the car. I am doing this. I'm almost . . . here.

Before I can knock, the front door flies open. There's a Latinx girl with two braids and purple lip gloss. Pilar Ramos. I know her, but she doesn't know me. Which is the case with nearly everyone in her friend group. "Oh, hey! You're . . . you!"

She doesn't remember my name. We've been in the same class twice and she doesn't know my name. If I tell her my name, will it make her uncomfortable because she knows she should know my name? Or if I *don't* tell her my name, will she think I'm snobby for not introducing myself? Two seconds in and there's already a stabbing feeling in my stomach.

"Hey," I say. And leave it there.

Pilar opens the door wider. Three or four girls are putting their shoes on, laughing and tossing their sneakers back and forth. Talia looks up and sees me in the doorway. "Stella's here! Everyone, let's cheer for Stella!"

The girls clap and chant, "Stella! Stella! Stella!" I float into the room and stick my present on the gift table. My head is blurry from the attention.

Talia grabs my arm and guides me into the kitchen. She wears her black hair in a high, shiny ponytail. She has on a gauzy tank over a bandeau top and loose pants with a funky print. I've documented each of Talia's seasonal style transitions this year, trying to match my own style without being too obvious about it. I had a similar look planned five outfits ago, but now I wonder if I overshot the whole thing.

"That shirt is cute!" Talia says. "Where'd you get it?"

I look down, like I can't remember what I'm wearing. I found this shirt in the garage last night at midnight after I'd gone through everything in my closet twice. It's my mom's old striped shirt, like nineties old. "It's vintage."

"Love that." She smiles and I realize she has on new coral lip gloss—I'll have to write down the brand when she reapplies. It's always a dance, figuring out which of her trends to follow and when I should stay basic and blend.

"You got here just in time," she says. "My mom is driving us in the minivan. My dad is bringing my sister in the truck, which is annoying, but he'll bring the gifts! Oh, grab a snack real fast." She rolls her eyes. "My mom wants everyone to eat healthy now since we're going to have sugar later. You know how moms are."

I try to remember the last time my mom bought carrot sticks and come up with nothing. I obediently eat celery and dip.

A black cat hops onto the counter and rubs against my arm. I stroke the cat's spine.

"Um, that's wild," Talia says. "Jasper hates everyone."

I shrug one shoulder. "I have a fawn pug named Pog. He lives for petting."

"My nai nai says that's how you pet cats. Up and down the back," Talia says. "It brings on good luck, brushes away the bad. Here people get scared of black cats, but in Chinese culture we believe they ward off evil."

"I should get one then." I give Jasper one more long, smooth stroke. "It might work on my brother."

"Ha, you're funny," Talia says. "You can cat sit for us sometime. Dad might try to trick you into keeping him."

"Sure! I *love* cat sitting." I've never done it, and Pog would hate losing any attention to Jasper, but I'm sure I would be a great cat sitter. But only for Talia's cat.

I'm feeling all the good luck. It's okay that Pilar didn't know my name because Talia is totally focused on me. And we're the last two into the van, meaning we get the captain's chairs. The girls in the back seat all lean in, stretching their seat belts, so they can hear whatever Talia says. "You guys know Stella, right?"

"Oh yeah! We had fourth grade together," Chloe says. She has red hair and pink skin. She has always been pleasant to me but not friendly. Like not rude, but not inclusive. I guess I haven't ever been anything to her either. I smile as big as I can, then worry it's too big so I put my hand over my mouth.

"We're all in choir together," Talia says. "What do you like to do?"

"For what?" I ask.

"For fun. Like an instrument, sports, draw?"

I used to have an answer for this. I used to do things, especially tennis. With tennis, you're on a team but you either play alone or play with a doubles partner. I used to play in junior tournaments—I *won* tournaments. My coach called me a "rising star."

But in fifth grade, I played doubles with a girl named Kate or Kathy, I can't remember. We were in a tiebreaker and it was my serve. I bounced the ball once slow, then two times fast, but on the last slow bounce the ball hit my foot and rolled away. So then I had to chase it and start my pre-serve bouncing pattern again or else I'd definitely miss the serve or lose the whole game. This time, someone coughed while I was doing the bounces. I worried they were coughing as a hint that I was taking too long, which I was, but it's a scientific fact that I had to do my pattern to succeed. Kate/Kathy looked back at me to ask if I was all right, which probably meant she was mad at me for missing the first serve. So even though I did all my bounces, my chest suddenly felt like it was being squeezed. My second serve soared into the stands and I bent over, gasping. We lost the next two points. I remember running to the bathroom, where I spent the next ten minutes crying and struggling to breathe.

So yeah. That's the last time I played tennis.

The girls are still looking at me.

"I like history?" I say. "Or learning new facts about something interesting."

Talia gives an aggressive nod, like she's hoping I can do better. "Fine, um, tell us something totally weird about you."

"Weird. Yeah." My throat constricts like it's being squeezed. There is nothing weird to say. Nothing *good* weird. I wish I had a birthmark of Montana or a celebrity uncle. "I like pickles. In chocolate."

I do not like pickles and have never dipped them in chocolate.

16

"That is soooo weird." Talia laughs. "How do you even know you like those together?"

I laugh. "Just got creative one day."

"Love it!" Talia squeezes my elbow and I'm good. I did that part right. I think.

"Wait, I remember. Didn't your mom get sick?" Chloe asks. "Cancer or something? Like in elementary school?"

"Yeah . . . no. I mean, not cancer." I tell my face not to go red, but based on the heat, I don't think my face listens. Sometimes I convince myself everyone's forgotten about that stuff. I mean, I want to be memorable for me, not for my family drama. "But yeah, she's alive. She doesn't live with us. She's . . . gone."

"Sounds like a disaster," Chloe says. She doesn't say it in a mean way. Only an honest way. And she is not wrong.

"Yeah. It is."

"Hmm." The girls in the back seat exchange a glance.

I've blown it. I should have stuck with dipping pickles! All hope of being part of this group is smothered now, thanks to Mom's ghost.

"You should come to the pool with us next week," Pilar says. "We go every Tuesday in the summer. We call ourselves the Dippers."

"Yes! Become a Dipper!" Talia says. "See? I've been telling them all about you, Stella. It's fate!"

Mrs. Huang looks at us in the rearview mirror. "You girls are whispering too much. We need to get pumped up for the party. Talia made a playlist. You ready?"

Talia lets out a whoop. "Yes, Momma! We are ready to move!"

Talia's mom turns the volume up, like all the way up. And

the girls start squirming and pumping their arms. They're so limp and squiggly, but they don't seem to *care*. I sorta toss my hair back and bop my arm in rhythm with the music. They roll the windows down and we shout along with an old Lady Gaga song.

The party hasn't even started yet, but this is the most fun I've had in, well, ever. Is this how the Dippers are all the time? Asking serious questions one minute, rocking out the next? I want to be like this, truly *like* this. I decide to dip pickles in chocolate tonight. I might buy some coral lip gloss too.

I will try . . . lots of things, all while I'm gone for the next two weeks. I'll talk to interesting people and visit enviable places and maybe get a second ear piercing. I'll meet up with the Dippers in three Tuesdays and tell them all my zany Las Vegas adventures while we soak in the sun. I'll be their effortless, sorta wild friend who is up for anything but also knows how to listen. We'll have a whole summer of Dipper days.

Talia looks over at me, all goofy grin.

And we burst into the crazed chorus.

Chapter 4

"**B**lue or green?" Ridge asks.

"Blue." I look out the airplane window. "Actually, no. Green."

My new favorite word is *actually*. Like, we are "actually" going to Vegas for two weeks because my dad "actually" took on a short-term project after he "actually" proposed to a lady he hasn't dated in twenty years and they "actually" think Ridge and I are going to fall in love with Whitney's daughter, Vivian, and "actually" stay in their house even though we're "actually" all strangers.

"Seven, one, six, or four?" Ridge asks.

I glance over at him. He made one of those origami–fortune teller things out of a barf bag. The Norths make do with what we have.

"Four."

"One, two, three, four. Pick your last one."

"I don't know. Seven." Pog snores, deep and rumbling. The lady in front of me keeps glancing back, but she's smiling so she must understand dogs. We got permission for Pog to sit on my lap, an emotional support dog perk. Actually, Pog might be the only anxiety relief coming with me to Vegas. Panic closets don't fit on planes.

Ridge lifts up the flap. "'You will lose something valuable.'"

"Seriously?" I say. "Can't you give me the you-will-win-a-million-dollars one instead?"

Ridge shrugs. "It's your fortune. You picked it."

"Actually," I didn't pick any of this.

My pick, obviously, would be to stay home. To go to the pool on Tuesday with the Dippers. Yes, I could be a brighter version of myself in Vegas, do thrilling activities to make the Dippers just the right amount of jealous. But staying in Washington was still the best option. We made at least four inside jokes already. A hangout immediately after the party would help my friend momentum.

But now . . . I might come home in two weeks and the Dippers could be like, *Wait, Stella . . . I think I frosted cupcakes with you once?* Going to that party and then leaving town was like getting one lick of an ice cream cone before dropping it on the dirty sidewalk.

"I can make you another fortune teller," Ridge says. "And only write nice stuff."

"But then it's fake," I say.

"Sometimes you pick the wrong number and get the bad fortune," Ridge says. "That's life."

"I guess." Pog snorts so loud that he wakes up. He smiles up at me—I can tell he's smiling because his buggy eyes go less buggy. It's nice to have someone always excited to see me, especially when he just woke up. I feed him two dog biscuits and pet him in my pattern—one long, two fast, one long.

Ridge lies down on the empty seat between us. We should

have packed more stuff to do. The only TVs on the flight are in first class. At least Dad gave us the row to ourselves. He's somewhere in the back.

"Do you want a snack?" I ask, rifling through my yellow backpack. Aunt Maggie got us so many snacks. I'm deciding between trail mix and a fruit bar when I see the purple envelope shoved inside the bag.

"Nah," Ridge says. "I'll make Dad buy us candy when we land. Hey, I'm gonna sleep now. Night." He wads up his sweatshirt and closes his eyes. He'll be out cold in two minutes.

Pog perches his wrinkly neck on the seat rest. The envelope has an orange sticky note on the sealed back flap. I read this first:

S—I TRIED TO GIVE THIS TO YOU IN PERSON AT PANDA EXPRESS BUT THE TIMING WASN'T QUITE RIGHT. THEN CAME YOUR DAD'S BIG NEWS AND . . . I CHICKENED OUT. THAT'S THE TRUTH. YOU, HOWEVER, ARE VERY BRAVE. OPEN IT WHEN YOU'RE READY. HERE IF YOU WANT TO TALK.

LOVE—AUNT M

At first I think it's strange of her to call a card *brave*. Then I flip it over and get an instant cramp.

It's my mom's handwriting on the envelope. I could probably live a hundred years and still recognize her handwriting—loopy and sharp. The card was mailed to me, care of Aunt Maggie, which tells me Mom didn't want Dad to see it. The return address is in Coeur d'Alene, Idaho, so I guess she left Washington. And she has an address, so she's living . . . period.

21

Pog notices how intently I'm staring and tries to lick my arm. I shift him into the middle seat, behind Ridge's head, so I can use both shaking hands to hold the envelope close to my face.

The handwriting triggers all of my senses. I think of the smell of her pineapple shampoo and how she could throw anything into a slow cooker and it would come out delicious and how soft her fingertips were when she'd tickle my arm to help me fall asleep.

But Mom vanished, all at once and little by little. She had a car accident. Took prescription pain pills. Too many pills. Went to rehab. Checked out. Came home. Sorta normal. Quarantine. Covid. Fighting. Alcohol. Pills. Divorce. Poof! Gone.

She went from doing everything all the time to guest appearances to not calling or writing. Until . . . now?

"This is your captain speaking. Prepare for landing."

Open it when you're ready, Aunt Maggie said. How does anyone ever get ready to see a vanished mom? I could hold on to this envelope for eight years and still never achieve "ready."

Eight years seems like a fair amount of time to wait until opening the envelope. Ridge would rip it open right away because his curiosity is so big. But worry beats curiosity. Worry beats most emotions. I shove the envelope into the inside pouch of my backpack, deep down where I can't see any purple poking out.

We're over the city. Las Vegas is open, brown, no trees, and clusters of identical boxes lumped in massive neighborhoods. The plane veers and there's the Las Vegas Strip, with rows of themed casinos, including a castle and a black pyramid.

We turn for the final descent, flying closer and closer to all those buildings, all that brown. My stomach pinches. I'm "actually" here. I'm actually here. I'm actually.

My backpack slides forward. I look at my feet. I think I hear whispering.

"You can't forget about me," the backpack says.

"Watch me."

And then I can't help it. I start on the catastrophic thinking.

There is no way I will ever get out of this airplane seat. I'll fly to Omaha or Milwaukee or wherever it's set to go until the plane finally takes me back home to Washington, where there are actually trees because it actually rains there and no strangers actually try to force my dad to marry them. Actually, I hate this place, and Whitney (what kind of name is Whitney?), and I *actually* hate hate hate my dad and my mom and this awful envelope and . . .

Ridge squeezes my hand. He's sitting up straight and looking at me intently. He has very big and calming eyes, my little brother. "Hey. Hey."

He hands me Pog. I hold my smiling dog with one arm and my sweet brother's hand as the plane gently touches the ground. A safe landing.

We are together.

Stable.

Calm.

Breathe.

"What do you think that fortune meant about losing something valuable?" I ask. "Do you think it had anything to do with losing our home in Tacoma? Or maybe friends?"

"You're thinking way too much about it. Here." He reaches

into the seat pocket and hands me a bag of beef jerky. "You almost forgot this."

"You mean I almost *lost* it!" I say.

Ridge shakes his head. "You need to stop trying to find answers in every little thing. It's beef jerky. That's it."

"Please remain in your seat until we come to a complete stop," a flight attendant announces. "And welcome to Lost Wages!"

Lost Wages. Blah.

I gnaw on the inside of my cheek as we walk off the plane, heat blasting us in the Jetway. There's more I want to say. I want to argue that when you have so many questions, finding one little answer would actually help a lot. I want to argue that he should make a new origami fortune teller that actually has a clue.

And I want to argue that slipping notes from absent mothers in a snack backpack is actually an unfair thing to do.

Chapter 5

I have never seen so many strip malls in my life. Intersection after intersection there's mall, mall, mall. All the trees and grass are landscaped with no natural forest. Empty land is simply dirt. Nothing growing. Is this my future? Dust?

"So I already have a sandwich platter at the house," Whitney says. We're in her practical blue car. She's blasting the air-conditioning and shouting over that. It's just pushing the hot air into the back seat. I move Pog, who is panting more than usual, right in front of the vent. "Vivian is going to meet us there—she had cheerleading practice. I got you toiletries like toothbrushes and deodorant in case you forgot, and—"

Dad pats her leg, which makes me actually want to throw up. "Thank you. It sounds like you've thought of everything."

"Just thinking about you, Micah." She leans over and kisses his cheek. "Always."

I have to get out of this house, and we aren't even *in* it yet.

"Can you not do that?" Ridge asks.

Dad turns around and smiles. "What?"

"Kiss." Ridge scrunches up his nose. "Please stop."

"Oh. Okay." Dad and Whitney share a secret smile, which is more annoying than the kiss.

More strip malls, more houses, more dirt, more blazing air until we pull up to a neat one-story with beige stucco and a brown roof. There's a stretch of fake grass in front, with a circle of rocks and a mini palm tree.

"Here we are!" Whitney says. "I know we'll be crowded for a bit, but it'll be a fun way to get to know each other."

Whitney's house is fine. Nice. Clean. A large painting of the Virgin Mary is paired with an ornate wooden cross. There are soft throw pillows and scented candles. I don't feel a connection to any of it, probably because I don't feel a connection to Whitney.

"You can drop your stuff off in the living room," Whitney says. "We'll talk about the kid space situation with Vivian."

Ridge takes the word *drop* literally and melts into a chair like we've lived here forever. I don't know where to leave my backpack, and when I say backpack, I mean letter. I finally settle on propping it against the blue velvet couch.

"You sure you want to leave me here?" the backpack asks.

"Super sure," I say.

"Did you say something?" Whitney asks.

Dad has business calls all afternoon, then an on-site appointment first thing in the morning. He pats me on the head three times, pat, pat, pat, before grabbing a sub sandwich and slipping into Whitney's office. Ever since the pandemic, he works more from home but is on-site for temporary projects like this. Once this assignment is done, we head back to real life. Dad and Whitney will probably get married after they sort out their jobs. I don't know when that will be, but I'm hoping it's a few years.

I pour a baggie of dog food into a white bowl. Whitney's kitchen is so clean that I wonder if she even uses bowls? I stare at the wipe marks on her stainless steel fridge.

"How are you doing?" Whitney asks. "What's on your mind?"

There are too many ways to answer. Like: *Why do I have to miss the Dippers Tuesday at the pool because you're playing house with my dad?* Or: *Why couldn't my dad check into another casino, like the volcano one, so you wouldn't have met him?*

The air grows expectant. I chew my sandwich. "Nothing?"

"Unless you're in a deep meditative state, it's pretty hard to think nothing." Whitney smiles. "That's what I tell Vivian."

I try to think of things my mom used to tell me. Pog snorts next to me, and I remember Mom saying people own dogs to use as excuses. Bad smell? Blame the dog. Don't want to go somewhere? Blame the dog. Want to get out of house? Blame the dog.

"Pog needs to go on a walk," I say.

"But it's two in the afternoon," Whitney says.

"Did we . . . is there something I'm supposed to do at two?"

Whitney laughs. "No, but it's Las Vegas in June."

"I don't understand."

"Tell you what—you go ahead on that walk," Whitney says. "You can go to the 7-Eleven if you can make it there. And when you get back, I'll take you and Ridge swimming at the community pool. You'll need it."

What I *need* is to get away from this house and away from the backpack and away from the letter. Actually.

27

"Do you want to come?" I ask Ridge.

"Whitney, what's your Wi-Fi password?" Ridge has already created a gaming corner in the living room.

Outside feels like that moment when you open a heated oven, except instead of taking the food out, you crawl *into* the oven. Sweat trickles down my back and armpits. My blood actually boils.

All my caring sweats right off of me in this heat. What does it matter what I do after this walk, or tonight, or tomorrow, or ever again? The Dippers or the letter don't matter at all. Actually, a Gatorade would matter. It would matter a whole lot.

Pog pants and pants, which I remember isn't good for a pug because of their cute little smooshed faces. I keep my head down as we walk the few blocks to the store. I make sure not to step on any cracks for superstition's sake, even though my mom already did break her back. The neighborhood goes from planned community to major street fast. Finally, there's the 7-Eleven in front of me, promising relief.

I run into the store, Pog trotting beside me. I yank open the refrigerator and groan when the blast of air hits. I pick up Pog and try to jam us into the icy air as much as possible, until I hear a shout.

"You know that isn't going to fly, kid. Out!"

I poke my head out, but not my body, because ahhhhhhhh. The counter clerk has her arms crossed in the universal pose of annoyed adult.

I shimmy out of the fridge and grab a green Gatorade. My mom used to call it a yellow Gatorade, and since we couldn't agree, we called it lemon-lime. I figure now I can call it whatever I want.

"Sorry!" I say. "I've never been in the desert before and apparently two in the afternoon is very hot and pugs overheat easily so we needed to cool off and don't worry I'm buying a Gatorade."

"You magically landed in the desert and your first stop is this 7-Eleven?" There's a jangling sound as the lady scans my Gatorade. Her arm is covered in crystal bracelets and a sleeve of tattoos, all different flowers. The art is beautiful, like her, with brown freckled skin and amber eyes. Her name tag says ZARA.

"Whitney—that's the lady I'm staying with, and also I guess my dad's fiancée—told me to get a drink. She said it was hot but I didn't get *how* hot." I know I'm talking a lot, especially to a stranger, but sometimes I do this when I'm nervous. "It's so dry here and sweltering. That's the word, *sweltering*. I don't think I've ever used that word before but now I understand it. I couldn't quit walking though, you know? Let Whitney know I can't handle this. It's like admitting that she won something."

"I don't know how long your dog will handle it."

Pog is panting, panting, panting. I grab a water and a coffee cup. Pog is good at lapping water out of cups, even if he's sloppy about it.

"You're not going to make me clean that, are you?" Zara asks. "It's a good thing I like dogs."

"I'll clean it. Just let me pay first." I slide a five-dollar bill across the counter. "Can I drink my drink real fast?"

"Sure thing."

I guzzle my green Gatorade. I don't know what electrolytes actually do, but they must work fast because I'm already feeling better. Plus, the store has air-conditioning, which is a nice follow-up to my fridge time.

"You've never been to the desert?" she asks.

"No. I hate it. Nothing is going according to plan."

Zara laughs. "I bet you're an earth sign. When's your birthday?"

I think she's talking about my zodiac sign? I don't tell her the exact date, in case she's trying to steal my identity. "September. Early."

"Yep. Earth sign. Virgo. Makes total sense." Zara counts out change but pauses before handing it to me. "Show me your palm real fast."

I'm already grabbing napkins and sopping up the water and drool Pog left behind. "My palm?"

"Are you right-handed?"

"Yes."

"How old are you?" she asks.

"Twelve."

"Okay, you're still a kid. Barely," Zara says. "So we read your passive hand. The lines in your hand change and form more often than adults'. Once you're a teen, we switch to the active hand."

"None of that makes sense," I say.

"Not yet, but it will," she says. "Let's look at your desert life, Virgo."

I reach my hand across the counter and she looks at my palm, nods. Maybe I shouldn't have told her all that stuff, like my dad's fiancée's name and my birth month. She's a stranger in a strange place and she's looking at my hand like the secrets of the world are buried in my skin.

"This is fascinating," she says.

"What?" I lean in, trying to decipher whatever it is she's deciphering.

"You just moved here, right?" she asks.

"Not moved. *Visiting*."

"See this line?" She points to the side of my hand. "It's chained low on the hand. That means change when you're young. You may have had some disappointments already—maybe a social or school success that didn't pan out. And there's more change ahead."

The door alarm jingles and a man in a tight teal shirt heads straight to the coffee.

My hand is sweaty and not because I'm hot. I look up at Zara's face but she's so intent on my palm. "And here—the heart line? You've had some challenges there too. Family, I think. It'll smooth out, but only after some conflict." She finally looks up. "Maybe there's a broken relationship you need to heal?"

"You don't know me." I drop my hand so fast it almost hits the counter. This was a waste. She's a silly cashier in a silly town. "I'm leaving."

"Okay." She shrugs. "I don't usually do that for free, you know. That's my side business to pay for college. And we didn't start on your lifeline."

I stare down at my hands, which have somehow betrayed me. I want to know what other mysteries are revealed. I want to know if she can tell me whether I should read my mom's letter, or if I'll ever be close friends with Talia, or if my dad is actually going through with the wedding.

I guess . . . I want her to tell me if everything is going to work out?

But instead I grab Pog and hurry out into the sweltering (that's definitely the right word) heat.

Chapter 6

Whitney takes Ridge and me to the neighborhood pool. When she asks about my walk, I don't tell her about the Zara stuff because . . .

      1. I don't know Whitney and
      2. I don't know how to explain what happened.

There aren't many big kids at the pool, mostly moms hanging out at the splash pad with their toddlers. Whitney waves at the other moms but doesn't go over to talk. Even in a swimsuit and cover-up, Whitney looks All Business.

"Sunscreen first. Sunscreen. Sunscreen." Whitney pulls out a massive bottle from her massive swim bag. "Come here, Ridge. I'll get you lathered."

Ridge's shoulders tighten.

"I'll do it." I grab the bottle from Whitney's slippery hand. "We like to put sunscreen on a certain way. It's okay, you wouldn't know."

Whitney stands there, confused and maybe hurt, but finally shrugs and heads to a table in the shade.

It's the first time Ridge and I have been alone together since we got off the plane.

"I don't want her touching my shoulders," Ridge says.

"I know," I say.

"But . . . I mean, do I let her? At some point? What are the rules?"

Ridge likes knowing the rules. So do I. But our rules keep melting. Whitney's not our stepmom, not yet. But when she's our stepmom and living in the same house, will sunscreen be her responsibility?

"We're too old to have anyone else put sunscreen on us," Ridge decides. "Only our family."

"I get it," I say. "But you might have a hard time getting *Whitney* to understand."

"But she has a kid."

"She had the kid but she didn't *have* us. So yeah, different rules."

We both look over at Whitney, who is thumbing through a book. She waves.

We walk over to the other side of the pool and soak our feet while we wait for the sunscreen to dry. Except we don't wait long because of the oven weather. The water is warm, too warm, but we jump in anyway and try to stay underwater as long as possible. When I pop out of the water, I pretend I'm popping into a new place each time. Pop, I'm at the Tacoma pool with the Dippers. Pop, I'm at the Disneyland Hotel pool. Pop, I'm at Grandma Whitmer's lake house in Michigan, which I haven't been to since I was seven, but it's all cooler than Las Vegas anyway.

I'm on my eighth or ninth pop when the gate to the pool

crashes shut. Four teen girls walk through in what feels like slow-motion. Like there's no way they're in the same heat as us because they're too fresh and breezy. They have on bikinis, sunglasses, and trendy sandals. They sit, almost in unison, on deck chairs. One of them—I'm guessing it's Vivian—walks over to Whitney. Vivian has her mom's same black hair with browner skin. Even from far away, her legs have visible muscles and . . . a shininess? Like she's shaved? She's old enough to shave her legs. Wait, when do I start shaving?

"Stella!" Whitney waves both arms and hollers. "Come over here, sweetie."

So I swim across the pool, but this dorky kind of doggy-paddle because now I'm aware of how I swim and they're *watching* me. This pool is seventy miles long. If I can cross in eight seconds, nothing bad will happen. Eight, seven, six, five, four . . .

I make it to the edge by three, stoked with my speed. But I don't want to get out because my swimsuit is small and young, especially next to Vivian's.

"Vivian, this is Micah's daughter, Stella Blue North. She's twelve, almost thirteen."

Vivian doesn't stop chewing her gum. She has big, pouty lips and white, straight teeth. "Hey."

I shield my eyes from the sun. "Hey."

"This is Vivian Angelina Marin," Whitney says. "I kept my maiden name so we have different last names, which gets confusing, but I think it's important for women to maintain—"

"Mom, what's with the big-deal introductions?"

Vivian's the kind of beautiful that makes me hyperaware of my regularness. I move my wet hair across my face.

"You're going to be stepsisters," Whitney says. "Big-deal relationships deserve big-deal introductions."

Stepsisters. *Stepsisters?* I haven't thought about this. I haven't thought about Vivian. There's been no time to think.

"Vivian is fifteen. She'll be a sophomore. Oh, and Ridge." Whitney waves at my brother, but he doesn't look at her. "Well. He's ten. I'm sure he'll swim over at some point."

He sits on the pool steps with a smaller kid. They talk animatedly, like together they are solving world peace. Ridge could start a conversation with a garden hose.

I, however, can't. I'm still blinking at Vivian, hoping she'll say something more.

"'Kay, Mom." Vivian turns to Whitney. "We're reading our magazines."

"Don't you want to—" Whitney glances back and forth between us. "Uh . . . hang? Together?"

Vivian chews her gum and I squint for ten more seconds. Then she walks away and I pop back under the water. I imagine myself in a few years with my own group of friends. Too cool for middle schoolers. Too cool for this heat.

We stay so long that my whole hand prunes. I wonder if Zara could still see the lines or if my whole destiny magically changed.

✳ ✳ ✳

The backpack greets me as soon as we walk in through the door.

"That took a while," the backpack says.

I jump. The voice is close because the backpack is. Right at the front entryway, not by the couch where I left it.

Whitney brushes a hair from her face. "Vivian, grab some of Stella's stuff. You guys can shower—I'm making stuffed peppers. Oh, and we're going out as a family tomorrow!"

"We're not a family." Vivian grabs my backpack before I can. I glance back at Ridge, but he's already raiding the fridge. I roll my suitcase into Vivian's bedroom.

It's a mess, with an unmade bed and heaps of clothes on the rug. The bedding is nice, as are the clothes, which makes me wonder why Vivian can't be bothered to keep nice things nice. There's a wall of pastel posters and exotic locations. Italy and Greece, unless it's Hawaii and Costa Rica? I don't know—they're peachy views of places I haven't been. There's also inspirational quotes mixed in, like "Be your own Shero!" and "Know your Power!" The kind of stuff you'd find on social media feeds, although it's clear Vivian's put a lot of thought into the whole display.

"You can shower first," Vivian says. "Don't use my shampoo."

I smell her shampoo in the shower. It's pineapple, like my mom's, which for some reason is the saddest thought I've had all month. Sometimes you're so sucked into living your life that you don't realize you've stopped recognizing yourself in it. That fact hits me in a pineapple-scented wave. I spend five minutes crying in a shower that isn't mine.

I turn off the water. Vivian walks right in. Luckily I have a towel around me but still, it's rude.

"Hey!" I shout.

"You were crying," Vivian says.

I push past her, catching a glimpse of my shoulders in the mirror and the red spots where I missed the sunscreen.

She must notice because she tosses a bottle of aloe lotion into the room. I rub it all over my arms and legs, which is maybe the best I've felt since arriving in Vegas. I put on a pair of black shorts and a T-shirt before clearing a spot on the rug, not sure what I'm supposed to do next.

If Dr. Matt were here, he'd help come up with a list of things to do in awkward moments like this. Making lists together was my favorite part of therapy, like our "Astronomical Anxiety Approach" (the guy really liked doing Stella/star puns). I forget everything on the list, but petting Pog was on there, plus giving signals and counting slowly. There was something about "fully feeling my feelings," so he'd probably think my shower crying was, like, healing. But now I have to guess what Dr. Matt would say since Dad stopped taking me last winter. Dad said my anxiety was doing way better, which . . . sure. But therapy is also super expensive. I think his bank account wanted me to be better too.

I roll onto my stomach. My backpack is now staring straight at me, so instead of staring back I grab the top magazine from Vivian's bedside stack. There's a hunched girl showing lots of teeth. An article catches my eye: "Are you ready for the summer of your life? See what the stars have in store for your hot months!"

I flip to the horoscope section, remembering other things Mom used to say. Like if she was fighting with Dad, she'd tell him, "Stop being such a Pisces," which I don't think you can help, right?

My finger drags down the page, stopping right on my horoscope.

And whoa. I am in for it.

Virgo loves, loves, loves control but Mercury is in retrograde, throwing everything into CHAOS! You may find all your carefully laid plans constantly interrupted. Guess what? It's time to double down on your control and make more *plans. Take charge of your destiny and give Mercury the business. This is true for love, friendship, or family. What do you want, Virgo?*

Now what are you going to do to make it happen?

Chapter 7

I sleep in the next morning, finally waking up to a text around ten. It's Talia! I sit up, trying to clear my brain enough to read the text.

How is Las Vegas?

I write **good**, then erase it. Write **cool**, erase that. Then I worry she can see a dot dot dot while I keep rewriting texts, so I open the notes app on the phone and spend some time carefully crafting the perfect reply.

It's sooooo hot but kinda fun. I'm sad I can't go to the pool with you tomorrow.

Talia writes me back so fast. **No biggie! We'll hang out when you get back.**

This reply takes less time: **Totally!**

Did you go to the Strip yet?

Dang, why didn't I asked Whitney to drive us down the Strip when we got here? I'm supposed to do every big and adventurous thing so I can have lots of stories to tell the Dippers when I get back. **Not yet, but soon.** Then I have a genius thought! **I'll get you a souvenir.**

Send me a postcard! Send me a bunch. I collect them.

Of course she collects postcards. I'd do the same cool thing but then she'd think I'm copying her. Which I would be. **Oh fun! We can be pen pals.**

She doesn't write me back for five minutes, the longest of my life. The pen pal line was sketch, right? Are pen pals even a thing anymore? Especially when I'm still geographically close. Why can't I be in Italy or Tanzania?

Dot dot dots. The glory of the dot dot dot! And then a meme of a surfer riding a wave with the words *Get On Board.*

We've gone meme, folks! Next-level meme!

I flop back onto the air mattress. My right hand throbs and I realize how tight I've been clutching my phone.

Talia: **Oh, my mom needs me to do chores. Don't lose all your money in a slot machine** ☺

Obviously, I'm too young to gamble, but Talia is funny like that.

I send a few thoughtful emojis in response and let out a relieved breath. This is positive. Good stuff. Leaving right after the birthday party didn't have to be the end of the world. This might actually help the friendship. By leaving, I'm playing it cool. Maybe Pilar and the other girls will text me too, inviting me to the mall when I get back.

But for now, I need to go to the Strip and find an amazing postcard to impress the Dippers. And I'll take some style notes here, maybe come back with a brand-new desert vibe. Wow, there's suddenly so much to do, which makes the next two weeks feel less like a punishment and more like a promise.

Whitney only has one car. Which means Dad, Vivian, Ridge, and I get to pick her up from work before the family meeting dinner thing. And the best part is Whitney works at Caesars Palace. On the Strip!

The Strip is a long street of flashy hotels. Some are pure gold, others all lights. There are mega screens advertising designer brands and concerts. There's also a poster of ladies wearing very little clothing—Dad tells us to try and focus on something else. A truck parks next to us at a light. Behind it is a trailer with a large banner for "Psychic Readings." Palm reading! Tarot cards!

I stick my hand in my pocket so I'm not tempted to look at the lines on my palm. Instead, I count the places I hope to visit during our trip. The Shark Reef Aquarium, M&M's World, Coca-Cola Store, the Pinball Hall of Fame. It's still blazing hot here, but at least there are all these exciting (air-conditioned) places to make up for it.

We drive into the concrete parking garage. Vivian knows a secret side entrance into the casino. Caesars Palace is designed to look like ancient Rome. We studied ancient civilizations in World History this year and now I'm seeing it come to life. Plus a lot of slot machines and cocktail waitresses.

Ridge runs right over to a *Star Trek* slot machine. A security guard appears within seconds.

"Casino floor is adults only."

"Oh, sorry," Ridge says. "Did I boldly go where no kid has gone before?"

Dad finally catches up. "Sorry about that."

The security guard points to the two types of flooring. "Kids are allowed to walk through the casino, but don't step onto the casino floor. Stay off the fancy carpet, all right, kid?"

Ridge scoots back onto the pathway. "Dad, please, please, please. Will you put a dollar into the *Star Trek* slot machine? Spock is speaking to me."

I fully expect Dad to say no. He has a swear jar in our kitchen, which is mostly empty. He buttons the top button of his shirt. The wildest thing he's ever done is sing along at a Grateful Dead concert. But he shrugs and says, "Sure, Ridge. If you're feeling lucky, so am I."

Slot machines don't have slots like I thought they did. Dad has to put money on a card and swipe to play. Meaning it takes a while, but it's also fun and not something we do every day.

Vivian rolls her eyes. "My dad says only fools play slots. There's no strategy. The real money is in poker."

I'm about to defend my dad's, I don't know, gaming honor when the little light on top of the machine lights up. WINNING SPIN LOOK UP. Some spaceships fire at numbers, adding more and more pictures that don't totally make sense but . . . we won!

"Whoa, buddy!" Dad says. "We won fifty bucks!"

Ridge and I jump up and down but do not cross the carpet line. Dad puts his winnings on the card. I wish the machine spit out a bunch of quarters instead, but money is money.

"You guys can split the winnings three ways, okay?"

"Three ways?" Ridge asks.

"Yeah, each kid gets about sixteen dollars," Dad says.

Vivian is already walking ahead of us. She shouldn't get any money if she can't bother to be nice to my dad.

"Dad, I want to buy a postcard to send to my friend Talia," I say. "Maybe we can buy a souvenir too?"

"Sure thing!" Dad's smiling super big. He's been smiling a lot lately. I'm happy for him, even if I'm still iffy on Whitney.

We stop at a kiosk and buy a postcard. I pick the one with a bunch of statues of gods by a fountain. I almost get the naked statue of Michelangelo's *David* as a joke, but I don't know Talia that well. What if her parents see it and say we can never hang out again?

Whitney is not at the front desk. Dad texts her and we wait at the hotel entrance until she comes down from the big office. She has on a black skirt and a silky pink tank. There's a headset thing in her ear too. She stops to say something to a large man in a beige suit before walking across the tile floor to greet us.

"Sorry, we had a VIP check in," she says. "Wanted two floors to himself."

"Dad won big at the slots!" Ridge says excitedly. This is maybe the first time he's spoken to Whitney without her asking him a question first.

"A gambler, huh?" Whitney slides her arm around Dad's waist. My stomach drops. "My man and Kenny Rogers, eh?"

Dad blushes. Like actually blushes. Kenny Rogers must be really handsome.

"Should we get to dinner?" he asks.

"Yes. I'm starving." Whitney unclips her earpiece thingy and sticks it in her purse. She is pure polish. Her whole vibe shouts *in charge*. "Oh, Ridge and Stella. I want to show you a Vegas trick."

She leads us over to a gold statue. We've passed all sorts of statues in the hotel—naked David, half-naked Cleopatra, and moving marble statues in a show. This one has on a gold breastplate with robes gathered around the waist. His right arm is raised like he's commanding an army.

"That's Caesar," I say. "We learned about this statue in school—well, the original one."

Whitney squints at me. "You studied Roman history already?"

"The place is called Caesars Palace," Vivian says. "It doesn't take a rocket scientist to know that's Julius Caesar."

"Actually, that's Augustus Caesar," I say. "He came *after* Julius Caesar. He was the first Roman emperor."

Whitney beams at me. "We have a master historian on our hands."

I don't really care about Whitney's attention. But I also really, really don't like Vivian's attitude. She was rude to Dad about the money, even though he was giving her part of it, and then acts like I'm the little kid when she's the one who doesn't know basic history.

"Here's what I wanted to show you." Whitney steps forward. "See how the finger on his left hand is shiny? That's because tourists rub it for good luck."

"Cool." Ridge jumps forward and brushes the thumb.

Dad waves his hand. "I've got all the luck I need today."

Vivian and I stare at each other, like we're deciding who goes next. She's older, so I wait even though she's too cool for everything.

She barely bumps the finger. "Fine. Done."

I pause, taking in the seriousness of the moment. Hadn't my horoscope told me to take charge of my destiny? I grab the whole bronze hand, cold and slick.

Caesar, I need a good story to tell the Dippers, okay? Make something exciting happen.

Chapter 8

Whitney takes us to a Korean/Mexican restaurant in one of the eighty billion strip malls. It's small, with brown tiles and a few simple tables—a no-nonsense, order-at-the-counter place. Much better than an order-from-menus restaurant. Those take longer. For our first "family" dinner, we don't need *long*.

"It's fusion food," Whitney says. "The bulgogi tacos are my favorite."

Dad squeezes her in a hug. "You're my favorite."

She pecks him on the cheek.

It's a good thing Ridge is in the bathroom. Instead, Vivian catches my eye. We don't make barfing sounds or anything, but our eyes communicate extreme disgust. My cheeks warm. This is the most acknowledgment she's given me all night.

I want to ask if she's seen her mom date a lot of men. Or if she's ever seen her mom kiss one of them. Does her dad date or have a partner? How long have her parents been divorced and does she go to both houses and is she close with her mom? Where does her dad live, does she like him, does she have a letter in her backpack that she's trying not to think about?

We're next in line. I look up at the menu, hesitant to try anything with "fusion" in the title. Haven't we done enough fusion between these two families? "I'll have chicken enchiladas with rice and beans. And can I have those all in separate containers?"

"What do you mean?" the cashier asks.

"Like, so nothing is touching?" I ask.

"It comes all together, honey," Whitney says.

Dad waves his hand. "That's how she likes it."

Whitney scrunches up her nose.

We pile into a table in the back corner. I sit next to Ridge and Dad is by Whitney, so Vivian has to pull over a seat. The chair scratches the tile floor, all loud. I can't tell if she's doing it on purpose.

Whitney reaches her hand across the table and squeezes Vivian's hand. Weird. Then she reaches her other hand across the table and squeezes Ridge's hand. Double weird. He bumps me with his knee but what am I supposed to do? Grab her leg?

"So here we are!" Whitney says. "I know this is a lot all at once for everyone." She gives Ridge another squeeze and lets go. He immediately sticks his hands under the table.

"Whitney and I have, er, news," Dad says. "And thoughts."

"Which one is it?" Vivian asks. "News or thoughts?"

"News first," Dad says. "So . . . well. This project I'm working on is going great. Really great. In fact, uh, well . . . my company asked me to stay until it's completed."

"How long?" Ridge asks.

"Two months."

"I don't understand," I say. "What does that mean?"

"I need to work here for two months. Whitney's offered to let us stay with her for the summer."

"For the summer," I repeat. The words slime down my throat. Two weeks was one thing. Two weeks was an interesting summer vacation. Two weeks was a missed hangout or phone call. But two months? That's the space in between sixth grade and seventh. That is swimsuits and Popsicles and late-night movies and secrets and friendship bracelets. That's the difference between Talia's friend group remembering my name and . . . not.

Two months is a *lifetime*.

"And *thoughts* means we want to have an open discussion about this," Whitney says. "Because we want you to have choices."

One time I asked Aunt Maggie what it was like growing up with her parents—my grandparents. Aunt Maggie is a lot younger than Mom, so by the time she was born, they weren't as hands-on. If she did something wrong, they'd get on her back. If she did something right, they'd smile next to her in a picture. But they didn't do much to help her in the moment. She called it "after-the-fact parents."

Whitney using that word—*choices*—reminds me of Aunt Maggie's phrase. Was it *our* choice they got engaged on a whim and shuttled us down here? Did anyone ask Ridge or me if we wanted to sweat the summer away in Vegas? She says we get a say in this situation, but it's only *after the fact*.

"But we don't," I say.

"You don't what?" Whitney asks.

"Have choices. You just told us our whole summer is basically canceled, right? We can't go home and stay with anyone else?"

Dad's voice wobbles. "I don't . . . I don't know if that's realistic. I thought . . . I thought you knew this was a possibility. I have to work. Whitney and I are engaged. We're going to have to make readjustments."

"So what happens after the two months?" Vivian asks. "Mom and I aren't moving there. No way."

"We aren't staying *here*," Ridge says. "Right, Dad?"

Vivian, Ridge, and I stare expectantly at Dad and Whitney. This is maybe the first thing we are united in, even though we all want this to go in opposite ways.

"We don't know what the future holds," Whitney says. "We'll see how things go this summer. Then we'll figure it out."

"Isn't this the stuff couples usually figure out *before* getting engaged?" Vivian asks her. "I mean, before they become a couple in, like, one day?"

Whitney ignores her. She does this a lot with Vivian, like she has no idea how to approach her so there is no approach at all. "We have a plan for the summer! And it's going to be super fun. I've created a schedule. Micah is going to be busy with his building project. I work different hours, often at night. So we will switch off who is in charge."

She's actually printed up the schedule, which feels very permanent. As much as I like charts and order, seeing our day-to-day spelled out makes this summer seem real. And long. Impossibly long.

Vivian scans the paper and slides it across the table. "I'm sorry. No."

"No?" Dad asks.

"I'm not babysitting your kids." She waves a hand toward Ridge and me. "No offense."

Dad tries to bury the expression, but he *is* offended. Ridge and I would never talk back like this. Did he think Vivian would act differently when they made all these big choices in a nanosecond?

"Don't start, Viv." Whitney shifts in her seat. "Everyone in this family needs to pitch in here."

"This family?" Vivian snorts. "I don't know these people. Stella, hey. Do you think I'm your family?"

I look at Dad when I whisper, "Nope."

Dad lays his hands on the table, as if in surrender. "Okay. Fair. It's all very . . . new. Whitney and I recognize that we're throwing a lot at you. But . . . I mean, it is what it is. We're here. Engaged or not, I still need to work. And Whitney works. You kids need someone checking up on you. Plus, Whitney has wedding planning."

"Wedding planning?" Vivian says it like a swear. "You really think you're *doing* this?"

Whitney holds up her hand with the ring. "Yes. August third. Marriage is the thing that follows an engagement, sweetie."

"That wasn't an engagement. It was a stunt." Vivian shrugs. "That's what Dad called it."

Whitney lets out a breath and looks up at the ceiling, like she'll discover all the right things to say in the cracks up there. Her ex-husband clearly has opinions about this change. I wonder if Aunt Maggie told my mom about Dad's relationship update.

I didn't tell Talia or anyone else at school about the engagement. I only said Dad was working on a project so we were turning it into a vacation, which was mostly the truth anyway. When they'd pitched the marriage idea, they made it sound like this faraway possibility, not an immediate *asteroid*.

I check myself, physically, to see how my body is handling this news. I don't always know what's going to set off my anxiety. One time we were in a corn maze and Ridge jumped out to scare me. I was so startled that I screamed and didn't calm down for two days. But now there's no tightening in my chest, the struggling to breathe, shaking, clenched fists. I don't feel like I'm in my own body hearing this. I'm watching this all from outer space.

I pick at my paper place mat. There's a red border around a bunch of animals and CHINESE ZODIAC in large lettering. I don't know why they are using Chinese place mats in a Mexican/Korean fusion restaurant, but they probably don't make Mexican/Korean place mats. I run my finger down the paper until I find my birth year. The Year of the Tiger. I wish I could roar.

Nobody talks, which is better than when they were talking, but still super awkward.

"Order for Whitney?"

The cashier slides our food in front of us, enchiladas now covering the information about my zodiac year.

"So there are three ways this can go, right?" Ridge asks. "You guys get married and we move to Vegas, you move to Washington, or you live in two different states?"

I pick at my place mat until there's a hole in the corner.

Dad wipes his forehead. Sweat marks ring his dress shirt. "I guess . . . yeah . . . I'm going to figure out long-term plans for my job. Whitney is going to look for jobs in Tacoma. We'll see what works out."

Everyone eats. So quiet.

I push my enchiladas away and rip more of the place mat. I rip, rip, rip until I've ripped out the whole section about the Year of the Tiger.

Tiger people are aggressive, courageous, candid, and sensitive. Look to the Horse or Dog for happiness. Beware of the Monkey.

"What year were you born?" I ask Dad.

"What? Oh." He scans his place mat, relieved with the change of subject. "Year of the Monkey. Same as Whitney."

I swallow—not food, because I still haven't taken a bite—but tears.

Vivian kicks me under the table. She juts her chin toward the front door. "Stella and I are going outside for a second. Uh . . . sister stuff."

"Me too." Ridge stands, but Vivian sits him back down.

"*Big* sister stuff. Like . . . how old are you, Stella?"

"Twelve. Almost thirteen."

"Yeah, almost-thirteen-and-up kind of stuff. Sorry, kid."

I don't look at Ridge because I know he'll be mad, but you don't say no to Vivian. I'll make it up to him. And it'll take a lot more than one win on a slot machine for Dad to make this up to us.

The door chimes. She pulls me over to a short bench in front of the restaurant. The trash can nearby overflows.

"Do you want them to get married?" Vivian asks.

"No way," I say, realizing it's the most decisive thing I've said in weeks. "And I don't want to stay here."

"Oh, totally. And it's impossible for me to move. I'm on the cheer squad." Vivian bites at a hangnail on her thumb. "I can't believe how rude they're being. This isn't like my mom. She's the most type A person I know."

"Well, it's not like my dad. He's the . . . He's stable. Like a regular person. He doesn't do stuff like this."

"Love changes you. Usually for the worse." Vivian's upper lip twitches. "Your brother forgot the fourth possible outcome."

"What's that?"

"They call off the wedding and no one moves. There's my vote." She blows out a frustrated breath. "I wish we had a way to know how this is all going to turn out."

I pull out lemon hand sanitizer and do one long squirt, two short, one more long. As I rub in the liquid, I notice the chains on my palms, the chains that Zara said meant change. Five minutes with a 7-Eleven clerk and she already understood me more than any adult in my life.

And then I realize—there *is* a way to know how things will turn out. I could make a Dr. Matt list! Instead of an Astronomical Approach, we could make an *Astrological* Approach. Our list could explore palm readings and magazine horoscopes and the Chinese zodiac and little paper fortune tellers. We could use crystal balls and fortune cookies. There is a whole world to predict—in fact, everything is already written in the stars.

Vivian and I might not have much in common, but we both don't want to be related.

Maybe if I learned more about being a Virgo or a Tiger, I could finally take charge of my own destiny. And by destiny, I mean: Make sure my dad doesn't marry Whitney. Then move home ASAP, back to Aunt Maggie, my panic room, and all the promising possibilities with the Dippers.

My horoscope said to double down on control this summer. Not only predict the future, but *change* it. And my Virgo brain is already formulating the perfect plan.

"I think I have an idea," I say. "But first, tell me—what is your zodiac sign?"

Chapter 9

Vivian and I are silent in the car back to Whitney's house. We don't want anyone to catch on to the vibe that we're teaming up. Or whatever it is we're about to do. My stomach has me doubled over and it's nothing to do with food. There's nowhere I can go to soothe my anxiety. It feels like the only option is to take immediate action to fix the thing that started my symptoms in the first place.

Whitney asks if we want to play a card game when we get home. Vivian makes a big deal of being annoyed. Such a big deal that I almost believe her.

"Mom, seriously," Vivian says. "No. We are not hanging out."

Whitney looks hurt. "Remember when you used to ask me to invite people over so we'd have enough players for Spit? Look, we're at five now."

"Stop doing family math," Vivian says. "I'm mad. I'm going to my room to be mad."

"But, honey." Whitney is reaching for straws. "Stella needs to sleep in there."

"Then I guess Stella is coming too."

I shrug at Dad and Whitney, like I have no choice. Actually, I don't. Vivian is my closest thing to an ally. When I poked Ridge in the car and pointed to Dad and Whitney, obviously in reference to the switch in summer plans, Ridge shrugged. "Dad's happy."

Traitor.

So I grab Pog and join my hopefully-not-stepsister. By the time I close the door behind me, Vivian already has a large poster board and markers on her multicolored rug.

"Do you have to bring the dog in here?" she asks.

"Where else would he go?"

Vivian tilts her head to the side. "I guess he could be cute on my social media posts. I'll allow it."

He's also the nicest dog on earth and a living, breathing *being*, but if a photo op keeps him close, fine.

"Operation Break Up Our Parents." Vivian draws an oval in the middle of the board. "Let's start."

"We can't call it that," I say. "We need a code name."

I kneel down on the floor. Pog jumps out of my lap and squeezes himself under Vivian's bed. Even he's scared of her. I curl into a comfortable ball on the ground.

"What are you doing?" she asks.

"My stomach hurts." I roll tighter. "And it's going to keep hurting so don't ask me about it."

"All right, geez," Vivian says. "Code name for this project. Hmm. Mission I'm Not Moving to Washington?"

"Let's do something with stars," I say. "Since we're using the zodiac stuff."

"Stars . . ." Vivian looks up at the ceiling, like she can see through to the sky. "Galaxies, constellations, spaceships, destiny . . . uh, Parents Go Kaboom?"

"How about Supernova Quest?" I say, already loving the idea of naming my new list after a star. Dr. Matt would be so proud that his Stella pun legacy lives on. "A supernova is a star that ends its life cycle with a big explosion that's brighter than the sun. But they also collapse. And we're trying to make our parents, you know, break up. That can be external or internal. And a quest is, like, our mission. Our purpose. Everything hangs in the balance."

"How do you know that?"

"Um, I read?"

"You put way too much thought into things." Vivian writes *SUPERNOVA QUEST* in large block letters in the center oval. "How do we use all this luck and fortune stuff against our parents?"

I roll a marker back and forth between my fingers. Focusing on one fidget helps me not focus on my stomach. "Here's what I'm thinking. We learn the future. I don't know how. Maybe google 'how to find the future.'"

"That's weak."

Whatever happened to "no ideas are bad ideas" when we're brainstorming? "I'm just saying—we need to find out what *is* going to happen with our parents so we can figure out how to mess it up."

"Yeah. Better."

We sit in silence, pondering possibilities. I've never had a boyfriend or even a big crush. I do not know how to make a relationship happen, let alone end it. I've only experienced my parents' divorce, which was long, sad, and not discussed. When they had problems, well . . . when Mom had problems, I tried to fix it. I would wake her up and help her get ready when she slept all day. I made meals and told Dad that Mom did it. I stayed quiet and took up as little space as possible so I wouldn't make things worse.

I glance at my backpack. It's silent. Probably because the letter knows none of it worked. I couldn't be the glue for their relationship. I wonder how my mom would feel about me trying to destroy Dad's new relationship. Would she be angry? Hopeful? Proud?

"What about a psychic?" Vivian whips out her phone and clicks around. "I bet we can find a website."

"Maybe." I think back to that truck with the billboard trailer we saw driving down the Strip. What did it say? Psychic Readers. "Actually, I saw this billboard on the Strip."

"Oh, the one with the eyes and a red hand in the middle?" Vivian asks. "I've seen that one all over. I'll look it up and . . . there! Let's call."

"Wait, now?"

"Why not?" Vivian hits a button on her phone. A recorded voice blares on speaker. "Welcome to Psychic Readers! Our services are twenty dollars for fifteen minutes, forty dollars for a half hour, seventy per hour with no required limit on sessions. We accept all major credit cards up front."

"Well, that plan is dead," I say. And good thing. Can't Vivian see how much is at stake here? We need to do this *perfectly*. Look up the different types of psychic mediums, the history of the field, the best strategy for our situation . . . maybe we'll be ready by Thursday. Next Thursday. "Do you know which cultures use fortune-telling? That would be fun research!"

"Hold on." Vivian rifles through her backpack. "My mom gave me a just-for-emergencies credit card."

"I don't think this qualifies."

"You don't think the most important thing in both of our lives *qualifies*?" Vivian pushes another button. Elevator music fills the room as we wait on hold.

"Hang up!" I shout. "Come on!"

"What are you so afraid of?" she asks.

What am I afraid of? This. All of this. What if the future is bad? What if it's good? What if it is regular? The better question is what am I NOT afraid of?

We have to stop. Collect. Weigh this out. Make a spreadsheet or PowerPoint. At *least* a basic list of bullet points.

"This is Mystic Shonda." This time the voice is live. Real. "Are you calling to book a session?"

"Uh, yes. Anything . . . now?" Vivian lowers her voice. Way, way lowers it. She's trying to sound like an adult, but it comes out more like an intoxicated frog.

"I had a cancellation so I would be happy to do a phone session with you," Mystic Shonda says.

"Oh, really?" Now her voice is high, like helium-balloon high.

It would be so much better to have an entire script written out ahead of time with questions that would help lead the psychic into saying exactly what we want so we can have the best future possible. Vivian is totally blowing this with her up/down voices. And we can't call back now, not when Shonda would see our same number on caller ID and think we're a bunch of kids wasting her time.

Even if we are.

I move, almost on instinct, grabbing the phone from Vivian.

"Excellent," I say, smooth and even. "Can I give you my credit card number?"

I tell her the card name, number, code, and expiration date. Vivian stares at me, mouth wide open. I wish I had more time to fully enjoy the look on her face.

"All set," Mystic Shonda says. "What are you hoping to learn today, Whitney?"

And yes. Of course she thinks I'm Whitney. I just said I was giving her my credit card. The name on the card is Whitney. And actually, the person messing everything up right now is *Whitney*. So isn't it Whitney's future we're hoping to change? We do that and Vivian and I are free from a classic case of Parental-Romance-Robbing-Kids-of-Their-Own-Destiny.

"Whitney?" Vivian whispers but I shush her. I know what I'm doing. Ish.

"Well, Mystic Shonda, what services do you offer?" I ask.

"I'm here to illuminate truth in any way you like. I offer tarot readings, dreamscape interpretations, psychic energy, mind readings—"

"Not mind reading!" I lower my voice. "I mean, I'm . . . interested in the psychic energy? I'd like to hear about my future."

"I enjoy this one over the phone," Mystic Shonda says. "I'm communicating with the universe. If we connect through trust, the waves of the universe are connecting us although we are separate in body."

"Sure," I say. "So, uh . . . what's happening in my immediate future. Like . . . this summer?"

"First I'd like us to sit for a few seconds of silence so we can go into our sacred spaces," she says. "This helps me clear my mind and energy before beginning the reading."

"Okay." I close my eyes. I try to empty my mind. I can feel Vivian shaking next to me. I'm pretty sure she's laughing. She said this was the most important thing in both of our lives, so why isn't she taking it more seriously?

Mystic Shonda stays quiet for a while. Too long, considering the cost. I don't know if she is looking into a crystal ball or cards or what. I could have asked for more specifics, but I don't care how she gets me the future as long as it's *fast*.

"Now let's touch on who you are as a person, because that's where I'm directed to go by the guides," she says. "The type of person you are."

"That's okay, I already know myself—"

"You are a helper," she says. "You like calm and order and you like to help other people achieve that too. You are very impacted by your environment. You find safety in routine. But when you do go out of that comfort space . . . you surprise yourself with your strength. Your time in this life is about exploring inner strength. Exploring and sharing that with others. You know what you want but you don't know how to get it. Use your spiritual guides and intuition to lead you there. Your journey will be surprising, but beautiful nonetheless."

This sounds like . . . me. Like she's saying things about me. It could be Whitney, but I don't think so. The fake name wasn't fake enough to throw off the universe. And let me tell you, it is not a comfortable feeling having the universe see you like that. Especially since I'm not sure I believe all those things about myself.

"You need to ask her about the wedding!" Vivian says. "Hurry!"

I glance at the clock. We only have a few minutes. I need the future. Whitney's future.

I sit up super straight, like Whitney. I think nitpicky thoughts like her. I visualize the man I love (yuck!) and how I don't care if I take him away from all these other people who love him more. I channel all I know about her (which isn't much) from my head to toes.

"Look, that's fabulous," I say. "But can I have you foresee something specific? I'm supposed to get married in two months. Do you see it happening? Or do you, uh, see anything getting in the way?"

"I'm trying to connect to another level, but I'll be honest, Whitney, I'm feeling some blocks. Do you know what those can be?"

The fact that I'm not actually Whitney, probably. "Nope. I'm, uh . . . connected here."

"Okay, I'm seeing some images. Let me zoom in there. I see . . . red stones. Some sort of rotating circle—I can't tell if that's a metaphor or not. Maybe a change of diet? Does this sound like anything to you?"

"No," Vivian says. I shush her. She grabs a sheet of paper and starts writing something.

"If not, it could be . . . do you have any health issues?"

"No," I say. Unless . . . Whitney does? Yikes, I don't want a health issue to be the issue. We want *other* issues. "Is that bad?"

"These predictions are just that. Impressions."

Vivian holds up the sheet of paper: *It sounds like she's making stuff up and waiting for you to react to it.*

"Hmm . . . you love this man very much, yes?" Mystic Shonda asks.

"I, uh . . ." How can Whitney love my dad? She doesn't even know him. They hung out, what, twenty years ago in college and now they're guaranteed soulmates? I mean, *I* love him. Of course. I've known him my whole life! "Yes. He is a good man."

"Lovely." She pauses. "There is also a . . . spirit or ghost from your past creating a sense of inner conflict."

Vivian nods and mouths, "Good."

Oh, now she thinks it's good. When it's something scary and dramatic.

"And tulips, I smell . . . they aren't a fragrant flower, but that's there. And. I can taste lime. There's maybe romance tied to the lime."

Most psychics on TV say super vague things that could happen to anyone. Like . . . "You will meet a person sometime this year." Or, "If you work, you will get more money!" But this is specific stuff. I have a smell, taste, feeling, and colors. But I still don't have the exact thing I need to know.

"But a wedding?" I ask. "Do you see a *wedding*?"

"I see a large gathering." Mystic Shonda's voice is wavy. Hypnotizing. "I'm not sure what it is. But beware a dark storm."

"Oh good!" I say. "I mean, bad? What kind of storm?"

"It's murky. Just like your feelings. Layered. Bittersweet, joyful. I don't know how immediate any of this is, but oh . . . what a journey you have!"

Ugh, ugh, ugh, ugh, ugh.

"And nothing can stop that gathering?" I ask.

"Everything can, dear. Divination suggests a potential future now, but it is not fixed. You have free will. Your future changes with you."

"Stella! Now!" Vivian grabs the phone and clicks it off.

I let out a surprised yelp. "Why did you do that?"

"Because our time was up!" Vivian says.

"I didn't get to say goodbye to Mystic Shonda. And what are you yelling my name for?"

"Mystic Shonda was bunk," Vivian says. "Mom just spent twenty dollars for her to talk about red stones. How is that helpful?"

But it was. Mystic Shonda gave us all the tools we need. "As long as we encounter everything she said, we know how the future ends: a dark storm over the large gathering. You add in a ghost and it seems like something or someone is going to stop the wedding from happening. We can check off each item as it happens. Then we know we're on the right track."

I grab a marker and construct a brainstorm web. I have a clear direction of where to go now. On one of the lines, I write *Psychic* and draw a stick out to each of her other premonitions. "So now we think of different kinds of fortune-telling that we can use to—"

"Sabotage?" Vivian asks.

"I was thinking 'make sure our parents have the best future for everyone else.'"

"Right. Through sabotage." Vivian stares at the board. "We can look at tea leaves? Do you know about those?"

"Not really." I add it to the board. "My mom used to have crystals in the house. And what are those cards with pictures on them?"

"Tarot. But those seem aggressive." Vivian scans our growing brainstorm web. "Let's keep it to fortunes. I don't want to cast spells or anything."

"Seriously?" I ask. "A breakup spell would save us a lot of time."

She ignores me. "I know a girl *super* into horoscopes. Anyone else?"

I don't offer up the 7-Eleven palm reader. Not yet. Zara saw too much of me too soon, and it's not like I know her anyway. I can call people in Washington but . . . how do I ask Talia for help breaking up a wedding when I haven't mentioned the engagement? She said she likes weird, but this is next-level *bizarre*. And beyond her, who do I have? Aunt Maggie? She's not the type to own a crystal ball.

"We have the internet," I say. "I'll start researching. We'll add ideas to the board as they come."

"Yeah. Okay." Vivian squints at me. I try not to fidget too much under her gaze, but it's not easy. Vivian's fierce. "I thought you were really, I don't know, breakable, when we met. Scared of the wind."

"And now?" I ask.

"Well, *Whitney*." She emphasizes my accidental fake identity. "You sure know how to handle a crisis. Our parents have no idea what's about to hit them."

Chapter 10

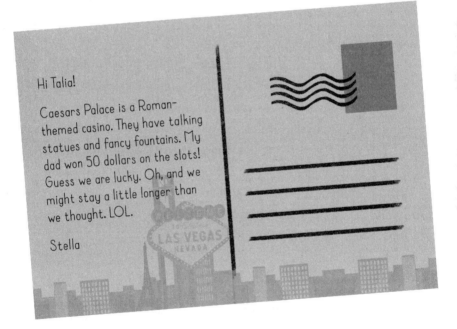

Hi Talia!

Caesars Palace is a Roman-themed casino. They have talking statues and fancy fountains. My dad won 50 dollars on the slots! Guess we are lucky. Oh, and we might stay a little longer than we thought. LOL.

Stella

Vivian has cheer camp that week, so we can't start Supernova Quest until the weekend. Meanwhile, Whitney posts the spreadsheet for our daily chores and home duties. I appreciate her bringing order in the home, but I don't want to be in this home. Or to mop this home's floors.

On Friday, I search through the piles in Vivian's room for my sandal. It isn't in my left corner, a small dwelling I've created in Vivian's domineering space. Having Vivian as a roommate is not the best living arrangement. What kind of person balls up her dirty socks and tosses them into the center of the room?

I have a blow-up mattress with mismatched bedding, a TV tray serving as my bedside table, and a small trash can. Part of me wants to hang a picture on the wall, something that says *Stella was here*. But that's something a person who is staying would do and *staying* is not the plan.

"Here we go!" I hold up my shoe, hidden under a stack of books. Vivian and I went to the library and checked out every book on crystals, dreams, astrology, hypnosis, palmistry, and metaphysics—whatever that is. "You and me, shoe. Let's go."

Oh. And I've also started talking to myself.

I grab my backpack, letter included, and run out to the car, where Whitney, Dad, and Ridge are waiting.

"Can you call the club and let them know we'll be five minutes late for the appointment?" Whitney asks Dad as she pulls out of the driveway.

Dad waves a hand. "Oh, I don't think five minutes will matter much."

Whitney glances at me in her rearview mirror. Five minutes matter to her *very* much.

Whitney has deemed Fridays "Wedding Planning Day." She doesn't want them to go alone because they're not the only ones getting married—it's all of us blending a family together. Even if three of us have no say in the blending.

 66

"Stella, I've been meaning to ask you what you're into?" Whitney asks.

"I don't understand the question," I say.

She juts her chin in Ridge's direction. "I found a gaming club for Ridge. Vivian has cheer. What are you going to *do* this summer?"

I'm guessing there isn't a Mystical Stop My Stepmom Camp. "I . . . I don't really do traditional activities. I like picking a topic and reading about it—usually something historical—but lately I'm . . . researching other interests."

"No sports? No music?" Whitney asks.

I hope Dad doesn't mention tennis or start on the whole if-you-stay-busy-maybe-you'll-do-better train he rode when my anxiety first started to get bad. Before he got me into therapy and understood that I didn't need to DO all these things to BE someone.

He finally answers. "Stella doesn't need to have an activity to have an identity, Whit. She studies history. Likes school. Keeps herself busy. No stress."

"Okay," Whitney says brightly. I don't think she means it though.

As a kid, my mom went to camp every summer for the whole summer. She promised she'd never do that to us. She didn't like preplanning things. Usually, she'd tell us to get in the car and she'd drive us somewhere without giving us a clue where we were going. I hated it then—hated not knowing what shoes to wear, how long I would be gone. But looking at it now . . . Mom never tried to make me into someone I'm not. That's saying something.

"Then maybe you should open me," my backpack says from

the car floor. Backpack has been quiet these last few days, only talking when I think about Mom.

"Soon," I whisper.

Whitney drives through the guard gate and up to the country club, an adobe building with crisp desert landscaping and a large veranda. Red mountains complete the striking backdrop. The tennis courts are right next to the building, and even from far away I can tell they're deluxe. One court has stadium seating. I'm tempted to sit in the shade and watch the team of ladies in matching pink snakeskin skirts.

"Stella and Ridge!" Whitney says. "You'll want to check out the bathrooms. They're so fancy. Showers, mouthwash, chocolates! I'm tempted to sneak in there for the full treatment."

Ridge and I follow behind. The floor is pink marble, the walls a dark green. The front lobby has a large library with a lit fireplace despite the hundred-degree heat. There are photos of hunting dogs and horses on the walls.

"This is . . . extravagant," Dad says.

Whitney waves at a short South Asian woman working the front desk. They squeal and comment on each other's hair before turning to Dad.

"And this . . . is my fiancé," Whitney says. "Wow. Can you believe I'm saying that *word* again? Micah, this is Jeeva. We did a hospitality internship together a gazillion years ago."

Jeeva winks at Whitney. "Well played, Whit."

Dad clears his throat, uncomfortable. "Hello, Jeeva. Are you giving us the grand tour?"

Jeeva leads us through the entryway, past a few smaller rooms with conference tables. A staircase winds downstairs—a group of men in polo shirts chatting below. There's a spacious restaurant with golf course views and waiters in black button-down shirts.

Jeeva stops on the large patio, overlooking the vividly green golf course. "That grassy spot over there is where the ceremony will be performed. How many guests are you anticipating?"

"Oh, not too many," Dad says at the same time Whitney replies, "One hundred fifty."

Dad turns to Whitney in a swirl of surprise. "One fifty? I don't have that many contacts on LinkedIn."

"Babe, my family is big. Cousins alone is thirty."

"One hundred fifty is totally manageable," Jeeva agrees. "Now what is the budget?"

"Maybe tell us your rates first," Dad says.

"Absolutely." Jeeva hands Dad an electronic tablet. "We like to create an experience that covers everything—less stress for the bride. The different packages and prices are featured there. And since it's a weekday in August, we can probably knock off ten percent."

"These prices are for . . . one day?" Dad asks.

"Honey, no worries." Whitney bumps his hip. "I've saved."

"I remember you using the word *casual*," Dad says. "It's our second wedding. None of this is casual."

"But it's our first wedding *to each other*." Whitney kisses his cheek.

I turn to say something to Ridge, but he's already abandoned us for the staircase, which apparently ends at the golf shop. Ridge is talented at sports, even though he doesn't do a lot of teams. The unspoken truth behind that is teams require rides to practices, and Dad is seldom home in time to get us places.

"I'm going to . . . explore for a bit," I say.

Dad and Whitney don't notice when I leave. I take this opportunity to follow Whitney's suggestion—check out the bathroom. She's right—this place is ridiculous. There's violin music playing in the grand space. The bathroom has a sitting area with a black leather couch and stiff chairs. Who sits around in a bathroom? I wander to the marble sinks, which include a jar of combs, razors, Q-tips, toothbrushes. There's mouthwash, deodorant, lotion, random perfumes, and a bowl of chocolate.

I spray one of the perfumes in case it smells like Mystic Shonda's tulips, but it's a heavy vanilla. I probably shouldn't search for the predictions—let them come to me. Otherwise I'll exhaust myself looking for tulips and limes around every corner.

I grab three Dove chocolates from the large bowl, unwrapping the first and balling up the tinfoil. Wait, don't these have little fortunes inside? I'm careful with the next chocolate.

Pamper yourself.

Sounds good, Dove chocolate.

Past the toilets is a small locker room. *Locker room* maybe isn't the right word, because this is nothing like the dank space in my middle school. The showers have multiple showerheads and soap dispensers built into the tiled wall.

Dad and Whitney could be another hour since they haven't even discussed details like how many people they are going to invite or how much money they are going to spend. Basically, all the details. I could sit in the lounge and read one of the coffee table books about hunting dogs. Or I could take Whitney's recommendation and give myself the *full* treatment.

My skin buzzes. I take a robe out of a locker, replacing it with my T-shirt and Vivian's hand-me-down corduroy skirt. There is one thing on the bathroom counter shouting at me—a razor.

I noticed Vivian's shiny legs the first time we met. Last night, she put on lotion in the bedroom—a long, luxurious process. I hid in the bathroom to examine my own leg hair—blond and fuzzy, but long. I'd almost used a razor right then, but I didn't own one and Vivian wouldn't want to share.

Now I take a razor out of the counter jar. No one has ever shown me how to use one of these. I've seen shaving commercials—the foamy calves divided into even lines as the razor rolls along the leg. The ritual seemed almost . . . poetic. So it has to be fate that I find myself in this elegant bathroom now with a whole bunch of razors and toiletries at my disposal. I'm almost thirteen—the time when the teenager things begin, right? If I start shaving now, I'll be an absolute pro when I get back to Washington. The Dippers will comment how Las Vegas matured me.

I get into the shower and turn on all three showerheads. The water coming from up high on the wall is like a beautiful flood. I scoot to the side so I can smooth on some shaving cream without washing it right off. One full breath. Calm my nerves. Calm my thoughts. Then . . .

I run the razor over my skin. I use the shaving cream as a guide—where I've shaved, where I haven't. The whole process is incredibly satisfying. Especially when I feel the contrast between the freshly shaved skin and the parts still covered in hair.

My first leg is a victory. On the second leg's third row of foam, the razor gouges my skin. Not a nick, two deep gashes. The blood pools instantly. I hurriedly rinse off the foamy soap and jump out of the shower. There, just below my knee, are two pebble-sized wounds. How could one little razor do this? The skin is whitish, but only for a moment before the blood rushes again.

I wrap myself in the robe and lunge for the fancy tissues. It doesn't matter how many times I try to stop it, the cuts keep bleeding. This is bad. I hope it's not *hospital* bad—could they even do stitches if I shaved off the skin? And how can I get Dad's attention to get help? He can't come into the ladies' bathroom! And Whitney will be so mad if I interrupt their Friday Wedding Planning. And the country club people might kick me out or try and sue me for using all their amenities when I'm not a member. I stole a shower and now the galaxy is punishing me.

It's difficult to calm my thoughts. If I can get the bleeding to stop for a few seconds, I can put on my clothes. But nothing will stop and this is bad and what should I—

Someone walks into the bathroom! I wrap the robe tighter and shrink against the wall.

"Stella?" Whitney calls. "You in here?"

I want to melt into a puddle of embarrassment. Embarrassment and this endless trickle of blood.

Whitney turns the corner and stops dead in her tracks when she sees me. The robe, wet hair, probably some panic in my eyes. She's holding a small glass of ice water.

"Shaving incident?" she asks. There is no surprise or scandal in her voice. Like it's totally normal for her fiancé's daughter to steal a shower in the middle of the day.

I fold my arms over my body. "Um, yeah."

She pours the water out of her cup and hands me the ice. "Put this on there. It'll constrict the blood vessels."

I do as she says. The bleeding slows enough that I can slip into a changing room and get dressed.

Whitney is reapplying lipstick when I return. She rummages

through her purse and hands me a small case of Band-Aids. "Vivian calls me Mary Poppins because I have everything in my purse."

"Thank you."

"Do you want me to put those on for you?"

"I got it."

I stick my leg up on the bench. We lean in close to examine the stinging wounds. Whitney fans the area, which actually . . . helps. I peel off the backs of the Band-Aids and get them adjusted. We both breathe a sigh of relief when I'm done.

Whitney makes eye contact with me. I brace myself for an I-told-you-so. Actually, she never did tell me so because it probably didn't occur to her to warn me about gouging my leg in a public shower so maybe more of a what's-wrong-with-you?

It never happens. She gives my shoulder a quick squeeze. "Meet us in the lobby whenever you're done, okay?"

When she's gone, I use one of the free combs to untangle my wet hair. My brain jumbles with thoughts and my heart pumps with feelings.

I have never shaved my legs because it didn't occur to my dad to tell me about it. These things will occur to him less and less now that he's distracted by Whitney and her one hundred fifty wedding guests. Whitney is . . . fine. Okay, she's better than fine. Sweet. Thoughtful. But she shouldn't be here for this moment. It's like the sunscreen at the pool—none of this is her job.

The person who should be teaching me to shave vanished.

"Are you ready now?" my backpack asks. It comes out muffled from inside the locker.

Sometimes my anxiety gets better from waiting, sometimes

it's worse. Right now it feels like I'll explode if I don't get this over with this very second. I'm alone, bandaged, and have plenty of chocolates to munch on while I read.

I tear open the purple envelope. The card inside is thick, cream, engraved.

Mom filled the card top to bottom. Her handwriting slopes up across the sheet.

Stella,

Yes, I'm alive! Huh, that's something I used to write in my teen journal when I hadn't written in a while. Still here! But maybe you didn't know I'm fine, maybe you're worried. So I want to make some things clear.

I'm in a treatment center. Your grandparents gave me another chance in a lovely facility in Coeur d'Alene. Seventy-six days sober. That may not sound big to you, but it's a lifetime for me. I eat oatmeal every morning. I feel things again, see things again. It's hard and wonderful.

Part of my work here includes making amends with the people I've wronged. This means you. I peaced out on you. As a mom, as a person. I became pain. Pills and pain. You didn't deserve it. You deserve homemade cookies and whispered secrets and balance. You should be focused on crushes and schoolwork and hobbies.

I messed up. I am sorry. I love you. I am sorry.

I sent a letter to Ridge too. Maybe don't compare notes, kids, because I said a lot of the same stuff. But here's what is different—you were older. You took on responsibilities you shouldn't have. You took on worry you shouldn't have. I wish I could wave *a wand and take that all away. But I can't. I live with that every day. I also miss you every day. Every minute.*

I have a cell phone again. When you are ready, I would love to talk. Here's my number: 206-555-9329

Mom

When Vivian and I thumbed through our library books, we read about something called graphology—the study of handwriting. Handwriting style can tell you a lot about the person's personality or skills. I trace my finger across the letters, wondering what I could learn about my mom besides all the words she just said. Heavy words.

I should have waited until I was home to read this, although home is not an option. My closet, my blanket, my security. I should at least have Pog. Maybe Dad? My shoulders are rocks and my chest is bricks. I fumble out of the bathroom, into the grandiose lobby. I collapse into the leather armchair and breathe, cry, breathe.

Dad and Whitney are there within minutes. Whitney waves but keeps a respectful distance. Dad doesn't ask why my hair or eyes are wet. He scoops me up into a hug, right in his lap. I curl into him and don't worry about the lobby full of people staring at us.

Dad knows how to be there without demanding any more.

I want to talk to him about shaving and other growing-up things we still haven't addressed. About the phone call with the psychic. About Mom's letter. The divorce.

But I stay quiet.

I don't know why.

75

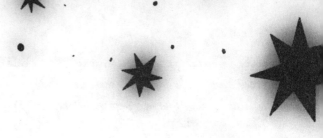

Chapter 11

Vivian's friend from her dance studio is our expert astrologer. How does Vivian have enough friends that she can separate them into different groups? When we were brainstorming people (okay, Vivian was brainstorming. I don't know anyone), she kept saying she could ask "my eighth-grade lab partner," or "this Braden kid from theater," like people are *that* easy to talk to. Or fine dropping everything to help random girls break up their parents.

Then again, Vivian is a Scorpio. She said it's a persuasive sign.

Whitney's so tickled Vivian and I want to "spend time together as future siblings" that she drops us off with limited questions. Gemma lives in a much nicer neighborhood than Vivian. It might be the nicest neighborhood I've ever seen. We have to wait at a guard gate to drive in. The sprawling houses are surrounded by towering palm trees and blindingly green lawns and tons of sprinklers to keep them that way.

I wear my cut-off shorts and a striped blue tank top. My leg is re-bandaged and smooth. I stuff my backpack with horoscope magazines. Ever since I opened Mom's letter, the backpack stopped talking to me. So that's a win.

"Just sit there, 'kay?" Vivian says as she rings the doorbell, which echoes across the huge home. We wait at the wide, metal door.

"Sit where?" I ask.

"Wherever Gemma takes us." Vivian smooths out her hair. "She's a junior and megapopular. She can be a *connection*, okay? And don't, like, kiss up to her."

I stand up straighter, trying my best to look old, or at least old*er*. Literally overnight, I skipped right over Talia's middle school birthday party into hanging with high schoolers. Which is great for my anxiety.

I half expect a butler to open the front door, but instead it's a teen boy.

"What do you want?" He's Black and maybe my age. He has braces and a scab on his chin. And he's . . . sorta cute. Don't tell.

Vivian smiles. "We are here for—"

"Gemma!" he shouts, basically in our faces. "Your zodiac zombies are here."

Gemma rushes down the spiraling stairs. Her hair is a mass of springy curls that fade from deep brown to white gold. Her makeup is an array of honeys and yellows—bright and bold against her dark skin. "Oh my gosh, Cooper. Why do you always have to be such a punk?"

Cooper grabs my shoulder and looks me straight in the eye. "This one is young. I can still save her. Listen to me, okay? Astrology is not science. Be free."

"Leave." Gemma shoves him. He stumbles to the side. Gemma grabs Vivian's hand and pulls her up the winding stairs. I follow, but glance back at Cooper. He gives me a wink before sauntering into the modern living room.

I hurry to catch up with Vivian. I realize I've been holding my breath since Cooper opened the front door. I exhale. My shoulder is warm.

"Sorry. My brother is *such* a Taurus." Gemma peers past Vivian to me. "Oh, is this your sis—"

"We aren't related," Vivian says. "That's Stella North."

Geez. We *aren't* related. So I don't care if she says we're not related. But maybe she could say it in a nicer way.

Gemma's bedroom has a full studio in the back corner. There's a vanity with two swivel chairs and three ring lights. A microphone is connected to a backlit mirror, and there's multiple webcams set up at different angles. The desk is stacked with a whirlwind of makeup jars and palettes, like a scientist's lab, except for your face. The midnight-blue wall behind the setup is decorated with star charts and zodiac signs, the room heavy with incense.

Gemma is clearly not casual about horoscopes. Or makeup. Or possibly anything.

"All right." Gemma rubs her hands together. "Give me the scoop."

"You aren't filming yet, are you?" Vivian asks.

Gemma laughs. "Your secrets are safe with me, Scorpio. But I need to know what you're both searching for."

Vivian chews on her gum like she's chewing over what to say. Finally, she gives a curt nod, like she's giving herself permission to trust Gemma. Then she goes full throttle, filling

Gemma in on our parents' quick romance, Whitney's summer spreadsheet, the wedding.

"So we need to break them up," Vivian ends simply. "I don't want to move to Washington. Stella doesn't want to move here. And we don't want to live together either way."

"Because I'm so horrible to be around," I say under my breath.

"What's that?" Vivian asks.

"Nothing."

Gemma looks back and forth between the two of us. Her eyelashes are so long—can she do that to mine? She seems to decide something, then grabs my hand. "You first."

"First what?" I ask.

Gemma busies herself selecting brushes and various makeup colors. "I match your makeup to your star chart. I mean, you can read horoscopes all day long, but I much prefer to see it painted across your face. What's your sun sign?"

"I'm . . . I'm a Virgo. What's a sun sign?"

"Ohhhh, Virgo!" Gemma rummages through her palettes. "Earth sign. Nature connection. Flowers . . . yes, blooms! Digging it."

"You are such an artist," Vivian coos.

I shoot her a look. Who is kissing up now?

"So a sun sign is the zodiac sign you know already, based on your birthday," Gemma says. "But if you know your birth time, we can figure out your ascendant and moon. Sometimes the ascendant feels more accurate."

"Love it." Vivian writes out a text on her phone. "I'll ask my mom when I was born."

"I'll . . . ask my dad," I add. Although I doubt he knows my birth time off the top of his head. His memory is so-so to begin with, but especially when he's working on something big. Like a work project. Or a wedding.

Gemma mixes some different beige foundations together and dips a sponge into her concoction. "Yeah, it's good to know your sun sign when you want to see how you match up with someone. But you also have to get their birth time to get the full moon/ascendant picture. Then again, I was dating this girl who totally thought I was a stalker when I asked what time she was born. She's a Taurus—they're skeptical about astrology to begin with. Although I also dated this guy, Aquarius, who got so into astrology that he wouldn't even talk to me if he thought our daily horoscopes didn't match up so . . . Oh, I almost forgot!"

Gemma wheels back her chair and starts flipping on switches. The space floods with light. I glance at my reflection. My face is hyper-defined, flaws and all. There's random eyebrow hairs and black pores, but also my eyes are bright and my skin already glows. "Okay, the camera is on, but don't worry about looking at the lens. I'll talk to you and to the camera and then edit it all together later."

"You're . . . you're filming me? Now?" I sit up straighter. This was not part of the deal. "Um, but we can't post this. We can't have Dad and Whitney know what we're doing?"

"Does your dad watch a lot of horoscope makeup tutorials?" Gemma asks.

Vivian snorts. I don't know why she's okay with documenting this, especially since she doesn't seem to want anything connecting us.

"You're not worried about this backfiring?" I ask.

"Gemma knows how to share this stuff without giving any

of the details of our parents," Vivian says. "Plus, she gives us a free makeover and horoscope info when she films us for her channel. Sounds like a fair trade."

"And, like, don't worry about my followers." Gemma beams. "They're tuning in for me." She turns to the camera and starts in on her spiel. "Hey, my little starbursts! Today I have my darling friend Stella. Stella is a Virgo, which is so perfect. If you're new, I'm a Leo—you know you love me! My horoscope said to share a connection with a Virgo today, so here we are. Stella has white skin with rosy undertones, total opposite of me, but I'm a pro with all skin colors. I'm going heavy on pinks and purples. Plus, Virgo's flower is the posy, which heals heartache. I'm so into this palette today. Earth signs, take note!"

Gemma spreads foundations across my face. She's going to speed up a bunch of the actual makeup application part, so we don't need to talk for a while.

"My mom texted me back!" Vivian pipes in. "I was born at 3:12 in the afternoon."

"Great, I'll punch that into my natal chart creator." Gemma steps back and stares at my face. "Thicker liner, I think."

My mind wanders as Gemma continues to layer powders and creams. It's been so much fun researching the history of horoscopes in the last few days. Astrology exists in multiple cultures and has been around forever—tracing all the way back to Babylon. It spread from there—to China, the Mayans, and Europe. Most of the astrology we look up on apps or in magazines started in the Hellenistic period—Egypt, Greece, then Rome. Twelve houses are divided into the year and change once a month. It's different from Chinese astrology, which has twelve animals, one for each year.

There are so many interesting nuggets I want to tell Gemma, but I don't think I should move my mouth too much. So I pick one of my favorite facts. "Did you know the first Roman emperor, Augustus Caesar, put the Capricorn sea goat on Roman coins? He said his horoscope foretold that he'd be a ruler of the world."

"Here she goes with Caesar again," Vivian says. "You read a book about Rome. We get it."

Gemma pauses, the brush inches from my face. "That's fascinating! I love Hellenistic history. I'm reading this book about the mathematics of astrology."

"Isn't it miraculous that ancient astrologers were able to organize their data into the houses so precisely?" I ask.

"Girl, yes!" Gemma says. "I have a total brain crush on Claudius Ptolemy. I could talk about his life all day."

"Um, that's okay!" Vivian interjects. "We know you're busy. We just need the zodiac info on our parents."

"Vivian's mom," I say. "My dad."

"Yep. Let me finish here." Gemma shakes her lion's mane and smiles at the camera. "Isn't Stella gorgeous? Here's how I channeled Virgo energy. You'll see I didn't smudge the lines too much because Virgos are exact. They are detail-oriented, analytical. And I used cool colors because Virgos are so aware — they don't like letting people down. They can be perfectionists and self-critical. Anxious. But they are gentle, kind. Their style is elegant and classic. That's why I didn't go too bananas on the shadow."

My stomach warms at these descriptions of me. She's totally right about the way my brain works. I can be a perfectionist and I get worried when things don't go according to plan. But I do like to connect with others. I hope I'm nice? And the word *elegant* makes me glow.

"Okay, now we're doing the family painting. I'm going to ask Stella a few questions about her family. Let's do your dad first. What's his sign?"

"Pisces." I'm relieved I came prepared.

"Interesting dynamic." Gemma gently pulls on my arm. She's moved from makeup to face paints now. She dips her brush into silver paint and draws a small fish on my right forearm. "You might get embarrassed by him because he's so changeable. Or he's always trying to invent something new, live in a different reality when you like certainty and knowing exactly what will happen."

"Totally," I say.

She fills in the fish with some purple and blue. "He's also caring and understands you. Sometimes he might get caught in an idea and go wild with it, or be inconsistent, but it's always clear he loves you. And tries to protect you. Pisces/Virgo."

She explained my dad so accurately and they never even met. I want to ask her a million more things. Like what is Talia's sign and are we compatible as friends?

"What about your mom?" Gemma asks.

"My parents are divorced," I say.

"Yeah, she's still your mom though, right?"

Technically? But not in practice for the last few years. Which is NOT something I want to broadcast on a makeup tutorial. I try to keep my face neutral, but I already feel control slipping away. "She's April. Early April."

"Aries," she says. "The ram."

She draws round, circular horns and a small brown face. It's more aggressive than the fish. I brace myself for details.

"They're extra spontaneous," she says. "Like they act and then they think. So they don't think about the future. Which is the opposite of you—you probably have a five-year plan and worry all the time. And she's self-focused, while Virgos are one of the most giving signs. I'm trying to think how you connect. Um . . . her energy and action can be a good motivator for you? Although they're also a fire sign so she can be quick to anger. Wow, and a Pisces with an Aries? That was probably a hot mess—whoops, sorry. Too honest." She finishes her ram with an orange flourish. "Anyway, does any of this sound true to your experience?"

"I, uh . . ." My eyes sting with tears. I swallow. Nope, nope, nope. This needs to go in a box. This does not need to spill out on my perfectly painted face. "Sort of."

"What about my mom?" Vivian asks. "Capricorn."

"I'm getting there." Gemma appraises me. She seems to notice the tears or maybe some fear in my eyes, because she holds an electronic fan up to my face. "Do you want to do the reveal first or take a short break?"

"Yeah. Can I . . . Let's do Whitney," I say. "Then we'll reveal."

"Got it," she says. "Take some deep breaths, okay? You just got tense."

I do, slowly. Breathe, breathe, breathe. Try to loosen all my muscles in my face, my neck, my hands. I refocus on our goals. It's good to know what I am. It's good to recognize how I think. It doesn't matter so much how I relate to my parents, but maybe it will in the future.

The whole reason we are here is to figure out Dad and

Whitney's compatibility. The makeup and the horoscopes are frosting on the cake.

Gemma turns her chair around so she's facing Vivian. "We'll go over this more when I do your makeup. But I'll tell you this much off the record: You are trying to take down a Capricorn. They're ambitious, determined. Relentless. And Capricorn with a Pisces? They might seem opposite, but they're actually missing pieces of each other's puzzle. They both like strong, grounded relationships and will do whatever it takes to make it work."

"Like force us to move out of state?" I ask.

"Uh, yeah." Gemma nods gravely. "I don't know what to tell you if you're trying to break them up. I guess . . . Pisces are emotional and caring. They like to go with the flow. Capricorns are practical, less emotional. They like to take control. So if a Pisces gets wounded, or a Capricorn feels like their partner can't step up, then . . . maybe a divide can start. Or Pisces might have a hard time staying on a path while Capricorns are planners."

"That's good." Vivian writes notes on her phone. "We can work with that."

"Maybe their moons clash?" Gemma dusts off one of her brushes. "Or their ascendant. But from what you've told me so far—it's a sweet match. I don't think you should mess with fate."

"They've dated for a month," Vivian says. "One month does not equal fate."

"But they've known each other for twenty years," I add. "They were college sweethearts."

"Reunited years later? Second Chance Love? Sorry, but I'm *obsessed* with that trope." Gemma pats my arm. "Can we finish filming now?"

She eases me back into the chair. She runs a brush through my hair, tucks in my shirt, makes me the best version of myself. Which I appreciate. I love attention to detail.

"You ready for the grand reveal?" Gemma asks.

"Yes. I can look now."

Gemma swivels me around. I almost cry again, this time in happy shock. My eyes are bright and magical, with a swirl of purple and pink topped off with long, thick lashes. The silver stars across my cheeks look like mystical freckles. My lips are shiny and pink. I resist the urge to blow a kiss.

"Stella, you're an earth goddess." Gemma puts her face next to mine in the mirror. "Now think about how to *own your light*."

Chapter 12

Stella!

I loved your postcard! I'm sending you a picture of the Space Needle because it's a symbol of Seattle, although I've only been there one time. I heard there is a hotel like this in Las Vegas. Have you been there? Did it feel like home? When ARE you coming home, btw? That's so random you went there for vacation and stayed longer!

We went to the pool last week and the new lifeguard is sooooo cute!

Send more postcards!

Talia

I spend the next few days going down an absolute wormhole on divination. (The practice of seeking knowledge of the future. Perfect!) It's so overwhelming that I finally stick my finger in a book and choose a random method, which lands me on "tas-seography," the practice of reading tea leaves. It seems easy enough—I drink tea with a question in mind, then look at the leftover leaves in my cup. I mean, I've never *made* tea, or drank it, but it seems cheaper than calling the psychic again.

I bang through the kitchen, searching for loose leaf tea. Whitney has herbal tea bags, which isn't great because I guess the leaves inside the bags are cut too small to "read." There's not a simple way to ask Whitney for the tea I need. Does 7-Eleven sell tea?

"What are you looking for?" Dad asks. He's in a dress shirt and tie with basketball shorts and droopy socks, his virtual business meeting attire. I didn't bother to look at Whitney's schedule to see who was in charge today. Vivian's at her dad's house and Dad leaves Ridge and me alone if we seem busy.

"Tea," I say. "Er, loose leaf?"

He chuckles. "How on earth do you know about loose leaf tea and why in the world do you want it?"

"I, uh, was reading a magazine article? About . . . the health benefits? And the flavor. It's better . . . flavor."

Dad reaches behind me and pulls down a copper canister. "Whitney likes English breakfast with milk and sugar. But it's strong stuff—I don't know if you're old enough for this much caffeine."

"Dad, I'm almost thirteen. Besides, you know Ridge drinks three Mountain Dews a day back home."

"What?" he asks. "When?"

"When you aren't looking." I reach for the canister and give his hand a little pat. "I'll give it a try. Unless you want to take me to Starbucks?"

"See if you like it." Dad checks his watch. "I've got another call in ten minutes. We'll do Starbucks another time."

"Deal."

"Stella Blue?"

I open the canister and sniff the tea. The scent is cozy and crisp, sorta flowery. "Yeah?"

"I know this is all hard. Thank you for trying."

Dad's misty-eyed, which I do not need. Emotions get in the way of goals. "Don't you have a meeting?"

I wait until he's back in his office to pull out the instructions I printed this morning. There's info on reading tea leaves—what kind work, the cup to use, how to drink it, everything. The main thing I need to do as the querent, or the person getting their leaves read, is to think about a specific question. I already got an answer about the wedding from Mystic Shonda. Should I ask something else? Think about a breakup strategy and start chugging to see if it will work?

I have the tea poured and I'm about to take my first sip when my phone rings. I would take it as some sign, but it's Aunt Maggie. She's called me three times this week and I keep sending it to voice mail.

"Hey, Aunt Maggie," I say.

"Stella!" Aunt Maggie sounds breathless and she's only one word into the conversation. "How's it . . . How's Las Vegas?"

"Hot." I keep my voice flat. "I read Mom's letter."

"Oh?" Aunt Maggie asks. "Do you want to talk about it?"

"You know I have anxiety," I say. Nothing else. Just that.

"I do, sweetie," Aunt Maggie says. "Pog helps. We all try to help."

"The letter did not help," I say. "Finding it in my backpack while I'm on a flight to a new town? Not cool, Aunt Maggie."

"Look, your mom surprised me too. I went back and forth forever how to handle it. I've settled on telling your dad about it, but I wanted to talk to you first. I've called you a few times?"

"I opened it a few days ago," I say, barreling ahead. I don't know why Aunt Maggie is talking about herself right now. "I left it in my backpack for a week but my backpack kept talking to me so I ripped off the Band-Aid. Or I guess ripped open the envelope. And I put on a Band-Aid. She left her number."

"How do you feel about it?"

I've sat in a lot of rooms with adults asking me how I feel about things. Therapists and parents and school counselors and teachers. Sometimes they ask me questions that are obviously steering me in a certain direction. Do I feel sad or am I scared or worried? Which is all so duh. Why do feelings matter so much anyway? What about what I *think*? It's a whole lot easier to control thinking anyway. A thought pops into my brain and I can either keep thinking it or let it go.

But a feeling? Those are gut punches, slaps, stabs. Sometimes they're warm or hopeful, but I rarely trust those. My body doesn't talk with me before it goes in whatever direction it wants. Like how my stomach has been twisted for weeks now, and the only time it untwists is when I start thinking. Plotting. Planning. *Doing*.

"Did she write you a letter too?" I ask.

"No," Aunt Maggie says. "She called me."

"What was that like?"

"Well, she's moving in with me tomorrow. She went to rehab again, totally without telling me this time. She's clean."

"Wow," I say. This is a big step into un-vanishing. First Mom had a return address on a letter she mailed to me. Then she sent her phone number. Now she'll breathe the same air as Aunt Maggie every single day. "How do *you* feel about that?"

"She sounds good." Aunt Maggie laughs. "More like herself. I'm hoping when I see her . . . I'd like to have my sister back in my life."

Now there's a thought I hadn't let form inside me. That my mom could someday un-vanish. "Cool."

"Look, I'm not calling to tell you what to do."

"Mom is an Aries," I say.

"Um . . . what?" Aunt Maggie asks. "Her birthday is April twelfth. I don't know what that makes her."

"She is." I take a sip of the tea. It's bitter, but I like that. Like it's pain with a reward. I think about how everything Gemma said about my parents' zodiac signs made sense. Aries and Pisces. Not a great match. Not as relevant as the Pisces and Capricorn match—our real mission. My mom and dad weren't going to get back together. So what does it matter where she's living. Dealing with Mom isn't going to get me back to Washington.

I take another sip of tea. Some leaves get in my teeth, but I swallow them down. "Aries are impulsive."

"That's true," Aunt Maggie says. "She's pushy too. I will hold her off if you want, but she's going to want to talk to you soon."

"It's just . . . we're staying here all summer," I say. "Dad and Whitney are getting married in August. Then they're going to decide where we'll live. Whitney's a Capricorn—did you know that?"

"Wait, they're getting married *this* summer?" Aunt Maggie asks. "You can't stay in Vegas for good!"

"Oh, I agree." I take a long sip of my tea, thinking about Aunt Maggie and Mom, Whitney and Dad. "But don't worry. There are forces in motion."

"Forces in moti—Look. I just need to talk to your dad. He can't take you out of state long-term. I don't think that's legal."

It never occurred to me to include Aunt Maggie in this madness, but her reaction is probably good for my case? Because we haven't considered the divorce rules. I have no idea what my parents' divorce rules are. "You should call him."

"I will." She pauses. "I'd really like to come see you. Especially if you're staying so long. I'll have to check, but I can probably work remotely. Maybe in two or three weeks?"

Why not? Vivian and I might have already broken up our parents by then. "Sounds fun. I have to go now. I need to focus on my tea."

"On your TV?" she asks, but I've already hung up.

I try to cleanse my mind of my mom moving in with Aunt Maggie so I can focus on the tea task at hand. But when I look down at my teacup, I realize I drank almost all of the liquid. I'll need to start over now.

I look at the instructions again: First the querent asks a question.

Well, I actually considered a question the whole time I was sipping the tea. I've been asking myself this same question since I opened the letter—since I got the letter.

Will everything be okay with my parents?

Question ready, I hold the teacup in my left hand. I swirl the last bit of water around three times, leaves floating or shifting on the sides of the cup. Then I flip the cup over on top of the saucer. The rest of the liquid drains out on the sides. I wait a minute or so, then rotate the cup until the handle faces me. I turn the cup back over and look inside.

There are leaves clumped together, mostly on the bottom with one glob closer to the rim. I stare at this glob first, trying to find an image in the murky leaves. The leaves curve into a semicircle. A sliver. Sorta like a crescent moon. Is a moon something I can look up?

There's a long list of possible images online. Next to the moon is the prediction: A change of plans. If the tea leaves are on the top of the cup, those things will happen soon. If they're toward the bottom, it's further in the future.

Well, duh. I moved here. Mom's moving in with Aunt Maggie. She reached out. I didn't plan for any of this. I mean, if we're looking back, we didn't plan for Mom's addiction either. Our whole existence is different than what we thought it was going to be.

The only other recognizable grouping is a square with a bit of a point on top, like a roof. It's a . . . house, I guess? I'll call it a house.

Which makes me super nervous. Does it mean I'll live in a house with Mom? Get a new house with Dad? I don't know what option I want. Definitely not another change of plans. I'm over change.

I scroll down and there's the info on house.

Safety and security.

Which is . . . all I've ever wanted.

I take a picture of the tea leaves. It won't mean anything to anyone besides me.

But right there, in this cup, is my hopeful future.

Chapter 13

Next Monday, I'm in the kitchen, helping Whitney pack a cooler with snacks, when the doorbell rings. Whitney freezes. Like literally does not move. Ridge is playing *Cosmo Kingdom*. We look at each other, neither wanting to get the door because it's not for us anyway. Dad whistles down the hallway as he passes all three of us.

"Did you not hear that?" Dad asks.

Whitney's face contorts into a strange horror. "Micah, don't—"

Dad swings open the door. A Latinx man in a fitted T-shirt that shows lots of muscles—I mean LOTS of muscles—steps into the doorway and grins at Dad.

"I'm glad I caught you guys," he says. "Heya, Whitney."

Whitney unfreezes real fast, covering the room in a few heated strides.

"Travis. You didn't need to come in. Vivian will be out in a second."

Travis holds out his hand, which is noticeably bigger than Dad's. "I wanted to meet the man of the hour. Or the summer, whatever. How's it going, Micah? Travis Marin. Vivian's dad."

Dad pumps Travis's hand, or maybe Travis is pumping his. It would be hard to hold back all that muscle strength.

"Thanks so much for saying hi," Dad says. "That's really cool of you."

"I'm always cool, right, Whit?"

Pog storms into the room and gives a low growl. I can't remember the last time I've heard him growl. Travis holds up his hands in surrender. "This your guard dog?"

"Emotional support," I say, although he was looking at Whitney.

Travis appraises me. "Okay. And you're the other kids."

I scoop up Pog. He's stopped growling, but his buggy eyes roll up at me as if to say, *So who is this dude?*

Pog is the smartest dog.

"Yep, that's our names." Ridge goes back to his game. "The Other Kids."

Travis lets out a laugh. "This one I like."

Vivian rushes out of the hallway wearing Whitney's same look of horror. "Dad, what happened to the honk and seat belt rule?"

"Relax, V," Travis says. "Micah's thanked me for doing an introduction."

"Okay." Vivian pushes him toward the door. "Now that we're all friends, let's go."

Travis pauses in the doorway, surveying the space. "You painted the living room gray. Huh. Interesting pick."

This time, Pog's bark is pure bite. The *smartest* dog.

"See you in a few days, Mom." Vivian gives Whitney a look before she closes the door. I think it's apologetic? But what would she be apologizing for? It's not her fault her parents aren't together anymore. Just like it's not our fault that our parents are together now.

"Well, that was a fun surprise," Whitney says. "Pog. You're a good dog."

Dad pulls her into a hug and kisses the top of her forehead. They stay like this for a few long minutes. Ridge searches the cupboards for chips while I stare at their moment.

"I know you get tense seeing him, but it could've been worse," Dad says. "I met your ex. We overcame a milestone."

"Thank you." Whitney leans her head on his shoulder.

"When's his birthday?" I ask.

"Who, Travis?" she asks. "Um . . . June. June seventh. Why?"

"Gemini." I nod.

I don't completely know what that means yet, but I'm excited I could match someone's sign to their birthday. I wonder if Geminis and Capricorns are good at agreeing on things like paint colors, because it seemed important to Travis to point that out.

"I'm so glad you're here with me," Whitney says, stretching out this not-really-meaningful moment with Dad. "I love you so much."

"Now Whitney can meet Mom." Ridge doesn't take his head out of the pantry. "She said whenever you're ready to give her a call."

"You . . . you talked to Mom?" I ask.

"Yeah, weeks ago," Ridge says. "She sent me a letter with her phone number and I called her right away. We send each other funny memes."

Whitney's smile is pure plastic. We haven't talked much, if

96

at all, about my mom yet. Mom is still vanished in Vegas. "Your mom reached out! That's so neat!"

"Sounds like we've got some big things to talk about tonight." Dad does not sound quite so surprised. Maybe Aunt Maggie called him already. And maybe . . . he hasn't told Whitney about it yet? "It's already eleven. If we don't leave now, the lines will be long."

I take Pog to his kennel in the laundry room. Part of me wants to interrogate Ridge about his whole correspondence with Mom. Ask what his letter said, what they talked about, if she's mentioned me. All of that. But even mentioning Mom is an adjustment for me.

Then I think about the differences between my brother and me. He's spoken to Mom. I haven't. Is that difference impacting our separate fates?

I know one person who could answer that.

"Before we go to the water park, can we stop at 7-Eleven?" I ask.

✳ ✳ ✳

Dad and Whitney stay in the car while Ridge and I run inside.

"I just need to talk to this clerk," I tell Ridge simply. I've decided not to tell him about Supernova Quest. He might try to give me the Both Sides talk, or have sympathy for Dad, or tell Mom what I'm trying to do since apparently they're chatting now.

"You know the 7-Eleven clerk?" he asks.

I open the door, enjoying the cool hit of air. "She's sorta my only friend in Vegas."

Zara is not at the counter. There's a man with a beard and a leather vest. His name tag says DWAYNE. "Where's your parents?"

"In the car," Ridge says.

"I'm watching you," Dwayne growls.

"Dwayne?" Ridge whispers as we walk down the candy aisle. "Your only friend in Vegas is *Dwayne?*"

"Oh my gosh, 7-Eleven has more than one employee."

I head to the back to get my Gatorade, grabbing a can of cheddar Pringles as I pass. A convenience store is more than convenient, it's familiar. I might not know what aisle I'll find SweeTARTS Ropes, but I know I *will* find them, somewhere in this contained space that reminds me of other contained spaces. It's not like outside, which is too dry and open.

Zara is back by the coffee machine, stacking Styrofoam cups. I overreact when I see her, waving furiously and running over.

"Hey there, Virgo!" Zara says.

"Oh, hi! Hey! Hello!" My voice is not normal. I am not normal. "I need to ask you something? Or somethings?" I grab Ridge by the shoulders and push him forward. "This is my brother. Ridge. This is Zara. She reads hands and stuff."

Ridge turns so he is standing square in front of me. His facial expression is clear. I've lost my mind. "That's great, sis."

"I was hoping . . ." I do not know what I was hoping. I guess I wanted to tell her everything that has happened with my family and everything I've learned and everything I think I should do in order to get everything I want. "I think you should tell Ridge stuff like what you told me."

Zara glances at Dwayne. He's reading a worn paperback. "Dwayne is my manager. I can't . . . get into it."

"Ridge is a Sagittarius," I add helpfully.

"A what-a-Taurus?" Ridge asks. "Can't we just buy some chips?"

"Tell me about him." I grab his left hand and pull it close to Zara. "He's my brother. Does he have the same family stuff as me?"

Zara rubs her lips. "Okay. Two minutes. I can't believe I'm giving another freebie."

"I can put my chips back and give you my change?" I offer.

"Next time you're in here, bring me a real gift, 'kay?" Zara says.

Ridge squirms under my grip. "Why are you acting so suspect?"

"Zara can read your palms. I'll tell you why it's important later."

Ridge rolls his eyes but stops fidgeting.

Zara lowers her face closer to his palm. "Huh."

"What? How?" I ask.

"You've got a cool future, kid." She smiles up at Ridge. "Long life. Lots of love. Focus on what matters and you'll be rewarded."

"Awesome. Thanks." Ridge drops his hand and heads up to the counter to buy his chips.

My mouth is wide open. This isn't what she does. This isn't why we're here. "That's it?"

"Basically." She shrugs. "Now I need to stock the coffee station."

"But . . . but." I stick my palm out in earnest. "We have the same mom. And she is . . . not like regular moms? And I found out he's talking to our mom even though I haven't seen her in a long time. If we have the same mom and we're stuck in Vegas together . . . shouldn't we both have chains or jagged lines or whatever you said is there?"

Zara lowers my hand and gives my arm a squeeze. "You can have ten people in the exact same situation and still have ten different ways to handle it. Ridge has smooth sailing written all over him. Besides, he's a Sagittarius. He'll charm his way in or out of whatever he needs."

"Okay." I try not to sound disappointed, but I am. I'm searching for answers and nothing is happening. "What are you, by the way? Your sign?"

"Libra. Obviously." Zara pulls a card from her pocket.

ZARA FLOWERS
TAROT READINGS * PALMISTRY * SPIRITUAL GUIDE

"Next time call me and schedule an actual reading. And, Virgo?"

"Uh-huh?" My voice comes out flat. Defeated.

"Fate is fate. You can't force the future."

Yeah. We'll see.

Chapter 14

Talia,

You said to send lots of postcards
so I will! Maybe one every other day.
This is a bighorn sheep. I guess it's
the state animal? Haha, I got this
postcard at 7-Eleven. I also met
this cool clerk named Zara there.
She has flower tattoos and can read
palms! My palm said ~~there will be~~
~~change~~ I will meet a cute boy. Maybe
I'll find a lifeguard too. ☺

Stella

The water park, Cowabunga Canyon, is a few minutes from
Whitney's house. Although I hate water slides (and roller
coasters and amusement park rides and the back seat of the

car sometimes), I love floating in an inner tube. The lazy river sounds promising.

Whitney's preplanning skills are coming in clutch. In addition to our cooler and 7-Eleven snacks, she's packed a beach bag with everything else we might need, from sunglasses to sunscreen. Dad could have had a week to prepare for today and most of this wouldn't have occurred to him. Whitney finds a cluster of beach chairs in the shade and goes about setting up our "home base" with towels and blankets.

"This is the coolest place I've ever been in my life," Ridge says.

Dad leans over and gives Whitney a kiss. "Thanks for taking time out of your day to spend time with us."

"With my family?" She beams. "Of course."

Dad lowers his voice and whispers something in Whitney's ear. She smacks his arm and laughs.

We've been here two weeks and I've yet to see them fight or disagree. Dad hangs on her every word. She seems so surprised and happy anytime he does something simple like take out the trash. They started watching a TV show together, sometimes at night, sometimes at seven in the morning, based on Whitney's work schedule. It's very normal.

Which is petrifying.

Dad and Ridge bolt for the Lone Ranger ride. I unpack Vivian's magazines. In fact, today I'm a Vivian twin. She lent me sunglasses and her old red swimsuit. It's a two-piece—stretched out in places that don't match my body—but it's still cooler than the old suit I packed (because I thought I was only coming for two weeks. Remember that?).

"The red suit." Whitney smiles. "I got that for Vivian from Target three years ago."

"Yeah, she lent it to me."

"What a compliment. Vivian's territorial with her stuff."

I pull down my hat so Whitney doesn't see the pink spread across my face. Vivian hasn't said anything especially nice to me yet, but at least I got a nice *gesture*.

"Hey, so the other day . . . at the country club . . . was that the first time you shaved your legs?"

I look down at the two pink scars on my leg. I haven't tried shaving since my rough start. "Sort of."

"I can give you the same tutorial I gave Vivi," Whitney says. "You might want to shave other areas too. And don't worry—I still nick myself sometimes. It's totally normal."

How did she know that totally normal is 100 percent the thing I want? And she waited until we were alone to bring up the moment. I would die if she said anything in front of Vivian. Imagine the eye roll she'd give me if she found out I randomly showered at a country club.

"I will let you know," I say.

"Great!" she says. "And not just shaving either. I'm here for *anything*. Puberty, goals. Your dad said you have some signals for when your anxiety is bad. Maybe we can come up with signals for moments when you need a female role model or—"

"I will let you know." I like Whitney better when she tries less. Like give me a Band-Aid. Check if I'm okay. Don't try to turn the whole thing into a Hallmark movie.

We sit in silence for a good ten minutes. Whitney reads a book and I thumb through a magazine.

"What are you reading?" Whitney asks. "Are you into astrology?"

I almost rip my page in surprise. Too bad Vivian's not around to change the subject. The chances of Whitney knowing about the Supernova Quest are slim, but I still don't want to clue her in. "Yeah, sort of."

"Read mine." Whitney lays out on her beach chair. She has on a cute yellow suit and a wide-brim hat.

I flip to the middle of the magazine. "Capricorn. Capricorn, your sign is in . . ."

"You know my birthday?" Whitney looks so genuinely flattered that I almost feel bad for the reason behind my knowledge. "So sweet. Yours is September sixth, right?"

She knows *my* birthday? We've known each other less than a month. How did she already collect and remember that info? "Uh-huh. I'm a Virgo."

"Ooh, I like Virgos. We're both organized. Analytical. Good energy."

"Yeah." This is a backfire. We are not supposed to be connecting. I need to think more diabolical here. "Do you want me to read your horoscope?"

"Absolutely!" Whitney cracks open a can of Diet Coke with painted fingernails. "Spill."

Whitney's horoscope is upbeat. It says, *Your relationship will see new horizons as you work together to build a foundation. You tend to put your romantic partner first, so make sure your needs are being met in the relationship too. Love will continue to bloom into something beautiful and bold!*

But this is not what I read to her. In fact, I don't read anything to her. Instead, I make up a horoscope right on the spot. "Your moon is in, uh, Saturn. Now is not the time to make big life changes. Now is a time for . . . uh . . . balance and harmony with yourself. Focus on your own path and . . . take charge. The more work you do, the better your career will be. Your heart should focus on abundance, not romance."

Whitney frowns. "Huh, sometimes they don't make any sense."

No sense? That abundance line was so good. And so obvious! "Really? It's better if you can sit with the words. Really try to listen, even when you don't want to."

"I *am* seeing a lot of opportunity at work right now," Whitney muses. "Although I'm not making big changes until the wedding in August. So I'm probably good."

I resist the urge to fling the magazine at her. There's an expression I learned in World History—Rome wasn't built in a day. I still have time to work on her.

Whitney rolls her head to the side and smiles. "Hey, Stella, I don't want to sound cheesy, but I want you to know I love your dad and I'm really happy that he's giving me these two cool bonus kids. I know you have a mom, and I'm never going to try to replace her, but I do want us to have a special relationship. It'll take time, but I see a lot of promise. I mean, we're both earth signs!"

I hate when an emotional moment happens and I have no warning. Or when someone tries to create an emotional moment that doesn't need to exist. These are all the things Whitney is supposed to say. I could google "how to be a step-mom" and her speech would pop up. I'm sure she means them too. Whitney may be a planner, but she doesn't seem calculating. Her authenticity is just . . . so much.

"Okay, thanks." I reach into the cooler and grab two ham sandwiches. "That's, uh . . . great."

"Toss me one."

I'm about to hand her a sandwich when I think about the thing Mystic Shonda said about a change of diet.

"Do you always eat ham and cheese sandwiches?" I ask.

"Um, I like them," Whitney says. "But sometimes I eat other sandwiches."

"And you always will? Like . . . you aren't changing your diet?"

"No, I try to avoid diet culture, but, honey, that's . . . not really a question you ask people."

My face reddens. Oh my gosh, I wasn't telling her to *go* on a diet. I want to figure out if Mystic Shonda's predictions have started yet. Guess I'm not asking her about health issues either. Or dark storms.

"Look." Whitney tears the crust off her sandwich. "I'm doing an engagement party next week. Well, it's a Fourth of July slash engagement party. Inviting some friends and family over so you guys can meet everyone. And to show off your cute dad."

"I didn't know people did engagement parties when they got engaged so fast after meeting?"

I swear I am not trying to be rude! Just honest. Sometimes those two things are the same. I should stop talking, but whatever I'm saying is also working because Whitney's smile looks like it might shatter.

"But we didn't *just* meet," she says. "We dated for two years in college. We almost got married back then. The groundwork is already laid."

"But that was like, what? Twenty years ago?" I ask. "Sometimes I see kids I knew in elementary school and I can't remember their name. Which was less than two years ago."

"We've kept tabs on each other with social media," she goes

on. "We stayed friends even after we married other people. So we aren't strangers. I know it might seem wild and spontaneous, but your dad and me . . . we're real, you know? I can't explain what it was like to see him again—it was like my heart floated right out of my body. I love him so much."

She is not getting it. "But if you don't always *feel* that way, that's okay too."

She reaches over and gives my arm a squeeze. I still don't like when she touches me. "I don't want you to worry about us breaking up, okay?"

"Okay. I will not worry about that." I stand up so fast that I'm instantly light-headed. "I'm going to watch Dad and Ridge on the slides. You're fine staying with our stuff?"

Whitney gives me an honest-to-goodness thumbs-up. "We'll have plenty of time to hang all summer!"

I did not factor her eagerness into this plan. Did not consider how sad she'll be when they break up. Dad will be too. At first. Then they'll see how bananas their whole idea was—mushing two families together in two different states! And then, way later, they'll find other people to date. Or they'll be one of those people "married to their job." That works great too, at least until I leave for college.

I wander over to the Dust Bowl and watch the ride spit out kid after kid. It's circular shaped—maybe this is part of Mystic Shonda's future? It's about time those predictions start happening. Except Whitney isn't on the slide, so this is nothing to do with her future. And Whitney's future is still the focus of our plan. Maybe I'm playing this smart—act like we're getting close so she trusts me. Then I can plant more horoscope seeds!

I know I sound shadier than a pool umbrella, but I have to

play tough to get what I want. There will be casualties, like Whitney's feelings, but better her than our whole family suffering.

I bite into my sandwich.

There are so many groups of friends at the water park. Swarms and swarms of friends. Instead of feeling wistful or anxious, I'm full of hope. I'm going to have this in Washington with Talia. I'll keep sending her postcards and texts. We'll grow this tight relationship the old-fashioned way—through letters! Then when I get back, I'll be super high up in her friend hierarchy. And we'll form a group of friends so big I won't even be able to remember everyone's name.

Dad spurts out of the slide. He waves at me as he trudges out of the water. He's so happy. Everyone is so happy.

"You having fun, kid?"

I paint on a smile that rivals the cheese in my sandwich. "So, so much."

Chapter 15

Dear Mom,

About a year ago, my school counselor gave me a worry journal. I could use it a few different ways. One was to write about gratitude. Something about focusing on the positive helps lessen the negative. That made me mad. Another was to write worry letters and then rip them up after. I didn't like the mess.

My favorite one was writing what she called "Lincoln Letters." I guess Abraham Lincoln used to write letters when he was angry or sad. Say everything he really wanted to say and then put that sealed letter in his desk drawer. When he died, they found a letter he'd written to a general, blaming him for losing a battle. Lincoln never sent it, but he still got to say it.

This one is my favorite. So I'm writing you a Lincoln Letter.

Do you remember the wax museum project we did in third grade? Everyone dressed like a famous person or historical figure. Some people were presidents and others were actors. I chose Jane Austen because we'd watched those movies together. *Emma* had the best costumes but *Persuasion* had the best ending. Anyway, you got so into it. Way more into it than any other school assignment. You found me a pink dress and a cream apron. I wore a green silk scarf with my hair in a bun. And you gave me your old college copy of *Emma* to carry around with me. We worked on my speech for a whole afternoon, making sure we included all the cool details about Jane Austen, like how she was independent and never got married but wrote all these stories. And at first the publisher put "A Lady" as an author because they weren't used to women being authors or even humans.

You were there, so maybe none of this is news to you. Or maybe you only remember some parts, so I'm giving you everything.

At the wax museum, we would stay frozen until someone came over and pushed a "button" to get us to speak (the button was actually a piece of paper but it was still cool). Obviously, a lot of people liked Jane Austen because a whole line formed in front of me. All the parents would nod and smile when I spoke. I'd get comments like, "I love the empire waist!" or "Those shoes are so perfect." I was more popular pretending to be Jane than I had been my whole life.

About halfway through I realized you hadn't come to my booth yet. I knew you were there because we drove together, although in the car you said your back was bothering you. Your back bothered you all of third grade and most of second, when the accident happened. I used to pray multiple times a day for your back. In fact, I got nervous when people said that rhyme "step on a crack and you'll break your mother's back!" because you DID break your back. Sometimes I closed my eyes and thought about how your face would pinch in pain, and how you'd try to cover it up with a smile, which never touched your eyes.

We rotated our breaks so we'd see everyone else's presentation. I really wanted to check out Albert Einstein, Bruce Lee, and Harriet Tub-man. I knew you would love the Einstein girl because she'd glued on bushy eyebrows. But instead I found you at Taylor Swift. You would not leave the kid alone. You kept pushing her button and asking questions. Stuff like, "Are you a nightmare dressed like a daydream?" or "Where's your red scarf?" When she tried to move, you shouted, "Shake it off."

You startled when I tapped you on the shoulder. Almost shrieked. It's not like I was running at you with an ax. Your eyes widened when you saw me (although your pupils were really, really small).

"Jane Austen? What are you doing here?"

"Mom, it's me." I squeezed your arm. Not hard, just to help you get back to me. "Stella."

"Jane, can you get me a Mr. Darcy?" Your eyes welled up with tears. "Or a Mr. Elton. He's cuter."

You burst into sobs, like shaking sobs. I tried to console you but people kept staring and whispering. Dad found us and rushed you out to the car. I don't know what happened when you were in the car because I had to go back to my station to give my speech. Except now the words were powder.

Then a few kids from my class—Vincent van Gogh and Serena Williams—came over to ask why you were crying and what happened. Someone asked if you were sick, and I nodded, and that's when people started to think you had cancer. Cancer seemed more explainable than what was actually wrong. I didn't have the words to explain your vanishing. More kids asked more questions, but I didn't answer because I wasn't supposed to be Stella right then. I was supposed to be Jane Austen and Jane Austen's mom didn't have a public meltdown in the middle of the school wax museum.

It wasn't my mom either, that person who'd interrogated Taylor Swift. That person had a disease that changed her whole personality. This was the first time I saw it. First time I realized how different you were from anyone else—too skinny, and crying when others were happy, or laughing when they weren't. I realized you were different from yourself, from the mom I'd known before the pills, before the accident. From then on, my life was split into before and after the wax museum. Regular Mom, Sick Mom.

Dad took you to Aunt Maggie's that night, who took you to rehab. He sat down with Ridge and me to explain that you were sick. You needed to go stay somewhere to get help. You couldn't overcome this addiction alone. He didn't tell us what the addiction was. Dad promised he would do everything he could for us. He's kept that promise, actually. He got us into therapy and found me Pog. Lately he's been on his own planet, but he's been through a lot. He'll orbit back to me soon.

You know all of the rest. The real low point happened in quarantine, which was hard for all of us, alone with our thoughts and ourselves. I know something big happened with you and Dad. I know you overdosed, which I luckily didn't see. You wouldn't go to rehab again. I don't know all the rest of the timeline—when the divorce started, when you got better or when you didn't. It's memory soup for me. But the wax museum? *That* I remember in crystal clear detail. The kids at school wouldn't let me forget it. My nickname after that was "Crazy Jane." The only thing that ended it was school going online for Covid. It's hard to whisper a mean taunt during a Zoom call. Then middle school gave me a fresh start. Sort of.

I guess I'm telling you all of this so you understand why it took me so long to open your letter. Why I'm not going to mail this letter or call your new cell phone. Why I started to shut down and worry and try to predict the next time my sky is going to fall. Why it took a while to figure out I was struggling.

Because there wasn't room for my problems. It's always you you you, all the time, even when you aren't here. It's like...even your ghost is more visible than me.

So please. Stop haunting me.

~Stella

Chapter 16

I change my clothes five times. Which is a lot, considering I only have about six outfits. But it's a big day for Supernova Quest—Gemma is taking Vivian and me to a crystal shop!

Gemma's mom picks us up. I thought Gemma's mom would have blue streaks in her hair, maybe extra piercings, at least funky clothes. But she is glossy. Designer. Natural.

Gemma is so lucky.

"Sorry, Stella. You need to get in the back with my brother." Gemma pulls up the seat and there is Cooper, playing a game on his phone.

"So give me a Crystals 101 before we go in," Vivian says. "Anything I should know beforehand."

Gemma starts talking about vibrations and frequencies, but I'm sorta distracted with Cooper being so close.

"What's up?" he asks as I fasten my seat belt.

"Nothing," I say casually like I sit in minivans with almost-eighth-grade boys all the time.

Cooper's playing *Tetris*, which is one of my favorite games. I can't help myself. I lean over to look at his score. "You're on level 108? Whoa."

He pauses the game. "What's your high score?"

"Fifty-two thousand," I say. "I like the timed round though."

"That's too much pressure." He smiles. He has blue rubber bands in his braces.

And then I'm talking without knowing what I'm going to say next, which is super rare for me. Super rare. "Did you know they've done studies that show *Tetris* is good for anxiety and trauma? Like if bad things happen in your life and you play *Tetris* right away, something works in your brain to help you deal with the hard thing. Everyone tells me I should tackle stuff head-on but I think it's better to breathe and zone out. Come back to it later. You know?"

"No." Cooper clicks back on his game. "I just like winning. But that's cool for you."

I sit back in the seat and focus on turning off all my awareness. It's not an easy process. When I go into a new situation, it's like every one of my senses shift at the speed of light. Like I can smell Cooper sitting by me, fresh eucalyptus, which is a way better smell than most teen boys. He breathes deep while he's playing too, like he holds his breath when he's trying to get a good move but then breathes out when he makes a Tetris. I also notice he has a lot of arm hair and a sharp jaw and wow, there's such a difference from almost-seventh-grade boys to eighth graders.

Anyway, I should train myself not to notice every little detail. I want to play *Tetris* on my phone, but that's too copycat. Luckily, we get to the mall pretty fast.

"I'm running to yoga," Gemma's mom says. "I'll pick you kids up in an hour."

"Two hours," Gemma says.

"You need to stay with your brother."

"I'm fine," Cooper says.

"I'll get him a nice cleansing stone," Gemma says. "He needs it."

We pile out of the SUV. Cooper is still looking at his phone as we walk across the parking lot. Gemma is in a short floral skirt and funky Mary Janes. I can see why Vivian wants to impress her. Probably wants to be her. There is no trying with Gemma. She just is.

"I'm going to the arcade," Cooper says.

"Not yet," Gemma says. "Mom's going to text me in ten minutes to ask for visual proof that I didn't ditch you. You're coming to the crystal store with me so we can take a picture."

Cooper blows a raspberry. "Fine."

Vivian falls in stride next to me as we walk across the outdoor mall. There's a large fountain with water pouring from a rectangular tower. Tent-shaped shades stretch across walkways. There's palm trees everywhere, which I know I keep noticing but it's cool and where did they all come from? Is there a palm tree farm?

"So we'll buy whatever Gemma tells us to," Vivian says. "And be nice to her brother. It'll help me get in good with her."

"Why are you trying so hard to 'get in good'?" I ask. "What does that even mean?"

"I'm trying to get into her friend group."

I'm surprised that Vivian needs to try for anything ever. "But you already have a friend group."

"Of sophomores, yeah." Vivian rolls her eyes. "But these are juniors and *seniors*. These kids can *drive*. Plus, she's really mature. Like me. Gemma said we're both star seeds, which are old souls that have lived lots of lives."

"If you've lived all these lives together, why are you trying so hard now?" I ask.

"You wouldn't get it," Vivian says. "Just . . . I'm asking you to be nice, okay? Be an asset, not an obstacle."

"So be my regular self because I'm actually way more chill than you think I am."

"If you say so."

I'll say it again—Vivian already HAS a friend group. I saw them at the pool. She also has a cheer squad, which means more connections. And now she's going after older kids. Some of us are trying to get *one* group of friends. One friend—one person to understand them and show they care. I'm not asking for the world here. Meanwhile, Greedy Vivian is asking for the stars and moon.

A bell tinkles as we walk into the crystal store. I'm not sure what I expected, but this place is . . . different. Lots of colors, strong fragrances. Light and meditative music. Like a fairy garden, but instead of plants there are rocks.

A wall holds clear boxes of crystals lined neatly in rows. There are short descriptions written out for each stone, things like PROMOTES PROSPERITY along with how the stone lines up with a chakra. Chakras have something to do with body parts, like hearts and throats. My favorite are the wire trees with tiny, multicolor crystals for leaves.

The woman who greets us has short, crisp hair with a visor on top. She's white, nearly translucent, and wears pink gingham capris and a sleeveless green polo shirt. She does not fit in with the funky wares. Maybe she's someone's great-aunt? Maybe she came into the store to use the bathroom?

She swallows Gemma in a hug. "My moon! How are you, dear?"

"Janice, I want you to meet some friends." Gemma motions to me and Vivian. "They were on the show. Vivian Marin goes to my high school and Stella North is visiting from Washington. Their parents are getting married."

"Maybe," Vivian says.

"Stella North? Now that's a cosmic name." Janice puts her hands on each side of my face and peers at me. "Oh, you are searching, aren't you? You're in the right place."

Her hands are cold and leathery. I don't pull away like I normally would with a stranger touching my face. She smiles at Vivian but doesn't call her cosmic. Vivian gives me a dirty look, like I can control my own name.

"Janice owns the store," Gemma says. "She's turned me on to crystals. And oracle cards, numerology . . . She's so good at helping you find your own spiritual path."

"Can we take a picture so I can go?" Cooper asks.

"That's my brother." Gemma turns around and snaps a photo. "Can we please find him a kindness stone? Or something that cleanses the teenage boy out of him?"

Cooper turns to me. "You want to get out of here? The arcade has a *Candy Crush* game. They might even have *Tetris*."

"Oh, I . . ." Of course I want to go with him. No one ever asks me to do something fun like this, especially something fun that we've already talked about liking. Both of us. Like . . . together. "I do, but—"

"Stella's on a *journey*," Gemma says. "She can meet you once Janice is done with her."

Cooper shrugs and turns to leave. Janice slips a rock into his hand. "This one is on me. Hematite. It's a great protection against EMF."

"Electromagnetic fields," Gemma adds.

"Whatever." He plops the rock into his pocket. "Stella, come find me once the pod people release you."

He's asked me to hang out twice in the last few minutes. I haven't even bought any crystals yet and already my manifestation is working! Not the one I planned, but I'm not arguing with the universe.

"Okay, girls, browse. Browse," Janice says. "See what stones call to you. Feel them in your hands. I know I have all these descriptions on there, but it's more about the intention you place on the stone. What cherry quartz does for Vivian might be different than what it does for Gemma. Be open, and you'll connect with something."

Gemma walks to the wall of gemstones and rummages around, picking out tumbled or rough stones and weighing them in her hand. Vivian speaks loudly to me. "We should find a sister stone! Something to connect us. Let's look over here."

A sister stone! I never knew this was a thing, but suddenly it's all I've ever wanted. At first, I didn't care if Vivian liked me because we planned to make our time together brief. But since we *do* have to work together this summer, and share a room, and be around her friends, having something that connects us is sweet. There's a pretty blue stone and some beaded bracelets. Maybe we could do stepsister bracelets?

"Okay, here's the deal." Vivian speaks in a low, hurried voice. "We're going to find a rock that works against both of our parents. Think *negative* energy."

"So you don't want a sister stone?"

"What?" Vivian looks confused. "No. I just said that to Gemma. She already made it clear she doesn't think we should mess with our parents' fate when she did our makeup. Keep up."

"Right." My heart sinks. Vivian's staying true to her mission. I need to stop hoping for something more. "So I'll look for my dad and you'll look for your mom?"

"Yeah." Vivian takes inventory of the store. "Although I don't know if it will make a big difference. No way these rocks have magical powers."

"It's energy, not powers."

"Sure." She snorts. "Should we find red stones so we force that prediction to happen?"

"I mean, if the red stones call to us, absolutely."

"Stella . . . stones don't talk. Please be chill."

I leave Vivian to her skepticism and take in the wall of crystal possibility. The first stone that catches my eye is purple and white. It's smooth and round in my palm. The sign by the bowl says AMETHYST. A STONE OF PEACE AND CALM. STRONG SPIRITUAL PROPERTIES. HELPS ANXIETY. WORRY STONE.

They make stones for worry? Where has this place been all my life?

I spend the next twenty minutes reading each description and feeling my way through different rocks. There are books on the glass counter we can thumb through, so I look up Dad's birthstone—an amethyst. No way I'm giving up my crystal! Plus, it does all these good things for him. Actually, the more

I read, they *all* seem to do good things? Where is the Stones That Will (Sorta) Curse Your Loved Ones but Only for a Little While section?

Finally, I read about black obsidian, which is a stone formed from lava. It's supposed to suck out all the negative energy, which might not seem helpful except Whitney *is* negative energy! Now he'll be able to see it. It can also "bring up past trauma" when it purges energy. Look, I know my dad has been through a lot. But . . . maybe he'll remember his divorce and think, *Wow, that was super hard! I definitely don't want to get married again.*

Obsidian "pairs well with clear quartz, because it brings clarity of mind." Perfect combo. Dad's been in this hazy love spell since he ran into Whitney. Or maybe a Vegas heat spell? Whatever is up with him, these will help him snap back to his senses. If he looked at our life, really looked at it, he would see how bonkers everything is. He'll want to go back to normal. To order. To rhythm and predictability. Two of my favorite things.

I find a table of charming heart-shaped stones in a rainbow of colors. I don't read the meaning behind the stones — just pick two rose quartz hearts. I'm giving this to Talia when I get home and tell her all about this store. All about Gemma. I won't mention the part about finding a rock to break up parents.

Vivian's made her purchases without showing me. What happened to being a team here? She's on a bench near the front of the store, scrolling through her phone. Janice might not like that, especially the electromagnetic waves, but Gemma is by the oracle cards, waving her hand over different decks, in no hurry whatsoever.

"Just these," I say to Janice. On the counter is a jewelry tree with a few different pendant necklaces. A milky, iridescent stone hits the light. I brush it with my fingers.

"Oh, moonstone," Janice says. "Good timing. Monday is a full moon."

"What does it do?" I ask.

"Depends on the intention you place. It is known as a stone for new beginnings. It can help with stress, give you calm. And when it's worn on a full moon, it heightens your intuition and psychic abilities. You'll be a moon goddess."

There are a lot of things I've been in my life, but a moon goddess is not one of them. "Psychic abilities? So it will help me predict the future?"

"You can use crystals for divination purposes, yes. We sell crystal balls over there. We have crystal maps for scrying. But, Stella?"

I jump, startled she's remembered my name.

"Set your intention, then let it go." She waves her hand. "With purpose comes peace."

Janice has a cool store with a lot of cool stones. But it doesn't mean she knows everything, especially about me. She doesn't understand everything at stake either.

When you're a kid, intention, or choice, is a luxury. I don't get to choose anything going on in my life right now. Where I live, who I talk to, where I go. Every detail of my life plays out on a spreadsheet that I didn't create. So she can go on about purpose and peace, but I'm throwing every ounce of belief I have into these breakup rocks.

Intention set.

Chapter 17

Talia,

I told you I'd send you lots of postcards ☺ This is from a crystal shop at an outside mall. They have a lot of outside malls here, probably because it's sunny every day? And they have misters in the sun shades because it's so hot.

ANYWAY! I got us matching crystal hearts. I'll give it to you when I get back. Which...will be even longer. My dad is soooo busy on this project. And he's maybe dating someone here, but it's not a big deal. And don't tell anyone, but I met a boy. He's probably not as cute as your lifeguard, but we both like *Tetris* and we went to an arcade. I guess it was sorta a date.

Oh, also! You're a Gemini. In case you're wondering.

~Stella

Vivian and I spend Monday cleaning her room to create space to meditate and set our intentions. I told her I read about the importance of clean bedrooms in a book, but guess what? I made this up so I could finally sleep in a clean bedroom. And it worked!

Afterward, we sit across from each other on the vacuumed carpet. Vivian plays some meditative music in the background. Our crystal collection is between us. Vivian bought a few more crystals than I did—she's got a green one, a yellow one, and a brownish sort of crystal with a point. I think because she wanted Gemma to understand she was taking it seriously? Although I don't think Gemma cares.

"This is the ring I bought Mom." Vivian holds up a silver ring with a green stone. "It's malachite. Stone of transformation and intuition. So she'll realize she's doing the wrong thing and transform herself into a normal mom."

"I'm not sure that's how it works?" I whisper.

"If it doesn't, I'm ditching all this fortune-telling for the next level."

"What does that mean?" I ask.

She says nothing.

I'm all mixed emotions as the five of us drive out to Red Rock Canyon late that afternoon. Going from the city to the canyon is like we've traveled by spaceship straight to Mars. The mountains are a mix of white, orange, and red sandstone—jagged and stark in the afternoon heat. It's not the first time that I've felt small in Las Vegas, although it might actually be realizing the world is so vast. Vast and ancient, with a million lifetimes carved into these craggy stones.

Vivian bounces along the trail, smiling and joking with her mom. Whitney was nice enough to pack Ridge and I walking sticks, which helps because we aren't used to this rocky path or dry air. Vivian sets a pace so fast that everyone else falls behind us. I barely manage to catch up.

"Viv . . . ian," I huff. "You . . . need . . . to slow. Down."

"We needed to lose the parents so we can talk," she says.

Although we've learned about our parents' horoscopes, Break Up Rocks is our first official mission. Knowing that makes us sort of buzz with electricity. Electricity that feels sorta like friendship.

"I know . . . but . . . give me a second."

"I thought you hiked like this in Washington?" she says.

"Not like . . . this," I say. "I mean, other people do. I take walks through the woods sometimes."

Vivian finally stops on a large boulder and takes a swig of her water. "What's it like? Going into woods?"

"What do you mean?" I chug my water. "Woods are woods."

Vivian is off again, scaling the rocks in quick, mountain goat strides. Every turn brings a new breathtaking view, sometimes of pathways carved into the mountain, sometimes of thin canyons.

"Tell me about your woods. How tall are the trees?" she asks. "And do you see animals and are there leaves or rocks on the ground?"

I slow my pace, too surprised to keep up. Spiky green plants jut out from crevices and circles of sand. Life here feels so unlikely, the opposite of home. "Have you . . . never been in a forest?"

"I've been to Mount Charleston. It's an hour away," she says. "That's got pine trees, but nothing like what I've seen in movies."

"No cedars? Maples? Huge douglas fir?" I am so homesick.

Vivian hasn't felt the dewy air, heard the forest sounds of a thousand creatures, so close and yet invisible.

"You're making me sound like a freak," Vivian says.

"No! Look." I pat one of the large boulders, my hand coming back with red dirt. "This is my first time hiking a red mountain in the desert. We all have different firsts."

"Wait." Vivian scoots close to me, rubbing her hand on the sandstone. "Stella. Red stones."

"The first prophecy," I say.

"We're not in a wizard movie so let's skip the word *prophecy*. But yeah . . . Mystic Shonda saw it." Vivian plops down on the boulder. "So does that mean it's happening? The future where our parents break up?"

"Giving them the crystals was a major part of the quest. So it makes sense that the red stones would happen today. We're on the right path."

"But the engagement party is tomorrow." Vivian picks up a pebble and tosses it into a crack. The sound echoes across the hills. "And having my dad show up didn't help."

"It bonded them," I say. "They were all blissed out at Cowabunga Canyon."

"Mom gets so aggravated when Dad is around," she says. "I thought Micah would see that and bail."

"My dad wouldn't ditch someone just because they're struggling with something."

"Isn't that what he did to your mom?" Vivian's voice is curious, not mean.

"No." I rub my moonstone pendent. "She ditched us."

"When did you last talk to her?" She shakes her head. "Sorry. Is that private?"

"No, it's . . . well, I actually got a letter from her. I guess she's moving in with my aunt—her sister. And Ridge talks to her all the time now. So . . . yeah. I should have found a crystal for Mom that makes her stay away."

"That's terrible," Vivian says. "I'm sorry. And then your dad moves you down here, away from all your friends. I can't imagine leaving my friends!"

"Yeah. I hate it." I'm talking about hard things but my body feels totally fine. No stomach or headaches. No tension. This place, this moment, is relaxing. Maybe it's because this is the most caring Vivian has been since I've met her. I don't know what crystals she got, but that energy is working for her.

I'm feeling pretty good, all open and connected with Vivian like this when Dad's and Whitney's voices carry through the mountains. They're carrying because . . . they're raised.

Ridge rushes toward us, not even looking up from his shoes. I have to call his name twice before he notices us.

"Can we go?" he asks. "I can't listen to fighting."

We've been here before. Adults fighting is the worst—especially when they are trying to keep their voices down to pretend like they're not having an argument. Or slamming doors. Or vanishing.

"We were just waiting for you guys." Vivian stands. "You want to hike with us?"

"Yes! Let's go." Ridge grabs Vivian's hand. She doesn't say anything about it.

"Pisces versus Capricorn!" Vivian whispers. "Go spy!"

I should follow Ridge. It takes a lot to ruffle him. And there's a beautiful moonrise to watch, and I have a moonstone and I am a moon goddess but . . .

I can't accidentally on purpose start conflict and not listen to what is happening.

"I'll catch up," I say.

Ridge rushes forward. Vivian gives me a conspiratorial salute.

The rocks are big enough to hide me from Dad's view. So I crouch around a bend. And just in time.

"It's too excessive," Dad says. "Twenty thousand dollars for a one-day event? We could spend that on a house, on a car. Your move."

"*You* aren't spending it," Whitney says. "I am. And what's this about my move?"

"We're putting all this time and money into a wedding and we still haven't agreed on what's happening afterward," Dad says.

"We're having the wedding next month so it's done before school starts," Whitney says. "Then we can get your kids registered for classes."

"You mean *here*?" Dad asks. The word is accusatory. "That's not settled. We could just as easily register for school in Tacoma. That would give them another month of summer."

"How is that easier?"

"Whit, it makes more sense. My kids are younger. There's two of them."

"And my kid has joint custody with her dad," she says. "Do you think he's going to let me leave the state?"

"I don't know what is going to happen with Clara either," Dad says.

"You said you could make this work," Whitney says. "The first day we ran into each other, you told me you'd do whatever it took."

"So did you." Dad exhales. "I think we both said things to help us get together. I didn't think about this enough. I only thought about you."

"I understand," Whitney says. "But your kids are doing great."

"No, they aren't." Dad snorts. "I caught Stella drinking tea the other day. The only place she wants to go is 7-Eleven. She gave me some magical rock. She had friends before she got here—I know she wants to go back."

Although I'm hiding behind a rock and doing my best to be invisible, I still feel seen. Dad might chalk up all my fate planning to middle school behavior, but at least he's aware. "Meanwhile, Vivian is way more adjusted—"

"And I want to keep it that way!" Whitney shouts. "She's in cheer. She's happy. I don't know why you're switching things on me. We had a plan."

"*You* had a plan," Dad says. "You always have a plan."

"You want me to apologize for that?" Whitney asks.

This is everything Gemma said about Pisces and Capricorns. Pisces not sticking to the path and Capricorns planning. I remember one line vividly: *If a Pisces gets wounded, or a Capricorn feels like their partner can't step up, then maybe a divide starts.*

"No. No." Dad lets out a sigh. It echoes in my gut. "I love that about you. I love *everything* about you. But I also love my kids and I don't know . . . I don't know if I can do this to them."

Whitney's voice is a feather. "Micah."

And then there's silence, the kind of silence that stretches across states and families and needs and wants. I don't know if they are kissing or turning away. I don't know if the crystals in their pockets are repelling or attracting. Did I win or lose? Or both?

When my parents got divorced, my mom took me to her favorite lake. We skipped rocks. She seemed sober. She kept telling me over and over that the divorce was not my fault. I already knew their divorce had nothing to do with me. I was not their scissors or glue.

But Dad and Whitney's breakup? It would have everything to do with me. Vivian and I shook hands on their destruction. Which isn't fair to them and isn't fair to me. There is no fair at all.

There's no great way to reappear after hearing what I just heard, but I do my best to pretend. I make a lot of commotion and then step out from behind the rock.

"Oh! Hey," I say. "Uh . . . nature called."

Whitney has her arms crossed and Dad's hands are in his pockets. They don't make eye contact with me. Or each other.

"We better hurry if we want to see the moonrise," Dad says.

We hike to the top of the mountain. The sky is completely starless despite being open and clear—even the North Star is gone. The moon dominates everything, glowing down on our faces. It's the saddest and most beautiful view of my life.

I pinch my moonstone and try to think psychic thoughts. Mystic Shonda saw these rocks. This hike was in the stars. The fight was too. A dark storm.

Vivian comes up and squeezes my hand. I want to pick apart our parents' conversation together. I want to ask her how many times she saw her parents fight, how she deals with it. Because I hate feeling it again.

130

"Supernova Quest is in full effect!" she whispers.

Dad and Whitney are stone silent on the car ride home.

I feel bad for Dad. Even Whitney.

But I have to get back to Washington. I can't live the rest of my life without seeing the forest.

I just . . . can't.

Chapter 18

Whitney makes a huge breakfast the next morning. I can't remember the last time I woke up to the smell of bacon. Maybe Grandma's house.

Vivian is still out cold. It'll take multiple alarms, shaking, and a bucket of water to finally wake her up. That's something I won't miss once we go home. Although now that we've cleaned this room, it is sorta cozy.

There's croissants, eggs, juice. It's like the breakfasts they eat on old TV shows. (Or don't eat. They just sit there talking and I'm always like *eat the food already*!)

"Good morning!" Whitney says brightly.

Dad reads a business magazine. Ridge is already dressed with his hair combed. Like parted and combed. Again like a TV show. Dad smiles when I sit down.

"How'd you sleep?" he asks.

"Great until the aliens came and replaced my family with clones." I lay a napkin across my lap. "What's with the spread?"

"I woke up hungry." Whitney slides some freshly cut fruit on the table.

Dad still hasn't looked at me. At least he's not all chipper dipper.

"Whitney and I went to Walmart this morning," Ridge says. "To get stuff for the party tonight. And she bought me a new video game. It's not as good as *Cosmo Kingdom*, but the theme and characters are cool."

"Here." Whitney places a wrapped gift in front of me. "An early birthday present."

Dad quirks an eyebrow.

I tear off the wrapping paper. A Magic 8 Ball.

"I was picking up a few things in your room and I saw the poster you did with Vivian. You listed horoscopes and psychics? What does SQ mean?"

"Oh, it's . . . a summer project I'm working on with Vivian."

I fix my face with a mask of calm, but inside I am freaking out. It's a good thing we changed the name of the project! But I still don't have a great explanation for all the divination practices we listed. Now I'm trying to remember what's on the poster.

"I read an article in the *New York Times* about why your generation is into all this stuff," Whitney says. "Zodiac, crystals, fortune-telling. It's grown a lot over the last few years, especially since the pandemic. We all want magic. We want to know our future will be okay."

I don't want her to ever figure out what we're doing. There's nothing magical about it, at least not the magic she's thinking of, all swirly glitter and hopeful dreams.

Dad puts down his magazine and side-eyes my gift. "I had one of those when I was a kid. Every time I'd ask a question, I always got BETTER NOT TELL YOU."

"Let's see if it changes," I say. "Ask again."

"Will my daughter help clean the house today?"

I give it a shake. "VERY DOUBTFUL."

Ridge peers over my shoulder. "That's not true! It says, IT IS CERTAIN."

I jerk it away from him. "Only the owner of the orb can decipher the true meaning."

"I think this 8 Ball might be even more magical than my broken one." Dad laughs.

"Thanks for the present," I tell Whitney, and I mean it. The words from their fight haven't left me. My needs are getting in the way of her wants, and still she's taking Ridge shopping and buying me this gift. She's a nice lady. Maybe I'll send her a postcard after we move home.

"You guys are going to help Whitney out with the house while I work," Dad says. "Her friends are coming at six."

"*Our* friends." Whitney looks at me as she says this.

Dad shrugs and goes back to his magazine.

It isn't until breakfast is over that I realize Dad and Whitney never actually said one word to each other.

✳ ✳ ✳

Ridge and I are in charge of bathrooms. Aliens really must have taken him over because he doesn't complain. He's cleaning a bathtub while I scrub a toilet. And the whole time Ridge keeps talking and talking, telling me more about the new game he got.

"It's different than *Cosmo Kingdom*. The economy is based on a barter system, but there's a black market for the magic.

Jake said the world building is more complicated but worth it if you can put in the time."

"Who's Jake?"

"Oh, the kid I met at the pool. He's got a whole gaming group. We game together all the time. We're hanging out tomorrow. He's rad."

"So you made a friend?" I ask. "Why?"

"I've made a lot of friends," he says. "Two skater kids down the street. A girl from Cowabunga Canyon. Because I'm a human and humans like other humans?"

"No, I mean why bother?" I ask. "We're going home next month."

"Maybe," Ridge says. "That's what Mom wants us to do."

I pause my scrubbing. "You told *Mom* about Dad and Whitney?"

"Yeah, of course."

"Aunt Maggie was going to tell her," I say.

"Mom was going to catch on." Ridge rubs his nose. "Obviously there's a reason we're in Vegas this long."

"It's not her business where we are!" I say. "We lived in the same house and she didn't see us. She doesn't deserve the details."

"What do you care what she knows?" Ridge asks. "You haven't talked to her."

"I don't . . . I don't want anyone to know!" I cry. "The wedding might not happen."

"Dad's engagement party is tonight. They're getting married."

"Perhaps."

"For real." Ridge goes back to cleaning. "That's why I'm focusing my efforts on a Back to Washington Plan."

I almost drop my toilet brush. "You . . . have a plan?"

"Yeah, and it's better than whatever you're doing with Magic 8 Balls and tea leaves."

"Our plan is working."

"*Our?*" He throws down his washcloth. "Don't tell me you have Vivian in on it. If she has her way, we'll live in Vegas forever. She's the one we're trying to beat!"

We aren't trying to *beat* anyone. Vivian, Whitney, or Dad. If anything, we're trying to heal.

"Ridge, I don't want to hurt Vivian."

"But you'll hurt Dad and Whitney?"

"What are you talking about?" I ask.

"If they break up, Dad will be crushed. Again."

"I know."

"Then don't stop the wedding," he says. "Only the move. Mom being in the picture helps us move back. Think about it."

We finish cleaning—bathrooms and bedrooms, trash out and vacuum. I spend as much time as I can getting the vacuum lines perfectly straight or else all of our cleaning will be an absolute waste.

The house sparkles, but our family is a mess. Dad and Whitney fighting. Vivian and I sabotaging. Ridge plotting.

I wonder if tonight's large gathering will include Mystic Shonda's dark storm.

Chapter 19

Stella,

Wait, you went on a date? You are the first of my friends to go on a date! How old is he? What does he look like? Does he wear cologne? I love cologne. Sporty kind, not old man stuff.

This is a vintage Yosemite postcard I found in my mom's desk drawer. Nothing exciting over here. I'm going to Cannon Beach for a few days. I might cut my hair. Pilar is mad at Chloe because she copies her clothes (I told them we're pen pals. They're super jealous). Nothing big like DATES.

Yes, I'm a Gemini, but more important—my Chinese zodiac is a Rabbit. My dad wanted to time things so I would be born in the Dragon, but I was in a hurry. Our zodiac years are different—you're a Tiger. The Rabbit is social and smart. And we love surprises! Like postcards ☺

Wow I wrote so much I ran outta ro . . . Talia

Whitney laid out matching red-stripe dresses on Vivian's bed. Our whole family is wearing red, white, and blue for the party.

"This is not happening." Vivian's hands ball into fists. "What is that fabric?"

"Seersucker," I say.

"Mom said I can leave early if I wear this."

"Where are you going?" I ask.

"High school party at Gemma's house. And she's filming for her YouTube video, so it'll be all zodiac themed."

"Oh. That's fun."

Vivian runs a brush through her hair. "Oh my gosh, don't beg me."

"Beg you for what?"

"To take you," she says.

"I'm not—"

"Fine!" She throws up her hands. "You can go, but you better not embarrass me."

"I don't want to go to a teenager party!" I say. "I don't even want to go to this backyard party."

"But I can't go alone."

"So you *do* want me to go." I am so confused. Does Vivian actually like me now? Are we hanging out as, like, friends? It makes no sense to invite me to a high school party.

"Yeah, like, whatever." She smears some lip gloss across her lips. "Cooper said you should come."

"Oh. Then maybe." I grab the dress to change. I need something to do so Vivian doesn't see how much I'm blushing. I don't know if it's because Cooper will be there or because Vivian went out of her way to include me.

The dress looks cute. I just can't tell if it's cute in a good way or bad. Like maybe I look too young? Too old? Too much, not enough, I know it's only a dress but I can't tell what this dress is *telling* me.

"Gemma texted!" Vivian calls from the bedroom. "Her tarot reader bailed. If a tarot reader is as expensive as Mystic Shonda, she's in real trouble."

"I know someone!" I run over to my backpack and look for Zara's card. "She reads palms too."

"How do you know someone?" Vivian asks.

"Long story."

To say I am dreading this Fourth of July engagement barbecue is an understatement buried under an understatement. It's hard enough for me to go to a social event where I know everyone. Now I have to meet people who are magically supposed to become family.

"Will you introduce me to everyone?" I ask Vivian.

"Of course! My cousins are going to love you." Vivian slings her arm around me. "And maybe we'll see another of Mystic Shonda's predictions tonight! Maybe tasting lime? I still don't get why that matters."

My heart zings. Right. Because Vivian and I are still hanging out so we won't later. I can meet every person at this party tonight, but if we crash the wedding, I'll never see them again.

Unless we do Ridge's plan. Then the wedding happens. Then Vivian and I are stepsisters. Then . . . Vivian might hate me for changing her destiny. And a Scorpio's wrath is extra wrath-y.

A group of people are already in the backyard when Vivian and I appear in our matching dresses. The reaction is a thunderstorm. There's cheering and laughter and waves. Whitney emerges from amid the throngs and pulls Vivian and I toward everyone.

"And this is Micah's daughter, my soon-to-be stepdaughter, Stella."

The first person to take my hand is Whitney's aunt Giana. She speaks with a heavy Italian accent. "You are so pretty. Whitney, you didn't tell me how pretty she is!"

"I told you she's darling."

But Aunt Giana isn't listening. She's looking me up and down. "The Lionetti women mature much sooner. You are a year away from becoming a woman, yes? Right on the cusp!"

"She's not a piece of ripe fruit," Vivian says.

"And this one." Aunt Giana pats Vivian's cheek. "Why are you being salty to your zia, hmm? You know it's my birthday this week."

"Oh, it's your birthday?" Vivian smiles with no teeth. "Then you're a Cancer."

Aunt Giana's penciled eyebrows shoot up in alarm. "I don't have cancer!"

"No." Vivian tries not to laugh. "I mean you *are* a Cancer. July birthday. That's your zodiac sign."

"None of this." Aunt Giana crosses herself. "The Pope said no fortune-telling. We are guided by God."

"Thanks for the advice!" Whitney links arms with Vivian and me. "I better show these girls around."

"Aunt Giana is bananas," Vivian says under her breath. "There's nothing wrong with wanting to see the future."

"That's nothing compared to your nonna. And Aunt Giana has the right to believe whatever she wants," Whitney says. "Same as all of us. Don't put down anyone for their religion or faith."

Another aunt grabs Vivian's shoulder and we're swallowed into a blur of compliments and questions. Someone says we already look like sisters (matching dresses will do that to you). Another asks if I eat enough, an uncle wants to know if my dad has a good job. There are so many hugs too, all from strangers who I guess wouldn't stay strangers if they became my stepfamily.

Finally, after an hour of shuffling and nodding, I end up next to Dad at the grill.

Dad is in a blue-and-white gingham dress shirt with a GRILL MASTER apron over the top. I don't know if I've ever seen him barbecue. He was always into making pasta back when Mom was home.

"Hey, Grill Master."

Dad flips over a burger. "Hello to you, Stella Blue."

"Did you meet everyone?" I ask.

"Mostly." Dad waves his spatula toward the backyard, which is filled with Whitney's people. Her life is so big.

"How will you remember everyone?"

"I told Whitney we should have name tags at the wedding." He laughs. "She said the sticker adhesive could ruin wedding clothes."

I actually thought the same thing as soon as Dad said it.

"They're all nice," I say.

"Think so?" Dad throws his arm around me and gives me a side squeeze. "Thank you for going along with this."

I shrug. "It's just a party."

"That's not what I mean."

"Then what?" I'd like him to say some of those things I overheard in his fight.

"I asked a lot of you, coming here. Actually, I didn't ask. It all just sort of happened. First the engagement, then the work trip, then the whole summer. I'm really sorry. I should have discussed this stuff with you all along. I was so, I guess . . . *relieved*, I didn't want to look at the bad when there was so much good. You know?"

Right now, Supernova Quest feels impossible. My dad looks so open, so tender. He was there for me during so many hard times. Maybe not *there* the way I wanted or needed, but he tried. He always tries. I don't know how to look him the eye and hurt him. Even if I would be saying the truth. "Coming here was messed up, but it doesn't mean my whole *life* is going to get messed up. Vegas is okay. Just for the summer."

Dad rolls a few hot dogs around on the grill. He wipes at his eye with the back of his sleeve. "I appreciate you talking to me about this. We need to talk more."

"Speaking of talking, did you, uh . . ."

"Hear from your aunt Maggie?" Dad laughs. "Boy, did I. Don't worry, I know she's coming. I know your mom is living with her. I think that's awesome. I'm rooting for Clara. We love you a lot. Everything is going to work out."

He doesn't know that. There's no way for any of us to know that. Maybe he needs to make himself believe it, though. Maybe I do too.

Whitney walks by with a platter of watermelon. She catches Dad's eye and gives a little smile. This might be the first time they've acknowledged each other since their fight yesterday.

The way my dad is looking at her—it's like she's the moon and stars. They're a galaxy.

"Can you watch the grill for a second?" Dad asks. "I need to tell Whitney something."

142

He hands me the spatula and strides right over to her. He cups her face in his hands and kisses her. In front of her family! They touch foreheads and whisper. I'm sure he's telling her sorry. Maybe she'll tell him that she will move to Washington.

Vivian appears next to me. She wrinkles her nose. "Why are you barbecuing? You're going to smell like hot dog smoke at the party."

I point. Dad and Whitney are holding hands and working the crowd together.

Vivian chews her lip. "One fight and one rock isn't going to break them up."

"Maybe that's a good thing," I say.

She looks at me with total disgust. "We have a deal and you better see it through. Fate is fate."

My stomach dips. "But do we really *know* what their fate is?"

"It's whatever we want it to be."

Dad and Whitney give some quick engagement toasts. Then Whitney escorts us to the cul-de-sac. She has a table arranged with all sorts of fireworks. Of course she does. There's also buckets of water to soak the fireworks afterward. And there's a fire hydrant. And fire-resistant gloves.

We put Pog in a kennel for the night so he wouldn't get frantic from the loud noises. Dad lights a few fireworks—nothing too wild—and the guests clap. I try to remember if I've ever had a Fourth of July like this. We always did things so small. Just our family. Maybe Aunt Maggie. Maybe a friend. We were fine with that.

But this is different.

I never knew there were so many ways to be happy.

Chapter 20

W e're late to Gemma's party because Dad has to drive us and Whitney doesn't want him to leave. Vivian is as hot as a firework, but she tells Dad thank you when we run out of the car.

Vivian sticks close to my side when we open the gate to Gemma's backyard. She's strung up bistro lights along the iron fence that looks out on the golf course. One half of her back-yard is a pool with a large rock waterfall. The grass is stiff—fake, actually. Before Vegas, I'd only ever seen fake grass on miniature golf courses. There's twenty or thirty teenagers here, which is a lot but not wild like the high school parties I've seen in movies.

Zara is set up in the back corner, underneath a blossoming tree. She's bent over a table, looking at cards and talking to a nodding guy. There's a line formed behind her table, waiting to see their fortunes. Gemma zips over.

"Zara is so awesome!" she says. "Thank you for connecting us."

"No problem." I realize the chances of getting a reading from Zara tonight are slim. I'd hoped to sit by her all night. This party is so cool and I am so not.

"Cooper is inside," Gemma says.

"Oh yeah?"

Vivian gives my back a big slap and pushes me toward the sliding glass doors. "Hope you brought the rose quartz tonight!"

It takes me a second to realize what she means—rose quartz being the love crystal. Oh geez.

Cooper sits at the black marble kitchen counter, eating chips and dip. He slides the bowl over to me. "I'm watching *The Office*. You in?"

The TV takes up half the wall. Michael Scott is yelling at the guy with glasses. Other kids can probably identify what season and episode this is, but not me. Because the thing is—*The Office* gives me major anxiety. The humor is too painful. And everything is too real life. Who wants to leave real life to watch more real life?

I don't tell Cooper any of this. "For a bit. Then I have to see Zara."

"You want a Coke?" he asks.

Caffeine is *another* thing that sets me off. So here I am, with people I don't know (at a party, which is worse), watching a show that makes me uncomfortable, sipping a drink that amps me up. At this point I'm sticking my thumb out and hitchhiking on the Anxiety Express. "Yes, please."

Cooper tosses me a soda before carrying the bowl of chips over to the long sectional. I walk over to join him, but I don't know what "joining" him looks like? Should I sit next to him or on the other side? Are we really watching *The Office* or is this code for something else?

I sit down on the other side of the couch and sip my Coke, trying so hard to come up with a conversation starter. I bet Talia would think of ten things to say if she were here. I want to text her and ask, but we still aren't I'm-sitting-by-a-boy-right-now-what-should-I-do friends.

Now the guy who always looks at the camera and the girl with curly hair are flirting at the reception desk. Ugh, now I'm watching a *romance*. With a *boy*.

"So do you miss Seattle?" Cooper asks me.

As much as I was searching for something to talk about, I didn't expect it to be this. "Oh. Yes."

"Is that why you teamed up with Vivian?" he says. "You're trying to break up your parents and go home?"

"Did Gemma tell you that?"

"Isn't it obvious?" He gestures outside at Zara. "You're trying to change the future, yeah? And learning all this stars and fortune stuff so you can."

"Oh." I shift on the couch. It's new. To be seen. "Yeah."

"That's cool." He shrugs. "So how's it going so far?"

And then I do something I really, really did not see coming. I tell Cooper. *Everything.* Even the stuff about Talia. Even stuff about my mom! He interrupts me here and there with a question, but mostly he's quiet. Listening.

". . . And so our parents made up, but the crystals clearly worked and now I'm not sure what to do next."

"Did you ever figure out that spinning circle?" he asks.

"No! Should I call Mystic Shonda again?"

"I don't know," he says. "It all sounds lose-lose."

"What do you mean?"

"I mean you break them up, you go home to Seattle. Fine, you see those friends and go back to normal. But with the stuff with your mom and your parents divorced—you can't completely go back to normal, yeah?"

My stomach somersaults. "I mean, no. But that's the closest to normal."

"It is?" He munches on another chip. "Because your situation here isn't bad. Vivian's mom sounds cool. And your dad's work is good. Vivian really likes you."

"No she doesn't."

"Uh, yeah she does. She talked you up to Gemma. My sister doesn't let just anyone on her show. And Vivian brought you to this party. She made sure I'd be home so there was someone your age. Plus there's all the fortune stuff."

"Yeah," I say. "I like Vivian a lot. She's closed off and sketch but . . . I like her."

"That's a Scorpio for you." Cooper's eyes go wide. "If you tell Gemma I said that, I swear—"

"I won't." I laugh. "I probably won't."

"And Vegas is tight. We have the greatest Chinatown, a million swimming pools, and you haven't even seen the Pinball Hall of Fame. Best of all? I live here." Cooper gives me this adorable grin and for the first time in maybe my whole life I think having space on a couch isn't always great.

"Good point." I smile. "About visiting the pinball place."

"Here to help." He turns back to the TV. "But that's the lose-lose. If you break up your parents, it means you don't see Vivian anymore. Or Chinatown."

I think Chinatown is code for Cooper, but he's right. If I change Whitney's future, I change mine. And going home would be like . . . almost like Supernova Quest never existed. Or the version of who I am in Vegas didn't exist. I would go back to Washington, back to my *before* life. And lose all the push and pull of my present.

We watch the show. The look-at-camera guy, Jim, is playing a prank on glasses guy. Glasses guy is totally falling for it. Cooper and I laugh at the same time, which makes us laugh harder.

"If you do end up staying here . . . you could meet my friends," Cooper says. "Our group is half Black kids, half everything else."

"Oh, I, uh . . ." We've never mentioned that we're different races. I'm not sure if we're supposed to? "I don't think about that."

"It's not about *thinking*. Race is fact," Cooper says. "Am I the first Black boy you've hung out with?"

I mean, yes. He is also the first *boy* boy I've hung out with. "Is that what is happening now? Are we hanging out?"

"Obviously." He swigs his soda. "Some of the girls are into astrology. Maybe because they all worship Gemma. But one of my friends creates zodiac spreadsheets. I don't want you to meet him."

"Why not?"

"You might want to spend time together doing something shifty. Like charting the stars." Cooper shrugs. "Oh, and we're all eighth graders. But I think you can keep up."

I could *totally* keep up. Even though I don't know what "keeping up" looks like. But I could read and rehearse everything. Prepare myself. Maybe write out some jokes and conversation starters.

If I stayed here. Which I'm not. I'm focused on going home. Back to the Dippers. I will 100 percent return to that goal, just as soon as I figure out why Cooper wouldn't want me talking to his astrology friend . . .

The sliding door opens. I shoot right up like I've been caught in the middle of something, although we are on opposite sides of the couch.

"Hey, jittery," Vivian says. "Zara says you can do a reading before she leaves."

"Oh." My face flames. "Yes! I want to do that."

"Can I come?" Cooper asks.

Vivian snorts. "No."

"Yes." What do I care if Cooper hears my card reading? I just vomited all of my secrets on him.

I reach out my hand to pull Cooper off the couch.

And even though we only touch for two seconds, my hand tingles the whole distance from the house to Zara's table.

Chapter 21

"Hey!" Zara reaches across the table and squeezes my hand. "Thanks for this gig! I made a lot of cash tonight."

"Oh, yeah. Money." I fumble in my pocket.

"Sit down, Virgo." She motions to a seat. "This is your finder's fee."

Cooper scoots in the chair next to me.

Vivian stays a few steps away, arms crossed over her chest. "Now ask how many days until our parents' breakup."

"Ask in *your* reading," I say.

"Oh, I'm not getting one," Vivian says.

"Why?" Cooper asks. "Gemma's probably done three readings today."

"Nonna wouldn't want me to." Vivian takes a step back. "She's really spiritual."

"Sorry, but . . . this *is* spiritual?" Zara says. I'd worry that Vivian is offending her, but I don't think Libras get offended. "Like it's called spiritualism?"

"Okay, then she's *religious*. We're Catholic." Vivian glances around the party like her nonna might be watching. "She told me once that fortune-telling cards are devil tools. Nonna's superstitious."

"I get it," Cooper says. "My gammie thinks Gemma is a witch."

Vivian has never brought up religion during Supernova Quest. I mean, we called a psychic, whose whole job is fortune-telling. But Whitney told us to respect others' beliefs. Sometimes we don't know what we think or feel until we're there facing it.

"I'm just respecting her wishes," Vivian says. "What if I get a card that says I'm going to marry a cowboy and join the circus?"

"I think I left that card at home." Zara shakes her head. "But no worries if you have reservations about this. Tarot is a device I use to self-reflect, but it wouldn't be effective if you're uncomfortable. We're all seeking in different ways."

"But Stella can totally tarot." Vivian takes a step closer. "Go ahead. Seek."

Zara levels her gaze on me. "Do you have anything you're contemplating or questioning you'd like to explore?"

Uh, does the Las Vegas Strip have a lot of light bulbs? "I don't know."

"Yes, you do," Vivian says. "How do we break up our parents?"

"Maybe you shouldn't give an opinion when it isn't your reading," Cooper says.

I like Cooper.

"Let's start simple. I've laid out three tarot decks," Zara says. "Pick the one you're vibing with."

There's a deck of bright colors with the tarot images I've seen in my library books. There's another one with unicorn cats, and another with pastel nature images. I go with that.

"Now we can go in any direction you want. Career, love, friendship, choice—"

"Yeah, that," I say. "Or, two choices."

"Two choices?" Vivian analyzes me. I try not to squirm. I don't want to say more than this. Cooper might know everything, but Vivian doesn't know I'm . . . considering my options.

"*My* reading," I say.

Zara shuffles the cards. They aren't like playing cards. She riffles the cards in and out of each other in a hypnotizing rhythm. "We can look at which path is best? Do you have something in mind there?"

I breathe out. "Yes."

Cooper kind of bumps my elbow. He gives me a look like Jim on *The Office* would give. Like, "I see you and I know what you're thinking and also . . . isn't life outrageous?"

"Great, let's look at your paths," Zara says.

My first direction is the quest: break up our parents and move back. The second direction is Ridge's approach: keep Dad and Whitney together and move everyone back home. I guess the third direction would be Cooper's plan: parents get married and we stay in Vegas. But then the whole go-back-to-Washington part is gone, which is basically the whole point of everything. Zara deals the cards facedown into two rows of four. She points at the first row.

"This line will tell us about your first path. These cards represent the past, present, future, and further future."

Zara turns over the first card. There's a man dangling by his foot from a gnarled tree. "The Hanged Man. Your past."

"Uh, that sounds scary," I say.

"None of this needs to be scary." Zara squeezes my hand. "These cards don't necessarily have good or bad meanings. They're personal guides, yeah? Images to help you understand inner truth. So this is a card of wisdom, but it's also a card for having your life suspended or in transformation. I mean, we all had our lives suspended during the pandemic. So it could reference that. But the Hanged Man is any turning point involving personal sacrifice. Can you think of something?"

"Yes." The hard times with my mom. Moving here with my dad. "It's the same answer for both paths, actually."

"That's cool. It's good to analyze the flow of the cards — to see where you were so you can decide where to go. Here it seems like this change set things in motion for more change. Which brings us to present." Zara flips another card. "The Seven of Swords. Huh."

"Huh?" I peer closer at the card. "What's the huh?"

"So whatever plan you have right now might be failing," Zara says. "It also involves spying. Secrecy. Look at the card and see what you notice."

Vivian nudges me under the table. I glance up at her, expecting to see annoyance or warning in her eyes. But no. It's fear.

"What?" I whisper.

"Nothing." Her voice wavers. "It's creepy, right? What she just said?"

"I'm guessing you're connecting to this?" Zara asks.

"Yes," I say calmly.

"This card might indicate you need to think things through," Zara says. "You might have arguments with allies, which means

153

limited success. You need to own your responsibility here. Otherwise—backfire."

Cooper lets out a low whistle. Vivian actually covers her face with her hair.

"How do I fix it then?" I ask.

Zara turns another card. Death.

Vivian falls down on her knees.

I push her with my elbow. "Viv. It's fine. Zara will explain."

"I liked the shiny crystals better," Vivian says.

Cooper shakes his head. "This is getting intense."

I hope Vivian and Cooper notice how *calm* I am, by the way. The very model of *poise* in the middle of *crisis*. I straighten my back and look straight at Zara.

"Zara, please tell me that Death does not mean death," I say. "I know you said there's secrecy, but I'm not plotting a murder."

Zara doesn't laugh or tell us we're overreacting. I like that about her—like she respects our worries and fears.

"We tend to fear this card, but there's so much beauty," she says. "And our reactions can tell us just as much about the card as the actual image. This means rebirth. Bright ideas, opportunities. New life. Promise."

"So . . . we like Death?" I ask.

"Duh." Vivian stands up and brushes herself off. "Like . . . obviously."

"*Possibly.*" Zara taps the card. "Before you get to the bright side, there's going to be a period of destruction. Out with the old. If you choose to follow this path."

Okay. Let's break this down.

So my present day, the Supernova Quest, is failing. But my

future card says my whole life is going to change for the better. But only after lots of hard changes (uh . . . destruction).

Does that mean I follow through despite hurting others? Because my new life is going to be so much better? In Washington. With Talia.

If so . . . I guess I have my answer then. Right?

Zara talks more about the last future card, but nothing registers. I don't want her to turn the cards for the second path. I should stick with door number one.

But Zara is already on to the next row. Option number two's past card is the Eight of Cups. She uses words like *misery*, *disappointment*. Super negative, but no surprises there. The present card is the Page of Wands.

"Tell me what you notice when you see this card."

I stare down at the image. There's a person holding a staff, looking up. They're dressed in mismatched clothes. "The person looks like they know who they are."

"Absolutely. This is a card of loyalty and honesty. New creative ideas. The Page can represent a person you already know, or a mentor entering your life. You can trust them. They are a true friend. They're going to help you along this path. Can you think of someone?"

A true friend! That's . . . incredible. This path would make Talia and I even closer. I'd have my own personal Page of Wands. So I guess I can at least *listen* to this second choice.

Zara turns a future card involving loss and betrayal. But the further future card promises fortune and change in environment—two positives that I am desperately seeking.

"Someone will be hurt," she says. "And I don't know what that will mean for the relationship."

Vivian. Vivian. She means I will hurt Vivian. "Anything else?"

"Along with this loss, someone from your past will come into your life."

"In the future?" I ask.

"Yes," Zara says. "Whenever that is."

"That's what Mystic Shonda said," Vivian says. "Remember? A ghost from your past creating a sense of inner conflict."

"But Shonda wasn't talking about *my* life," I reason. "That was for Whitney."

"Oh, you've had your cards read before?" Zara asks.

Vivian ignores her. "Wait, I'm confused. The first path is obvious. That's the quest. What other choice is there?"

My palms are sticky. I try to clear my throat but it's too dry. There is no way she would go for Ridge's plan. No way. She'd chain herself to a cactus before leaving Vegas.

"I don't know," I say. "I guess . . . the second choice is no plan? Or not . . . our plan?"

"So you're thinking about skipping out on the deal?" Vivian asks.

"That's not what she said," Cooper says. "She could be considering other options."

Now he thinks I'm talking about staying here! Which, future aside, I don't know if Vivian would like. I would be around all the time, and I'm younger and not popular and . . . wait. Who cares? Staying in Vegas wasn't even a thought before Cooper brought it up an hour ago. I can't let him cloud my judgment.

I analyze the spread of cards. Do I have any say in this? Mystic Shonda said agency will change our future, but my fate feels completely sealed right now. Both fates.

All fate.

No choice.

"How are you doing?" Zara asks.

"I'm still lost," I say. "What am I supposed to do? Path one or two?"

Gemma flickers the bistro lights and calls, "Party ending, everyone!"

Party ending. Card reading over. I could stop right now. I don't need to give any *meaning* to this. We could shuffle the cards. Leave. Forget.

"The cards aren't here to make a choice *for* you." Zara gathers her things. "It's to give you clarity in choosing your path. Are you leaning toward one or the other?"

I scrunch up my eyes super tight. So tight that I see little pricks of stars. One, two, one, two. Both paths had good and bad. But if I were to line up every person hurt on each path, the numbers don't compare. Dad, Whitney, Ridge . . . all impacted by path one. And me. Because then I actually wouldn't see Vivian again. Or have a chance of seeing Cooper. Gemma. Zara.

The second path hurts Vivian. She'll hate me. She'll make things impossible for Whitney. Maybe move in with her dad. But . . . I'd still have her? She'd be my stepsister. And Dad would have Whitney. And Ridge could see Mom and . . .

"I don't know why we turned over those other cards," Vivian says. "That path is nasty. Except for the ghost from the past part. Do you have an ex-boyfriend you never told me about?"

My phone buzzes. I figure it's Dad coming to pick us up. Or maybe Ridge checking in.

Nope. It's a group text with Aunt Maggie, Dad, and a number I don't recognize.

I read the first line of the text. And instantly abandon all thought of choosing a path.

"Whoa," Cooper says.

"Ghost from the past?" Vivian scrunches in close. "Let me see."

Hey Stella.

It's Mom :) I'm coming with Maggie next week. My sponsor thinks it would be okay as long as Maggie is with me and we stay off the Strip. Everything I wrote before stands. You don't have to see me. I would love if you did, but this is your choice. You can also keep your original plans and only see Maggie.

I talked to your dad on the phone. Ridge is coming to stay for a few days. Let me know if you want to come too.

I love you.

Chapter 22

Talia,

I don't want to write too much on this Hoover Dam postcard. What if the mail carrier reads this? They might be like, oooh, "who is this boy?" Or "whoa, that's some big drama!" So two things: He's older and like whooooaaa on the cute scale. What's above cute? Fine? Yeah, he's fine. And we hung out again, this time at his house during a high school party. No big.

Obviously, it's the best summer ever, but I miss home. I miss my clean bedroom and my favorite blanket. I miss the forest. Rain. Friends. I miss normal. Not that I ever had it.

Whew, downer. Seriously, I'm having fun. I'll be back in a few weeks. Now stop eavesdropping, mail carrier!

♡,

Stella

I manage to avoid all discussion of Mom for the rest of the week. Vivian and I go swimming, we watch a movie with Gemma and Cooper. She doesn't bring up the text. Dad doesn't bring up the text. Even Ridge is quiet. There's a family game night in there too.

The whole house waits.

Dad finally bursts on Tuesday, waking me up at 8:00 A.M. for a chat.

"Look, we have to talk about this." Dad doesn't define the obvious *this*. "Whatever you want to do, I support you."

"I don't know yet," I say.

"Your mom is still your mom," he says. "She'll always be your mom. I may not agree with her sometimes, but I think it's important you have a relationship with her."

I wonder if this is what Dad really, *really* thinks. Because my mom was still my mom last month, when he decided we were staying the summer in Vegas. She was still my mom three months ago, when I tried calling her and she never picked up. She was still my mom last year when she showed up at the house high, begging to tuck us in. If it's so important to have a relationship with her, why didn't he say this any other time when she wasn't being a decent mom?

"So you're saying I need to see her," I say.

"I'm just laying the facts out there," Dad says. "You can decide. And . . . soon."

"I'm going back to sleep," I say.

My stomach is a permanent knot. They've added chaos on my chaos. My only solution—the best solution—is to shut it all out.

Vivian comes into the room around eleven. "Mom and I are meeting with her florist today. Since you're here, you can come."

It's not exactly my dream day, but I also don't want to talk to Ridge or Dad.

Vivian and Whitney sing to music as we drive along the freeway. I am here but I'm not. I'm nowhere. Gone.

Whitney turns down the music. "I'm sending invites out this week, but I canceled the country club," Whitney says. "Micah was right—it's expensive. So now I have to look at some cheaper venues. And it's last minute."

"I still think you should go with one of those little chapels on the Strip," Vivian says.

"Just because we're getting married in Vegas, it doesn't mean I want a Vegas *wedding*," Whitney says. "And I got married in a Catholic church when I married your dad. It was lovely, but I want to do something outdoors this time. I just hope the whole wedding doesn't melt."

Vivian laughs. "What does that mean?"

"Or wilt," Whitney says. "Or sweat. I'm trying to factor heat into everything. I was at an August wedding once and the cake melted. Like the layers of the cake slid off the top and onto the ground. I don't want that happening to the cake. Or Aunt Kate."

"You guys should get married in a swimming pool!" Vivian says. "You can get synchronized swimmers to dance around you."

"With one of those flower bathing caps as my veil?" Whitney erupts into a fit of giggles. "Can you imagine?"

Vivian turns around in her seat. "Do you think Mom should get married at Cowabunga Canyon?"

I live with so many opposite feelings at the same time. I like Whitney and Vivian, but I don't like the idea of them? I'm glad they're being nice to me, but I also want to be mean to everyone and everything.

"You're being ridiculous," I say.

"Mom, Stella thinks your pool idea is *ridiculous*." Vivian turns back around. "She thinks a Viva Las Vegas wedding chapel is way classier."

"Hey, do you need anything?" Whitney looks at me in her rearview mirror, worry crinkling her eyes. "I can stop at your 7-Eleven?"

"I'm fine." I ignore them the rest of the car ride. Every one of Zara's cards turns in my head on repeat. Because I did choose a path. I made up my mind based on which journey would hurt the fewest number of people. And I'll probably have Vivian guilt until the day I die and beyond because she'll haunt me in the afterlife.

I chose path two, and fifteen minutes later the future card happened. Which is the card I'm trying to avoid. My mom is here. Close. Somewhere. My whole body buzzes with that knowledge.

Whitney parks the car in an upscale strip mall. Vegas might look the same on the outside, but Bloom boutique is darling inside. There's blue-and-white tile and bistro tables and paintings framed in gold. Very French and fancy, but also inviting and sweet.

The florist, Veeda, leads us to a small table in the back. There are floral arrangements all around and a large binder of photos. Whitney flips through a dizzying variety of centerpieces and bouquets and altarpieces.

Veeda sits close to us, laptop open. She's Asian, around Whitney's age, and super stylish. She has on three different floral patterns, which you might think is too much, but her style is Goldilocks right. She also has on rose perfume—the lady clearly likes a theme. "So you filled out our form but left a few parts blank. What's your venue?"

"Well, here's the thing. Micah and I had a bit of a disagreement about our initial location and well . . . he's made some good points. The country club wasn't our style and it's pricey so I'm thinking about switching to another venue. But no wedding chapels on the Strip."

Veeda pauses her typing. "You're getting married in a month?"

"I know it's soon, but . . ."

"It's August." Veeda stares at the screen. "Maybe. Maybe you could find another venue. Midweek. But August is so . . ."

"Hot," Vivian says. "Mom doesn't want anyone or anything to melt."

"That's a good plan." Veeda slides a magazine over to Whitney. "I'm sure you've looked at a million of these bridal magazines, but I would get back on the venue hunt before you settle on flowers. Is there any other theme I should know about? Colors?"

"I want a mix. Wildflowers." Whitney's face reddens. "Because we both kind of grew in less than ideal conditions? And we're blending a family? So I want to show beauty in surprising ways."

"Charming. I can work with that." Veeda searches her bookcase and comes back with a worn blue book with intricate gold detailing. *The Language and Sentiment of Flowers.*

"You'll like this book from the Victorian era. They really got into the meaning of flowers. A yellow rose means friendship or a bluebonnet means bravery. I tell my brides to make sure they aren't accidentally giving their bridesmaids something that says they hate them."

"I want my bouquet to be massive," Vivian says. "Bigger than Mom's. We're talking a *bush*."

I'm the only one who doesn't laugh.

"It's a satisfying project, coming up with the words you want to communicate through plants," Veeda says.

"I love that!" Whitney clasps her hands together. "What do I want my bouquet to say? I got it." She opens her eyes. "Cherish. He makes me feel cherished. And I cherish him."

The word slices through me with its strength. Everything would be a lot easier for everyone if Dad and Whitney weren't so in love.

"What do you want the bridesmaids' bouquets to say?" Veeda asks.

"Connection." Whitney puts an arm around each of us. "Vivian is my world. We have a thread connecting us to each other always. And now we get to have threads with Stella. Aren't I lucky?"

"I think I have some ideas already." Veeda beams. "But if we're looking at a month away, I need all the info from you by Sunday—the wedding venue, number of guests, your colors, favorite flowers, the whole bit."

"Okay." Whitney nods. "By Sunday. I'll get it done."

And she will. With color-coded notes, no doubt.

Whitney and Vivian flip through the bridal magazine, discussing pros and cons of different places. Why is Vivian being so nice to her mom, so *into* this idea of their wedding, when the Supernova Quest is supposed to end it?

I browse the floral displays, smelling the different flowers before looking them up in Veeda's darling book. Bluebell—humility. Iris—hope. Daisy—innocence.

My mom wanted to name me Marigold and call me Mary. Or Goldie. But I had a lot of dark hair when I was born. Mom said the name didn't fit me. She chose Stella Blue because of the Grateful Dead song, but she also said I glowed like a star. I look up marigold in the book. Jealousy. Grief. Good call, Mom.

Watching Vivian and Whitney chat and giggle makes me miss Mom, even if we never had a relationship like that. Now Mom's coming here, close, and looking for . . . something.

Maybe I'll text her back. Or talk to her. I can't picture us sitting close. I can't picture what she looks like now.

Vivian waves me over. "What are you doing over there anyway?"

"Just looking up flowers," I say.

"You better not pick a flower with a scary meaning."

"Viv." Whitney rolls her eyes. "Stella wouldn't."

"You're right," I say. "I wouldn't." At least not on purpose.

Then I see the large bunch of pink and yellow tulips, the scent light and sweet. I stare open-mouthed at the cup-shaped buds. Another Mystic Shonda checkmark.

I flip around in the book to find the meaning of tulips.

Forgiveness.

I roll my eyes. Okay, universe.

I'll see my mom.

Chapter 23

Dear Mom,

~~What are you doing?~~
~~Why are you such an Aries?~~
~~Are you trying to ruin everything?~~
Are you okay?

I tell Dad and Whitney I'm ready to see Mom. They have everything scheduled within an hour. I'll stay with Aunt Maggie, in a room separate from Mom and Ridge. Vivian's with her dad. Pog will go to a fancy pet hotel. This is the first time Dad and Whitney have been alone since they got engaged. Whitney's friend has a cabin somewhere in Utah, which means I can't back out. They try to hide their excitement about the weekend getaway, but not so well.

Anyway. I guess I'm seeing my mom.

On Friday, Dad drops me off at Springs Preserve, a desert wetland with museums and trails. From the parking lot, it looks big and boring. How long can you really spend looking at cacti and dirt?

"Why this place?" I ask. "Isn't there a mall down the street?"

"Your mom read about it online." Dad opens his car door. "She wanted to go somewhere unique."

"Oh good. Because I haven't had enough *unique* lately."

Dad hands me my suitcase. "I can walk you in."

I thought about this. Thought about what might happen if they saw each other again. Like in this old movie *The Parent Trap*. Twin girls who didn't know the other person existed meet at summer camp and decide to get their parents back together. It's sweet and funny but not what I'm trying to do. Vivian and I are basically pulling a *reverse* Parent Trap with Dad and Whitney. And my parents? I don't see how they would be good together again. For them, for me, for anyone.

"I think I'll have less anxiety if I go alone."

Dad gives me a hug—a long, clinging hug—like maybe he's more anxious than I am. I wheel my suitcase and watch my feet as they carry me across the parking lot, a long concrete walkway, past boulders and plants, right to the ticket booth. I hardly notice the surroundings.

I've spent a lot of time picturing how and when I would see my mom again. I figured she'd come to our house, our Washington house, maybe for dinner but in the backyard because it might be uncomfortable for Dad to see her in their old kitchen. They would have a strained conversation before Dad went inside. And then Mom and I would do something oddly connected, like in the movies. We'd both accidentally wear the same shirt, or discover that our new favorite food is Thai despite never eating it together. And we'd laugh. Genetics!

I did not picture our reunion here, in the Las Vegas desert, my dad driving away for a romantic weekend with his soon-to-be wife.

Mom sits on a bench near the entrance. She's looking in the opposite direction so I have a few seconds to take her in. She's in a powder-blue sundress. Her arms are sculpted, tan but thin—bones. Her curly hair is swept back in a high ponytail, and she has highlights, which means she's doing well enough to remember things like hair appointments. When she turns to see me, I immediately look away, but not before I see her expression burst into joy.

There have been times over the last few years where I leave my body. Like I float away and watch everything happening around me, totally detached from any events. This would be an ideal time to do that. To remove myself from the flash flood of emotions. But it wouldn't help. I need to get this over with.

I stay. Present. Here.

I don't run over. I stick my hand inside my pocket and squeeze my amethyst. My stride is steady, calm. I kind of don't know what to do with my arms though? Like do I swing them or keep them straight? How does walking work again?

She stands. I stop a few feet away.

"Hey, Mom."

"Hey, Twinkle."

Her voice is so clear. I don't know a better way to explain it. When my mom was high, she sounded like she was underwater. Or nasally. Or far away. My nickname snaps across her tongue. Twinkle, as in Twinkle Little Star. It's cheesy, but normal. And the thing about normal is, when you haven't had it in a long time, you don't know what to do with it when you do.

Like the hug. She holds out both arms while I turn for a side pat. What results is a three-quarter hug with some of her hair in my mouth. I pull back first.

She laughs. "I am so nervous! Are you nervous?"

"I'm always nervous," I say.

"You got taller," she says. "Did you get your period yet?"

"Mom, seriously?"

She looks me up, down, sideways. "You are so beautiful. And clever and kind and real."

It's what she always said in response to random comments people made when I was little. Like if a lady in the grocery store complimented my baby curls, Mom would nod and say, "She's also great at solving puzzles." Because she didn't want the only compliment to be about my looks. So she didn't weigh in on my style. Which used to be such a safe thing with her. I don't know what it is now.

She probably wants to hold my hand or link arms, but Mom knows better than to start strong. We circle around a paved path and check my suitcase at the desk.

"Should we walk the trails or a museum?" she asks, looking at the map.

"Wherever there's air-conditioning," I say.

The trails are twisty with a variety of desert plants. Any other time I would take pictures of the bold flowers and broad branches. Today it's all a heated haze. I can't believe I'm here. That she's here.

Inside the first museum is the skeleton of a woolly mammoth with impressive tusks. We wander through the *Natural History* exhibit, all dinosaur bones and taxidermy animals. I stop at some placards and pretend to read, but it's more to get into a rhythm with Mom suddenly so close and . . . un-vanished.

"Thanks for coming today," Mom says.

"I wasn't going to," I say. "There's a reason I didn't respond to the letter."

"Do you want to respond now?" Mom asks.

"No, thank you. Let's look at the Las Vegas exhibit."

The *History of Las Vegas* exhibit is all flash, with vintage slot machines and black-and-white posters of famous entertainers on the Strip. There's western wear! Horse saddles! Old-fashioned music and antique neon signs.

"If you're not ready to talk, can I?" Mom asks. "I spoke to Ridge about some of this and—"

"I'm not Ridge," I interrupt. "He's, like, forgotten about all your issues."

"He was a lot younger." Mom is too close, but that's how she stands around people. A few steps too far into personal space. "It's not about forgetting. He never saw . . . the things you did. And you took on a lot at a very young age. More responsibility, more trauma."

"I wish I hadn't."

"Me too," Mom says.

I turn the corner and stop in front of a pink sequined wall. There are huge, bubble-shaped windows displaying wild and loud fashions. Feather showgirl fans and extravagant costumes from different plays and concerts. We stand in front of a bejeweled southern belle dress with a wide purple bonnet.

"Do you want to talk about something else?" Mom asks. "I'd love to hear about school."

"It's summer. I'm not *in* school." I gesture to the wall. "That's why we're on this funky field trip."

"Good point . . . what about your friends? Boyfriends? Girlfriends? Or . . . Ridge said you've been working on some project?"

I laugh and cover it up with a cough. Imagine. *Imagine* if I told Mom about the Supernova Quest. If she was into the idea, I'd get super defensive about Whitney. If she was against it, I'd tell her Dad wouldn't need a breakup if she hadn't already broken us *all* up.

Anyway, I came to see her. That's all she's getting.

"Let's go outside," I say. "These sequins are giving me a headache."

It's jarring, the switch from the exhibit's frenzied colors to the barren landscape. Maybe *barren* isn't the right word. Once my eyes adjust to the sun, I can take in the rainbow of desert colors. The alarmingly blue sky and draping green branches and tiny purple flowers and large boulders. (Red stones. Okay, prediction, we get it.) When we first flew in, all I saw was blah brown, but now I see shades of tawny, syrup, tortilla, hickory. Vegas has its own aesthetic.

But these colors dull to Tacoma's shine. The cherry blossoms at Point Defiance Park, the grays and blues of the ocean, Mount Rainer glowing purple in a sunset, and a normal city full of office buildings, bridges, or arts centers instead of one infinite stretch of neon casinos.

We enter another museum, this one devoted to development and water. I read another placard. "Water is a rare treasure in the desert. Springs Preserve has been a vital natural springs throughout history . . ."

"Can I say one more thing?" Mom asks.

171

She's not going to quit. I can't hear her. Armies of kids bounce around us. No focus. We should have stayed in the other museum.

"It's loud in here, right?" I ask. "And . . . busy."

I spin in a circle, searching for something calming in the crowd. But spinning in circles *creates* chaos, so now I'm dizzy and panicking about the dizziness. Why did I agree to this? I need out, out, out and space, space, space and—

"Hold tight." Mom leaves me in a quiet, private corner.

I focus on my breathing. Mom is back in a flash with a cup of water. I sit down on a bench and sip.

"Let me know when you're good."

I count a few more beats. Sip. Wait. "Yeah . . . it's fine. Go."

"Sweetie." Her hands are shaking. "I had this whole . . . talk ready in my head and, uh, I'm not explaining this right. Are you sure you want to do this now?"

"No, I never want to do this." I close my eyes. "But if we don't, the moment is going to get bigger and scarier so . . . can we get it over with?"

"Absolutely. Look, it's fine about the letter. I owe you a *million* letters, a million apologies, a million attempts at making this right. I messed up everything, I totally own it."

"How?" I ask.

"How?"

"*How* are you going to make it right?"

"That's a fair question. Yeah." She runs her hands up and down her legs, finally sliding them under her thighs. "How. Well, I'm going to try every day. I'll talk when you want. See you when I can. I'll be sober and present. I got a job—it's copyediting for Aunt Maggie's website. Her company has really grown and I'll

stay busy. I'm broke, but I'll start saving some money. I know . . .
I've done a lot of damage. Some things can't be fixed." She's crying now. Her shoulders hunched, hands still under her legs.

I don't move.

"I can't give you the life you had," she says. "That *we* had.
But I want to start being the kind of mother you need, whenever you need it."

I feel like a rude robot, sitting here all mechanical and cold.
Because it's just words. Words are words. Easy. Shaky. Untested.

But they're also—heartbreaking? Because if you looked in
my worry journal, you'd see a lot of words in there too. Words
written in dozens of Lincoln Letters. Words saying "I love Mom
no matter what" and "I would do anything to have her in my
life." Words detailing the whole layout of my panic room with
cut-and-pasted pictures of Pog as a puppy. Words comparing
our childhoods. Words asking how to make friends. Some of the
words might be bad words, but my counselor said that was okay.

I've said so many words to my mom when we weren't even
speaking. Right now, the best I can manage is two.

"Sounds good."

"Sounds good," she repeats. "Yeah?"

"Yeah."

I squeeze her hand. And we walk outside.

We eat lunch there, at the Divine Café.

The conversation starts to resemble a conversation. The
topics stay safe. The weather. Mom's new job. Ridge's favorite
video game.

Everything in my life is tied to everything else and I don't know how to discuss one thing without the other. Like I can't talk about Talia's postcards without bringing up the move, or Cooper without mentioning Vivian. Or Zara, who, oh yeah, predicted Mom's reappearance.

But I need to give at least one real thing. I pull my crystal out of my pocket and hold it out to Mom. "I collect crystals."

"Like for science or healing?"

"Both."

"It's gorgeous." Mom smiles encouragingly. "Is that an amethyst?"

"Yeah. Do you like crystals?"

"One of my friends in rehab was into Reiki."

My mouth drops open at the mention of rehab. We've never talked about rehab.

She sees my look and says, "One of the Alcoholics Anonymous steps is to turn our will over to a higher power. Most people use God. My friend was into the power of Mother Earth."

"Oh, I don't . . . I think earth is great, but I haven't thought about higher powers."

"I didn't connect to mine until I was thirty-eight," she says. "But God got me through the darkest years of my life. I pray all the time now, especially for you and Ridge. You should try it."

"Praying?" I ask.

"Yes. Or meditating or manifesting. Whatever connects you to your higher power."

I tried chatting about the weather and now we're into a discussion about God? I change the subject the first direction that comes to me.

"I've also gotten into astrology," I add. "Tarot. That kind of stuff."

"Wonderful." Mom's smile is serene. "One of my therapists at rehab told us that scriptures, crystals, anything religious or spiritual has one universal purpose."

So I guess we're staying deep. But one universal purpose? Who wouldn't want to know that?

I lean forward. "What is it?"

"To learn how to give love and learn how to be loved."

She doesn't say anything else. Just takes a mouthful of salmon. I think she's done being profound until she points at me with her fork. "Some people are fine taking love, but don't know how to show it. Or they could be loving to others but hard on themselves. Like they don't think they deserve love either way. You know?"

Does she know she's describing me? Is that why she's telling me this—so I'll receive her love? Or love her? Love myself?

There's a flurry of activity outside in the large amphitheater. Employees in black bow ties lay white tablecloths across round tables. Bistro lights string across rows of white chairs. A calligraphy sign says CLOSED FOR A WEDDING.

Springs Preserve would be a stunning wedding venue. This whole place is—wild and flourishing. And nothing like the wedding chapels on the Strip.

"A butterfly habitat!" Mom looks down at her foldable map. "Remember when you went through a butterfly phase in first grade?"

I do remember, and I'm glad she does too. But there's something else I want to see first. "Yeah, let's run into the museum before we leave."

"What?" Mom asks.

"I need to grab a brochure."

Mom follows my gaze outside. "Ah. A *wedding*. Maggie told me about the quick engagement."

"It has been short," I agree. I don't know where my allegiances lie in this conversation. I'm not sure if I'm supposed to have allegiances. "Whitney was a big surprise."

"Vegas was a big surprise." Mom drags her napkin across her mouth.

"It just sort of happened that way," I say. "We're probably coming home in a few weeks."

"*Probably?*" Mom asks.

There's my open door leading directly to plan two. Mom won't like it if I tell her Dad is making us stay. And if Mom doesn't like it, she could work to get us back to Washington. Then I wouldn't have to be the bad guy with Dad. Or Vivian.

"Yeah, like . . . Whitney lives here?" I start off tentative. I haven't talked to Mom about something this important in months. Maybe years. "So . . . I don't know what is going to happen after . . . the wedding, but . . . maybe they want us to stay? Whitney wants to stay. It's sort of a touchy subject."

"I bet." Mom pushes her plate away. "Look, I don't want you to worry. It's going to work out."

"*What* is going to work out?" I don't like vague answers. Give me an outline. Action. "Coming home to Washington?"

"I've known your dad for over fifteen years," she says. "The wildest thing I've seen him do is leave a used cereal bowl in the sink. No way is he spontaneously moving here for good."

"Dad proposed after *one day*." Mom flinches when I say this. I don't want to hurt her, but truth is truth. "And he took the work project down here. And then *stayed* down here. Dad isn't thinking the same way the Dad you know thinks."

Mom reaches across the table and squeezes my hand. "What do you want?"

It's almost funny that I see Dad every day but he hasn't asked me this question. A few hours with Mom and she's right to the point.

"I want to go home," I say. "I don't want to make things hard for Dad, but I really miss my friends and Tacoma and my Christmas pajamas."

"You've had a lot of change in your life."

Totally. Just check my palms.

"You could talk to him, yeah?" My mind windmills with problem solving. "Maybe we can find Whitney a job in Seattle—there are hotels in Seattle! And you can point out how excellent the schools are. We can wave a box of Pao's Donuts under Dad's nose. And . . . Mom! We could stay with you while they try to get everything organized and moved. It's perfect."

"You want to live with me?" Mom asks.

The idea didn't occur to me until a few seconds ago, but . . . we could. Part-part-time. That's the natural next step. We lived with her when she was sober before. We can live with her sober now.

"Yeah, like once you move out of Aunt Maggie's," I say. "Not all of the time, but I bet you can get lawyers to figure that out and make it all fair, just as long as I can keep Pog with me. Ridge wants this too, he told me his plan and—"

"Take a breath," Mom says.

I gulp in air. My negative thought patterns have flipped over to positive possibilities. Mom's visit was written in the stars. All the pressure is lifted off my shoulders. I can skip along path two into the Washington sunset.

"I clearly need to talk this out with your dad," Mom says.

"But you're better now, right?" I ask. "So you can do it."

"Better isn't the word . . ." Mom's voice trails off. I can't tell what she's thinking. Maybe she's going down a possibility path just like me. I hope her new house has an extra coat closet I can turn into a panic room. "But we will definitely come up with a plan that works."

I did not predict that my ghost from the past would be the one to turn things around, but if I've learned anything this summer, it's not to question fate.

Well, favorable fate.

Chapter 24

Talia,

Did you get my last postcard? I sent it a while ago. Maybe the mail carrier really did read it, LOL (but isn't that against the law?)

You're probably busy so no biggie, I totally understand. Actually, you can text me again if you want. It's a lot faster, obviously. Like ...if you remember.

I had some bigger stuff happen. I mean, besides the boy? Remember how my mom was sick? Well, she came to visit. It was ...positive. And unique.

Are Pilar and Chloe getting along? How was Cannon Beach? Are you excited for school to start?

I think I'll be home soon.

Stella

Ridge and I walk to the hotel pool with Mom and Aunt Maggie. They should have another name for it besides "hotel pool" because those are usually one long rectangle with a few lounge chairs and a sign saying NO LIFEGUARD ON DUTY. This place has loud music and a DJ and a million people in small swimsuits and alcohol, so much alcohol.

My mom is sober. In Las Vegas. Bad combo.

Aunt Maggie flags a waitress. "What's with the club in a pool?"

"It's the weekend." The waitress shrugs. "Always a DJ on the weekend."

Mom adjusts her beach hat. "Maggie, I'm okay."

"We don't have to swim," Ridge says.

"I bet the water is gross," I add.

Mom chews her lip. "Don't you want to dip your toes in the water?"

"Good point." I hold out my elbow for Ridge to escort me. "Shall we?"

Ridge hooks his arm into mine. We make a big deal of sashaying all the way to the edge of the pool. In unison, we ceremoniously dip our big toe into the water. Mom and Aunt Maggie die laughing. Like bent over, tears streaming.

And it's funny, probably not *that* funny, but who cares when we're all relieved and happy?

"We can leave after I talk to the DJ," Aunt Maggie says. "I'm building an entertainer section on my website, and I think she'd help boost our social media following."

Aunt Maggie marches over, all business.

Mom turns to me. "Is there anything new you want to see?"

I think about the Stratosphere, the tall tower that looks like the Space Needle. I could get a fun postcard there for Talia, but otherwise I don't want to go. There's supposed to be roller coasters that dangle you over the edge. Take two guesses how my anxiety would handle that.

"There are so many awesome things to do here, it's hard to pick," Ridge says. "What about the High Roller? It's that big Ferris wheel that's like the London Eye."

It's the first time it's occurred to me how much of the Vegas Strip is "like" something else. The Stratosphere, the High Roller, the Eiffel Tower at the Paris hotel, or the Egyptian pyramid at Luxor. So many impressions. Copies.

"That's probably expensive," I whisper to Ridge.

"Aunt Maggie is sponsoring this trip." Mom's eyes are soft. "Thanks for considering cost, but don't worry."

"Rad!" Ridge says. "The High Roller is on the bucket list my gaming club gave me."

"Are you okay with the heights, Twinkle?"

"We're in huge pods," Ridge says. "It's not a rickety Ferris wheel."

I smile brave as can be. Sometimes people check to see if you're cool with something while still begging you to accept it.

"Let's High Roll," I say.

✳ ✳ ✳

The LINQ Promenade is filled with themed restaurants and popular stores. And bars. All kinds of bars—pubs and an ice bar and margarita slushies. I watch Mom to see if she, I don't know, falters? Pauses? Springs into the bowling alley and starts chugging a pitcher? When your sky has already fallen, it's hard not to look at all the angles it can fall again.

We ride escalator after escalator until we get to the loading area. The cars are big round balls with sliding doors. There are several monitors overhead narrating facts about the High Roller and Las Vegas. The cars seat thirty to forty people, so I guess we're lucky there's only one other family with younger kids and a couple who must not have dated very long because they are very kissy.

Ridge was right. The pods aren't too bad for my anxiety. It's better than a roller coaster, but not as good as standing on regular ground. The car moves slowly, with roof views of nearby hotels. It's dusk, so we can still see the outline of the surrounding mountains. Ridge sits by Mom with his head on her shoulder. So natural, like we spend every day with her. Like she's not a recently un-vanished ghost.

"Did that DJ sign up for your website?" Mom asks Aunt Maggie.

"I got her card," Aunt Maggie says. "Vegas might be my next focus city."

"You totally should," I say. "Whitney works in hotel administration. I bet she'd help you find more clients."

Aunt Maggie snorts. "Whitney's not going to help me."

"Why not?" Ridge asks.

"Because I'm related to your mom," Aunt Maggie says.

"So?" I say.

"So that's *wrong*," Aunt Maggie says. "You don't go into business with your ex-brother-in-law's new fiancée."

"Whitney is a nice lady," Ridge says. "And it would be one phone call. Chill out, Aunt Maggie."

Mom barks a laugh. "My sister hasn't known chill for thirty years."

Aunt Maggie sits primly on the edge of the smooth orange bench. "That's because you took up all the chill in the room, big sis."

"Well, now you can have all the chill in this pod." Mom waves at the other family. "Excuse me, do you mind if my sister uses all the chill in here? I apparently stole it from her when we were kids."

Aunt Maggie reddens. "Sorry, my sister is a nuisance."

"A nuisance?" Ridge laughs. "Stella, are you a nuisance too?"

"No, I'm more of a bother."

"An annoyance," Ridge adds.

"An irritation," Mom pipes in.

"A menace," I conclude.

"Oh no." Aunt Maggie wipes her forehead with a tissue. "The synonym game. I forgot how you Norths act when you get together."

We're grinning. All three of us.

Mom's the outgoing one who never gets embarrassed. She strikes up conversations in elevators. We used to come home with new friends after every family trip. Not just acquaintances either. Legit *friends*.

She's the sun. When Mom shines, you bask in the glow.

Ridge and Aunt Maggie get wrapped in the narrated history of Vegas. Mom bumps her shoulder softly against mine. "So what's the consensus?"

"For what?"

"Are you glad I came?" Mom asks. "Did I make the right call?"

I don't say anything for a bit. I usually rush my words when I'm anxious, but I'm working on taking my time and considering. It's a big question. I want to have the right answer. "I'm glad we got over the not-seeing-each-other part. The longer it went, the bigger it felt."

"I get that," Mom says. "I should have called you once I got privileges in rehab. I even dialed your number a few times, but stopped myself again and again."

"Why would you tell me that?" I ask. "It's like giving someone an okay present and then telling them all the better things you were going to buy them instead."

"You're right," Mom says. "The point is—shame kept me from reaching out. Shame guided a lot of my choices. Not only did I lose who I was, but I wanted to escape what I'd become."

"I mean, you are my *mom*," I say. "That's not something you can escape."

I know, that's sorta what my dad told me and I sorta got annoyed with him, but it's also true.

"Yes. I am your mom." Her eyes are shiny. "And I always will be. Things will be different now. We're going to have a lot more time like this."

"What, learning Las Vegas history?" I ask.

"No." She brushes a hair out of my face. "Together."

And I can see it. Not fully formed, but an unfocused view of what *together* could mean. Beach picnics, bike rides, baking brownies . . . I shake my head. I never go on bike rides. The idea of Mom is so new it's like I have to borrow a highlight reel from a mom/daughter commercial.

The sun is almost gone. The spokes of the High Roller light up the night. The monitor shows old photos of Vegas until we are at the top, when a woman's voice says, "Congratulations, you've made it to the top. Five hundred and fifty feet above the Las Vegas Strip. You are now a true High Roller!"

"How far can you see on this?" Aunt Maggie asks.

"Into forever," Ridge says.

"Then look away." Mom scratches her arm. "I don't want to know my forever, do you?"

I know they're having a moment and all, but I have to jump in. Because this is *exactly* what I would want. "You're saying you don't want to know how things are going to turn out? Like if I had a crystal ball in my pocket, and I could tell you the future, you'd say no?"

"Sheesh, Stella. Don't make this a thing," Ridge says. "All I was trying to say is you can see far away."

"I'm with Stella on this." Aunt Maggie readjusts her blouse. "I would give a million dollars to know my forever. In a color-coded binder, if possible."

"What's the fun in that?" Mom asks. "Isn't the point to life the discovering? Being surprised and amazed? Like seeing a gorgeous sunset in a new place with people I love. Shock and awe!"

My merry mood dissolves. I have to bite my tongue to stop myself from saying anything. Not figuratively. I mean, I bite down on that fleshy muscle in my mouth until I taste metal. Blood. Because look at who is saying this! The person who flung herself into the future without thinking one tick how it impacted us. The person who forever changed our forevers! If she'd actually seen all this—the drugs, the divorce, Dad remarrying—wouldn't she want to do everything in her power to change it?

"Shock and awe," Ridge repeats. For some unknown reason, he likes this phrase.

Aunt Maggie puts her arm around me. We look at the sky together.

"If I'd known this summer was in your future, I would've told you," she says. "Whether you could change it or not. I'd still warn you."

I give her a hug. The biggest hug. "That's the nicest thing you've ever said."

The sky inks. All this talk about seeing into the future makes me wonder about the next step in my hazy plan. Because now that I'm thinking about it, I am in a literal rotating circle. Although I'm not sure if this is Mystic Shonda's same circle, since it's supposed to be Whitney's future and she's not here.

I get out my phone to text Vivian but stop myself. Following the predictions means I'm still doing the Supernova Quest. The kindest option is to avoid the topic completely for as long as I can.

But Cooper would want to hear about this. Maybe hear about anything. I open our text chain. He wrote three days ago: **How is your mom?**

And I wrote, **Good.**

And that is . . . it.

I decide to start things off slowly. So I type: **Hey there.**

He doesn't respond immediately. So now what? I have never texted a boy who isn't Ridge or Dad. Or my partner on school projects. Do I text something meaningful? Flirty? A question?

My text looks lonely all by itself, so I add a heart emoji. Except a heart emoji all alone is way too forward, so then I add a flame, but that's double flirty so I add a baby angel. Dog. Skull. Ghost. Brain. Firefighter. Money sign. Fish. Thumbs-Up. Kissy lips.

I'm about to erase the disturbing emoji train but then I hit send.

Send. SEND?

I hold my breath and watch for dots but nothing comes. He doesn't write back. Maybe he doesn't write back because I'm the worst texter in the history of the world.

Cooper is a nice guy, but even nice guys think random emoji texts are nerdy. Cooper's going to rethink the whole "you could hang with eighth graders" thing. He'll block my number and I'll shrivel into a pile of awkward dust.

Mom slides into the seat next to me. "You okay?"

I push my forehead against the glass of our car. The lights of Vegas glimmer around us. We're surrounded by a glowing valley, all glittering lights and flashing entertainment. Above us there's an eerie, glowing blackness. The sky is cloudless and bright, but despite the brilliant view, I can't see one single star.

Chapter 25

D ad and Whitney meet us in the hotel lobby. Which is very nice but very sticky because my mom is standing very close and there is something very thick in the air.

"Micah." Mom says Dad's name like it's dipped in diamonds. I realize she probably has not seen him since, well, even longer than Ridge and me. After their divorce, we often met Mom at the park or Aunt Maggie's house. Maybe she wasn't allowed to drive us, I don't know. My parents didn't speak then so . . . this could be their first interaction in more than a year. And maybe she's still in love with him? I mean, they got divorced because of drugs. Not falling out of love.

Life is messy.

Dad has on a button-down shirt and dress slacks. He stands upright, like a pencil. Whitney's smile is ruler-long.

"Hey, Clara," he says. "I'm glad we caught you. I want you to meet my fiancée, Whitney."

Mom nods, which is a little royal of her, but what is she supposed to do? Kiss Whitney's hand? Hug her? Pass over a Future Mrs. North baton? "We've met before. Remember we ran into each other in a grocery store right after Micah and I got married?"

"Oh," Whitney says.

Because what is Whitney supposed to say? Thank you?

"Well, it's nice to see you in the present," Whitney says.

"Indeed," Mom says.

"Great! So . . . thanks, Mom!" I turn and give her a quick peck on the cheek. "Fun visit. We'll see you in a couple of days."

"Bye, baby." Mom tucks her hair behind her ear. Twice. "Micah, we'll bring Ridge home Tuesday, yeah?"

"Fantastic," Dad says.

Whitney has this smile on her face, like she might spew a bunch of things she wants to say to Mom, good and bad, so I start walking toward the parking lot.

"And can we talk Tuesday?" Mom asks. "Alone?"

I stop walking. Getting back to Washington hinges on Dad's reaction. They're behind me now, so I can't see any expressions. I don't know if they're staring at each other or avoiding eye contact.

"Absolutely," Dad says.

Jackpot.

I wheel my suitcase out to the car. Dad and Whitney are behind me, whispering to each other, probably dissecting why Mom wants to talk. Maybe talking about how wispy Mom looks. Maybe assessing her sobriety. At least they don't bring her up once we're in the car.

Whitney turns around in her seat. "You are a genius! I talked to the wedding coordinator at the Springs Preserve and it's a perfect fit! And the fact that they had an opening this close to the wedding! It's fate."

I smile. "I thought you'd like it."

"You know me," Whitney says.

Dad looks in the rearview mirror and winks. The handoff was hard even before Mom vanished. The few minutes between leaving one parent and going to the other. There are questions in his eyes. I miss Mom and miss whatever Dad stuff I missed while I was with her. I know Whitney doesn't mean anything by it, but bringing up the wedding the second after I said goodbye is rough.

I lay back in my seat. Dad turns up the music. The wedding is two and a half weeks away. Nothing has changed. Everything is changing.

You would think having my Formerly Vanished Mom meet my Possible Stepmother would be the oddest part of the day. But then I walk into the living room and there's Cooper, playing a video game with Vivian's dad, who has Pog on his lap.

I stop in the doorway. My rolling suitcase gets stuck on the doorframe and does one of those death wobbles, crashing at my feet.

"That's an entrance," Vivian says.

"Cooper. Hey." I kick my suitcase across the threshold. "What, uh . . . What are you doing here?"

"Vivian and Gemma are hanging out later. I asked what you were doing. She invited me over."

Vivian beams at me like she's done me the world's biggest favor, but the truth is I *hate* surprises. Even good surprises, like parties or presents or a new friend showing up in the living room.

My body doesn't know the difference between good surprise or bad surprise. I automatically go into full adrenaline alert.

Whitney and Dad walk up behind me. Dad stumbles on the same step. Whitney, who I'm guessing isn't a big surprise person either, actually gasps.

"Sorry, I asked Vivian if I could come in." Travis gives Pog a little pet and stands. "I, uh, well . . . I got you a wedding present."

The gift, wrapped with ivory wrapping paper, sits heavy on the kitchen counter. Travis hoists the box on his hip.

"I was a jerk when we met." He slides the box over to Dad. "Vivian says you've been good to her. And Whitney. You seem like a decent dude so . . . here."

"Wow." Dad smiles huge. "Yeah. Of course."

"It's a blender." Travis shrugs. "Viv said it'd be funny, since you're blending a family."

"That's so considerate." Whitney moves to the side to open the doorway. Her voice is void of emotion. "Thank you for stopping by."

"Sure." Travis points at Cooper. "You have my screen handle, kid. I want a rematch."

Dad shakes Travis's hand in this strong, meaningful way. Dad might actually hug him if Travis doesn't leave soon. Vivian rolls her eyes. Almost every kid of divorce wants their parents, and stepparents, to get along. But it doesn't make it any less awkward to witness.

Pog whines when Travis leaves, which isn't very emotional support dog of him.

Whitney collapses on the couch.

"Sorry, Mom," Vivian says.

"Oh! No apology. Your dad was so gracious. I'm just over-whelmed." Whitney offers a weak smile to Cooper. "You must be Ridge's friend? He's not here."

"No, uh." Cooper shuffles his feet. "I was . . . stopping by to see Stella?"

Then every person in the room turns to look square at me. Being stared at by a large group is fantastic for anxiety, by the way. Two pivotal interactions with exes and yet I'm suddenly the focal point.

"I need a minute," I say.

I grab Pog and my Magic 8 Ball and lock myself in the bath-room. I sit on the toilet and pet pet pet Pog. Breathe breathe breathe.

My breath echoes across Whitney's bathroom. I never heard breath echoes in my panic room. My panic room doesn't echo; it cocoons. I might as well be sitting in a black hole right now, that's how huge and hollow this bathroom is.

By the way, I don't care about the Travis thing. He was nice and we needed a new blender. But the first surprise? Cooper in the living room? Why why why?

Breathing isn't doing anything. I grab a towel and try to swad-dle myself tight tight tight. Pog licks my arm, which is sweet, but he's never understood that licking is actually gross. At least he sees how bad this situation is.

Unless it's good?

Is this good?

I shake the Magic 8 Ball.

"Is it good that Cooper is here?"

The triangle reads SIGNS POINT TO YES.

I shake again. "What should I do with him?"

The ball answers, CONCENTRATE AND ASK AGAIN, although it doesn't matter because I didn't ask a yes or no. I toss the toy onto the bathroom rug.

Pog hops off my lap. I pace pace pace. I need to talk to someone, like a real person, not a plastic fortune teller. Vivian is the right answer, but Vivian is sitting next to Cooper and actually she's the reason for this freak-out and why didn't she send me a warning text? This is totally something I should meditate on for days. Research! Spreadsheet! Graph! ANGST!

Whitney? Do I ask Whitney? But she might Make It a Thing, like when she got all emotional about our bridesmaid bouquets.

I curl into the bathtub. Water drip drip drips from the faucet. I turn it tight, then reconsider because the *plop plop plop* gives me something to count.

Not Dad, right? Too uncomfortable. Aunt Maggie would have smart advice, but Mom would want in on the action and I'm not opening the door that wide this fast.

That's the hard thing about a situation that looks good but is actually bad. Or maybe it's bad but actually good. If I were writing this on a postcard to Talia, I would make the Cooper visit sound amazing, everything is amazing, just like people do on social media . . .

Wait.

TALIA.

I click on her contact info.

I call. Hang up. I call. Hang up. Call and . . . my thumb freezes. Phone rings.

She answers on the second ring. "Hey, girl! Did you call me twice?"

"Hi!" My voice is chipper. Too chipper. I did it. I called her.

Out of the blue. Like a . . . like a friend. "Hahaha, whoops. Yeah. Anyway, I need help."

"Is this boy stuff?" she asks. "Tell me it's boy stuff."

"It's most *definitely* boy stuff." I let out a breath. "Okay, so Cooper."

"Your boyfriend."

"What? No." Pog scratches on the tub. I rest him on my belly. His weight is wonderful. "He's not my boyfriend. He's a . . . friend. I think. Like, he must be my friend because he just randomly showed up at my house!"

"Where is he now?" she asks.

"Living room."

"Where are you?"

In the bathtub with my emotional support pug and a Magic 8 Ball. Duh. "I went in the other room to call you."

"Okay, sooooo what's the problem?" she asks. "Like, don't you guys hang out all the time?"

"Yeah, but . . . um, I sent him this text? And then he showed up?"

"What did the text say?"

"I'm so embarrassed." I swallow. "I was sort of practice texting and then I hit send."

"Read it to me."

"I wrote, 'Hey there' with a bunch of, uh, random emojis!"

"Which emojis? Any kissy lips?"

I want to disappear. "Yes."

"So flirty!" Talia squeals. "This is better than our lifeguard gossip! You're living a romance novel."

I instantly regret all the postcard drama. Cooper is an actual person—using him to create juicy postcards wasn't smart. What if he'd *seen* those postcards? I would turn to dust. Dustier than dust.

"So what do I do?" I bite on a nail.

"What do you mean?"

WHAT DO I MEAN? Isn't it obvious? I need a minute-by-minute plan here.

"I don't know," I say. "I don't know what I'm doing. Most of the time. All of the time. I wake up every day and I'm not sure what I should do or even who I am. And I would talk to Vivian about it, but she sprung this on me after I'd been gone for days."

"Who is Vivian?"

"She's my stepsister. Well, potential. We're trying to break up our parents' wedding using divination. I mean, sort of. The crystals seemed to work. Horoscopes not so much. Tarot was dead-on. Oh, and this psychic gave us all these predictions, and they're all coming true, so I don't know if fate is fate no matter what you do or if there is any say in our destiny, you know?"

"Whoa." Talia giggles. "You did *not* cover this in your postcards."

"I tried to lead with the exciting stuff."

"You might get a *sister*!" Talia says. "That's so much cooler than a boy. Cooler than a lifeguard."

"Really? You think?"

"Look. Relax," Talia says. "This is all good! You have the Dad-getting-married stuff *and* a cute boy visiting! Go talk to him. Get him a snack so he's chewing. That saves you from talking. But he's not the important thing here, is he?"

"What's the important thing?" I ask.

"Oops, I owe you another postcard! Sorry, we were out of town and then this new girl moved in down the street. Molly.

You'll like her—she'll be on our same bus stop. Oh wait, unless you live there now. Do you?"

First of all, *what's the important thing* and why is this girl Molly moving onto *my* bus stop and I don't know where I live but I do know there's a boy in the living room of the house I'm in right now.

After we hang up, I grab my backpack and dig around until I find my crystals. I squeeze the rose quartz and amethyst and try to set an intention.

"Okay, universe. I would like some calm please. And friendship. Whatever kind you want. If there is some *like* liking friendship in there too, that's okay." I open one eye and look around the bathroom, trying to remember how to end the meditation. "So yeah. Go team!"

The universe doesn't respond.

But I still get out of the bathtub.

Chapter 26

Cooper sits at the kitchen table. Whitney has already loaded him with snacks. She gives me a thumbs-up behind his back. Will she ever not be embarrassing?

"Well, I'll let you kids get back to your *video game*." Whitney puts way too much emphasis on the words, like it's code for something else.

"You want to play *Cosmo Kingdom*?" Cooper asks.

"I don't like that game," I say. "We can play *Tetris* on our phones?"

"Sure."

So we sit on the couch. I find the perfect position. Comfortable now. Way less freaked out. Breathing decent.

We don't play against each other, but we start our games at the exact same time to see who can play longer or get the higher score. What I told Cooper a while ago is totally true. Focusing on *Tetris* makes all the other stuff melt away. It's just me and those cubes.

Cooper. I'm still aware that he's here. But I can almost forget the text I sent him. It's not like he brought it up. Maybe he

didn't read anything into it. Maybe Talia is right. This is . . .
fun?

After *Tetris*, we play Scattergories. We eat more snacks. We
play fetch with Pog, who runs in circles until he almost falls
over from being dizzy. I have never hung out like this. With a
boy—with *anyone*. No plan, no agenda. Super chill.

"Do you want to go outside and do something?" Cooper
whispers.

"Yeah, but why are you whispering?"

"I think your stepmom is listening to us."

"Yeah, there's sports stuff in the garage."

The garage is hot—maybe at some point Vegas people stop
being surprised every time they step outside into Satan's armpit,
but I'm not there yet. Whitney has a large bin of random stuff—a
skateboard, balls, whatever. Cooper picks out a badminton kit.

"I flipping love badminton!" he says. "Can you play?"

"If it's like tennis, I can."

"You play tennis?" Cooper asks.

"I . . . used to."

"Grab the tennis rackets. We'll play in the street."

And here's the thing—I do it. Whitney's in a cul-de-sac, so
we can spread out far. Cooper drags a trash can into the middle
of the street, calls it our "net," and we hit until the streetlights
come on. Cooper pretends like he's a sports announcer at Wim-
bledon, shouting things like "North with a backhand volley" in
a British accent.

It's nothing like the tournaments I'm used to. My mom isn't
whistling in the stands, a Gatorade by her side. I'm not wearing
a white skirt and there's no coach silently appraising each play.
No order, no precision, no rules.

198

But there is the song of a swinging racket. The bounce of the ball against the strings. Tennis shoe squeaking on the street. That green fuzzy smell. A dry breeze. Throaty laughter as the ball whirs past.

I could have picked and plotted for days and still not have created a more perfect return to this sport. It's a gift. Truly.

We shake hands across the net (again, a trash can) and flop onto the neighbor's grass while we wait for Cooper's mom. The day started out tense, but now I'm relaxed and . . . free? I'm not worrying about what Cooper is thinking or what is happening with my parents.

This rose quartz is truly working its powers tonight.

"I'm glad you came over," I say.

"Well, you texted me."

I sit up on my elbows. "You saw that?"

"The text of a thousand emojis? Yeah. I figured you were playing around."

"Totally." Playing around? That was code. *Eloquent* code. "Actually, it was a butt emoji."

"I've done that."

This isn't a date. But it's something, right? The streetlights are bright, so are the houses, so is everything. I love Las Vegas at night. I love *this* night. The non-night.

"You have to come to the country club with me," Cooper says. "We'll play tennis and swim at the pool."

"I'm . . . sort of busy?" Tennis at a country club is a different level. I'm not ready yet. "The wedding is in a few weeks."

"Then after that," Cooper says. "Once we start school."

"I move before my school starts," I say.

"Oh, I thought . . . Vivian made it sound like you'll stay."

Cooper looks down at his phone. He pretends to read a text, but I didn't see any new texts on the icon. I think he's reading an old text to avoid looking at me.

"My mom said we're going back to Washington," I say. "She's talking to my dad about it soon."

"That's great," Cooper says. "You'll have to keep sending me your *Tetris* scores so I can feel good about myself, 'kay?"

"You mean so I can destroy your confidence? Sure."

Then he does the oddest thing. He slides his hand across the grass until our fingers touch. His hand isn't sweaty, despite the summertime tennis. It's actually cold. And soft.

I don't say anything because if we start talking, I'll mention the hand holding, and I'm pretty sure you're not supposed to draw attention to it. In fact, I think I should pretend like we aren't touching at all.

"You're really good at tennis," he says.

"You're better."

"Why'd you quit?"

I never told him I quit, but Cooper's a kid who reads between the lincs.

"It was too much pressure," I say. "At tournaments . . . there's not a huge crowd, but the people there are watching you, only you. I hated being in the spotlight. I'm just better at blending in."

Cooper laughs. Hard. So hard that he drops my hand and sits up. He starts choking and coughing and it's a whole minute until he can talk again. "Blend in?"

"You shouldn't laugh at me." I pull my knees to my chest. Here I open myself up and he *laughs*.

Car headlights shine down the street. It's Cooper's SUV. He

needs to drive away and never talk to me again. I don't care how high his *Tetris* scores are.

"I'm not laughing *at* you." Cooper leans in. The streetlights are behind him, so his face is shadow with halo all around. "I meant—you don't blend in. Your name literally means star."

"So?"

His mom honks. Cooper gets on his knees and bends down close to my ear.

"So Stella North. You . . . *shine*."

And then he's up, opening the car door, waving, driving away.

Leaving me alone in the dark that's not really dark, my heart once again racing but finally, finally, finally in a thrilling way.

Chapter 27

I float, flutter, fly back into the house. We've been outside long enough that everyone is back to their normally scheduled activity. Whitney and Dad watch a show while Pog sleeps in between them. Vivian's in her room, painting her toenails.

She brightens when I walk in. "That was a long playdate."

"We're just friends."

"The way he looks at you is not *just* friends."

"I thought you were hanging out with Gemma?"

"We just said that to get Cooper over here," she says. "She's filming tonight."

I sit on her bed and start rifling through her bin of nail polish colors. I haven't painted my nails in years. It's too hard to do it myself and usually there's no one home but Ridge. I don't see him as having a steady hand or attention to detail, you know.

"Want me to paint?" Vivian asks.

I run into the bathroom to wash my hands. I stop myself right before I turn the water on, considering the earlier hand holding. I put my hand close to my face and sniff. There's nothing Coopery in the scent. I wash, dry, and run out to Vivian, who gets to work with a nail file.

"So do you like him?" Vivian asks.

"I don't know. Sort of?" I split into a grin. "Probably."

"Oh, I love it!" She claps her hands together. "If you two get married, then Gemma is your sister! And I'm her . . . what would it be? If she's my stepsister's sister-in-law—"

"Slow it down." I hand her a pink nail polish—Flashbulb Fuchsia. For a quick second, I wonder if Cooper would like the color. Except I doubt Cooper would notice the color. Although he did say I shine! Should I switch to gold instead? "Seriously, we hung out. That's it. He's a good friend."

"Okay, fair. Fair." She fans her toes. "Wait, he's a Taurus, right? Let's look up Taurus and Virgo compatibility."

I already have and we're both earth signs, but I'm not going down that road. "How was your weekend with your dad?"

"Ahh, changing the subject, are we?" She winks. "Okay, fine. It was awesome. We golfed. Drank boba. Shoe shopped."

"You golf?" I ask.

"Dad-Vivian does, yeah." Vivian unscrews the nail polish. "What did you do with your mom?"

"Wait, I'm confused. Who is Dad-Vivian?"

Vivian scoots in close and starts swiping the polish on my pointer finger. "That's the person I am with my dad. We had to find things we both like doing to bond us. And I act different over there. I don't know why—I heard that a lot of divorce kids have to shift some of their personality into the different homes." She looks up at me. "Don't you? I mean, weren't you different with your mom?"

I think about the last few days and yes, I was different, but I can't tell if that has anything to do with seeing my mom or just all the differences that have happened overall. Like Zara said,

I have change written all over me. I can't separate where and why it's happening. Meeting Vivian has changed me. Living in a new place. My summer research has changed the way I think and act. Like all the high vibration stones and mindful meditation has helped? A little?

"You might not know how you are with your mom since it's so new." Vivian dabs at some skin with a Q-tip. "That had to be intense. How'd it go?"

I'd thought about telling Talia this stuff. You tell friends big things. But I also had no idea where to start with Talia. How much backstory to give her—backstory I'd rather leave, well, back. Her parents are still married. She lives in the place she's always lived with friends she's always had. Talia would be sweet about it. But she might not get it.

Vivian is, however, *involved*. Heavily involved. She might not listen to everything I say, might give her blunt opinion, but the person who understands what I want most right now is the person I've shared a room with—shared a plan with—this entire summer.

"It went better than I thought," I say. "Mom looks healthy. She seemed honest. But I couldn't tell when she was lying when I was little. So I don't know how to tell now."

"Did you forgive her?" Vivian asks. A gut punch question only she could ask.

"Halfway," I say. "I forgot how much I love her."

"It feels good, huh?"

"It really does."

"And it hurts," she says.

"Uh-huh."

"Well, congratulations." Vivian drops my hand and motions for the other. "And I'm sorry."

"Ha, yeah. It's both."

We stay silent as Vivian paints my other hand. I watch her, the way she focuses on each nail like it's a canvas. Then I let my gaze wander around the space. Vivian's room has stayed clean since the Fourth of July. Not only clean but organized. And that's when I notice it. A small white side table by my bed. She's put my crystals in a bowl next to a green lamp. My library books are stacked neatly on the bottom shelf.

"Did you . . . did you get me a nightstand?" I ask.

"Now you notice." Her cheeks go pink. "Dad had to run to Target for the blender anyway. It was easy to put together."

But this isn't an easy thing. Or a small one. Vivian got me a gift. Not only got one, *made* one! It's thoughtful and perfect but also odd and impractical. Why get me a nightstand in a room she wants me out of? Just over two weeks for us to cancel the wedding and go our separate ways. A piece of furniture isn't very separate, is it?

"I like it," I say. "I won't need it for long, but it's perfect for now."

"Oh, that's only half of it!" Vivian slides her hand under her bed until she finds a smooshed brown gift bag with purple tissue. "Here's the other present."

"Why are you getting me so many presents?"

"Scorpios are excellent gift givers." She shrugs. "Love language or something. Open it!"

I wave my wet fingernails around. "I can't."

"I got it." She pulls out the limp purple tissue and plunges her hands into the bag. There's two sticks. No, candles. Silver and elegant with small carvings on the base.

"They're manifestation candles!" Vivian says. "Dad took me to a spell store. He was sketched out, but lucky for us his love language is doing things I want even if he's not into it."

"Geminis are followers," I say.

"And Virgos like to keep the peace. So I know you'll do this with me."

I blow on my nails. A few more minutes and I'll be dry. "I'm not in a mystical mood tonight."

"Hey, the clock is ticking on this wedding. We need all our focus and bravery."

Mention of the wedding floods me with guilt. I'm done with the Supernova Quest. I can't keep investing in these cosmic strategies to break up our parents because I don't want them broken up. And Mom is taking care of the Washington work.

But I can't tell Vivian any of that.

"Focus and bravery," I say. "Got it."

"The lady at the spell store said Monday is the moon's day for the week. The moon is good for domestic matters, which I think means house and family stuff. And the silver color is to refresh relationships with family. Oh, and it's a new moon tonight. It's a good time to bring energy in."

"What does that have to do with us?" I ask. "What's our intention?"

"Hold on. I have a whole speech ready for this." She pulls her legs underneath her. "So obviously, my dad is on board with the wedding. He was so cute picking out the blender, by the way. I made sure it had a smoothie setting."

"Is your intention about the blender?" I ask.

"No. Dad gave me advice that switched my brain around. He said I need to get more loose about my definition of family. Oh, I need this lit while I say this next part."

She strikes a match and lights each of our candles. The flames sparkle white.

My eyes sting. Is she saying what I think she's saying? Has Vivian come around to this idea—to *me*?

"We don't have to be blood-related to be family." Vivian's eyes shine in the candlelight. "This wedding . . . it's okay. I'm not going to try and break them up anymore. We can be sisters."

Sisters. I never let myself realize how much I wanted this exact thing.

And I don't have to quit the Supernova Quest—Vivian's quitting it for us! Not that I regret doing it, not one bit, because this was in the cards for us. Maybe Mystic Shonda saw this too. Actually . . .

"Viv." I wave the candlelight in a circle. "Here's our rotating circle. Unless it was a metaphor."

"Prediction complete." She grins. "Our destinies are entwined."

"My sister the Scorpio," I say. "My step-Scorpio-sister. I'll play with it."

"And our first order of sisterly business will be to make some closet space in *our* room."

The last line sucks the air out of me. Out of the house. Out of the universe. "Our room?"

"Yeah, that's why I got you the nightstand." Vivian points to the corner. "Mom said we can get you a real bed. A dresser. I'll move some of my stuff. Give you space."

"Space?" I close my eyes. I feel like I'm floating. Like I'm out of my body. Like we're two different planets. "Vivian. Who says we're staying *here*?"

"Mom does." Vivian's voice is flat. "Me."

"I'm sorry, I don't know how to tell you this, but . . . my mom won't let that happen." We have a plan. She has a job and sobriety. Mom might have messed up before, but that doesn't mean Dad can move us without her blessing.

And it doesn't mean everyone gets to decide my life for me either. That's the whole problem with the summer and engagement and life. No one asked me. Vivian switched her plans and assumed I would go along with it. My horoscopes keep telling me to take a stand. To control my fate. And I'm finally at a point where I can.

"Let's make sure you're not setting expectations too high." Vivian places a hand on my shoulder. "Just because your mom blows into town like Mary Poppins on her umbrella, it doesn't mean she's not going to disappear again."

I can't decide what bothers me more—the words she's saying or the way she's saying them. All earnest and superior, like I haven't had people say mean things about my mom for years. Like Mom deserves this treatment after all her hard work. When Vivian's dad talks about family, it's an epiphany. When my mom does, it's nonsense.

"Well, Mary Poppins said she's going to make Dad bring us home."

"Your dad can get a lawyer." Vivian analyzes her nails. "I bet he'll win. Your mom didn't talk to you for months. That won't look good in court."

I snub out the candle. "This isn't your business."

"Hey! We're supposed to put out the flame together." Vivian

reaches across the bed and pats my knee. "We can relight it. And I know this mom stuff is hard. No one knows that better than me. So I'm here for you. Sister's promise."

I jerk my knee. Her hand flops off. It's dark in the room, so dark she probably doesn't see the darkness sparking out of me. The betrayal and hurt.

Fury.

"I want you to listen closely," I say through clenched teeth. "We will never, ever be sisters. I don't live here."

"What in the world?" Vivian jumps up and flips on the light switch. Her face is a storm of shock. "Of course you're living here! That was your second path. I know you couldn't tell me during the card reading. The ghost from the past showing up right at the moment made it so obvious—"

"Shut up about the predictions!" I feel under her bed for the poster board, holding it triumphantly in her face. "I quit the quest, okay?"

"What do you mean *quit*?" she asks. "You can't quit your fate."

"But this isn't my fate!" I wave the poster board. It flops up and down. "This isn't *my* life. We're in your room! Your town. Your rules!"

"Bull! Everything on that poster board was your idea."

"Well, it's trash. The whole plan was garbage." And then I rip the poster board in half, banging my nails in the process. Swipes of pink run across the ripped paper. "My second path wasn't about staying in Vegas. I was trying to move everyone to Washington!"

"*Washington?*" She snorts. "You see your mom one time and you think we're going to change everything in our lives just for her?"

Now she's up in my face, really close. I want to punch her, to shove her, to make her stop *being*. Because if she didn't exist, then Whitney would have moved to Washington anyway. If Vivian wasn't here, I wouldn't have to share a room or feel like a baby. The quest got in the way of seeing the truth.

"You make one cheap nightstand and you think I'm going to change everything in my life just for you?" I ask.

Vivian steps back, like I hit her. She didn't see things going this way. Because she never sees *me*.

I almost snap the manifestation candles in half, but even in my rage, I can tell I've done enough.

"Keep your room." I grab my pillow, my blanket, and my Magic 8 Ball. "I'll sleep on the couch."

"Why don't you go sleep on the couch in *Washington*!" she shouts.

The most confusing thing is: I don't want to. I want to stay in *our* room. I want to go home. I want to be with Dad. I want to be with Mom.

Mostly, I want to fast-forward to the far future, a kind future, where none of these problems exist.

Where I didn't just lose my best friend.

Chapter 28

Stella,

The High Roller looks fun. But I'm confused—why was your mom there? You didn't mention that on the phone. I don't know what the story is with her? Is she sick? Is she moving there too? And what's up with Cooper?

I have other news too (although the lifeguard was important!). My nai nai is sick. We are going to San Francisco to stay with her this week. I've never seen anyone I love this sick. It hurts so much that I try not to think about what might happen but you can't turn off your brain, you know? Anyway, I'm telling you because I think you'll understand.

Please pray for her. If that is your thing.

Love,
Talia

I wake up to Pog on top of me, his drool dripping on my neck.

"Pog. No." I push him away. There's sunlight, so much sunlight.

"Your dad already took him on a walk this morning," Whitney says.

She's at the kitchen table, a mountain of ribbon and tulle spread around her. There's a large bag of candy and tiny boxes. Whitney has on a stained sweatshirt and cut-off plaid pajama pants.

"Um . . . looks like you've had a busy morning," I say.

Whitney flops her head down on the table. "I've been doing this since five A.M. I'm surprised you slept through it."

"I've been really . . . tired."

"You and me both, babe." Whitney sits up and cuts the tulle into small squares. I watch her from the couch, transfixed.

"Do you want to help?" she asks.

"Oh, sure." I'm light-headed. I cried so much last night . . . Maybe I'm dehydrated? "Let me brush my teeth."

Whitney organizes stations for us, with piles of tulle and ribbons. "These are called *bomboniere*. It's an Italian wedding tradition. You put five Jordan almonds in each bag and tie it up."

I slide into the chair next to her. "Why five?"

She digs around until she finds another pile of printed cards. "We attach these cards. 'Jordan almonds are an essential part of every Italian wedding. Traditionally, each guest receives five almonds symbolizing Health, Wealth, Happiness, Fertility, and Long Life.'"

"Would you rather us assemble these one by one or take jobs? Like I can put the almonds in the tulle and you can wrap it with the ribbon and card?"

"Organization! Order!" Whitney pushes a mass of knotted hair away from her face. "Finally."

We hit our stride quickly. I bite on an almond, but it hurts my jaw.

"Careful. My nonno lost a tooth on one of those."

"Which almond was it?" I ask. "Happiness or Health?"

Whitney smiles as she ties another bow. "I don't like how they taste either, but our family always has these at weddings. And your dad is supposed to carry a tiny piece of iron in his suit pocket. And I need to rip a bit of the veil."

"Why?"

"For good luck. Italians have all sorts of superstitions." She drops an almond bundle in a box. "Mom still thinks Travis and I had bad luck from the start because someone didn't clink a glass when Dad gave a toast at our wedding."

"I'll be on Mom duty all day," I say. "Make sure she's happy."

"That's a task." Whitney cracks her neck. "My mom likes your dad. She liked him the first time we dated. But she'd like it more if he was Catholic."

Wait, is she going to make Dad Catholic now? Am I Catholic now? Is that how this works? "So she's mad about the wedding?"

"Oh, not at all." Whitney grabs a Post-it and jots a note. "But it wouldn't hurt to add some more traditional elements for her. Maybe we'll do a reading."

"You guys haven't ever been traditional." I shrug. "Why start now?"

"Your dad made the same point."

"Where is Dad anyway?" I ask.

"With your mom," Whitney says.

"Oh."

"It's been a long time." She scrunches her nose. "There's a lot to discuss."

Discuss is a soft word. Mom is fighting for my middle school future right now. And Dad is . . . I don't know how he'll respond. Maybe he'll be receptive. Relieved. They're probably hammering out a custody agreement right this very second.

Whitney keeps tying ribbons, which has to be hard. Not the tying, but the Not Talking about what is happening right now. Not Talking about everything that happened in the past. She's not a go-with-the-flow person.

"And, uh . . . where's Vivian?" I ask.

"She left early. Had to blow off steam after your fight."

"She told you we had a fight?" I ask.

"Sweetie, the whole neighborhood knows you had a fight."

"Oh."

"I put my head next to the air vent. Vivian used to do it when she was little so she could overhear my TV shows." Whitney stands and stretches. "I think we all need to have a talk tonight, 'kay? There's a lot of uncertainty. Let's get everything settled before the wedding."

She's vague here. What is the "everything" that's going to be settled?

"You good on the almonds?" I ask. "I need to do some things."

"Yes, oh!" Whitney clangs around the kitchen until she finds what she is looking for. "I found this when I was running wedding errands."

It's a beige cafeteria tray, the kind with the three different food compartments.

"Interesting wedding china," I say.

"No, I thought . . . you don't like your food touching, right?"

She pushes up a droopy sleeve. "This should help when you're eating at the house. If you want."

I can't handle thoughtfulness this early in the morning. Not from the person my mom might be starting a custody fight with as we speak. "Great! I'm, uh, actually going to head back to Vivian's room while she's gone. I need to . . . I have lots of research."

I don't wait to see the expression on her face. I'm starting to care about her expressions. About her reactions. About . . . Whitney.

In Vivian's room, I scour through the books and magazines—up, down, sideways, backward—searching for something I missed. A sign or clue to make everyone happy.

I spot one magazine shoved under Vivian's pillow. The August issue, dog-eared to the horoscope section. Of course mine is accurate. And of course, it's annoying.

You're rolling into August with major Leo energy. This fire season means things are heating up in your love life. Be bold and confident—Virgo season is next! Finish off your year around the sun with strength and wisdom. Now is the time for self-reflection. To ask yourself what you want to happen next. You might face conflicting paths. Choose wisely—this will set your course for years to come.

Chapter 29

I take a snack break after a few hours of unhelpful research. Whitney and Vivian sit at the kitchen table, which is scattered with printed photos. Whitney has her head in her hands. Something's wrong.

"Hey, Stella." Whitney swipes at her eyes. She's been crying. "You're probably starving. I ordered a pizza."

"You got pepper and sausage, right?" Vivian asks.

Nobody likes pepper and sausage but her.

I pick up one of the printer-quality photographs. There's a finger blocking half the image. The other part looks like it's outside of a Starbucks.

"What are these?" I ask.

"I'm still figuring that out," Whitney says. "But you don't need to worry about it."

"She won't worry, Mom," Vivian says. "This is exactly what little Miss Stella Blue wants."

"Vivian Angelina Marin," Whitney says. "Stop it."

Vivian thrusts a photo into my hand. It's Mom sitting at a table outside of Starbucks. She hands me another with Dad next to her. It's sorta blurry. Are they hugging? Or are they . . . kissing?

"Where did you get these?" I ask.

"I took them." Vivian snatches the photos. "They didn't even notice me. Your mom and dad were so intent on each other."

"So you're spying on my family now?" I ask.

"Girls, please." Whitney stands between us. There's a current in the air. "I'm going to talk to Micah. This is an adult issue."

The garage door opens and Ridge slides into the kitchen, Dad not far behind. They freeze when they see us.

"What's . . . going on here?" Dad asks.

"Adult issues," Vivian says.

"Micah, can you come talk to me in my bedroom?"

"No way," Vivian says. "I deserve to know why you're cheating on my mom."

"I am?" Dad takes the photo from Vivian and stares close. "I don't speak teenager. Is this a joke?"

Whitney looks steady, but I have no clue what she's feeling. "Vivian followed you today to take those photos."

"You took *Mom* on a date?" Ridge snatches the photo from Dad. "Is this when I went to breakfast with Aunt Maggie?"

"We weren't on a date!" Dad's voice shakes. "We had a coffee and hugged goodbye. Obviously."

"And kissing!" Vivian says.

"I don't think they're kissing." Ridge turns the paper upside down.

"I hugged her to be nice." Dad's voice is higher. Louder. "We'd just had a hard, important talk. Whit, this isn't what it looks like."

"It's exactly what it looks like," Whitney says. "You talking to your ex-wife about co-parenting. Which is hard, so really? I should frame that photo."

"I love you." Dad crosses the room and bear hugs Whitney. "You have no idea how much."

"I know," Whitney says. "But we still need to talk about this."

Oh, they will. Dad will explain whatever Mom explained to him, and Whitney might be just as shocked by the Washington news as she is by the pictures, but . . . everything is going to work out. I'm at peace with it.

"No. Nuh-uh," Vivian shouts. "I showed the photos. The proof. Now you're supposed to break up. *Purge your toxic relationships.* That's what my horoscope said."

"Sweetie, we're blending a family," Whitney says. "I'm glad Micah talked to Clara. Your dad and I talked last week too. It's not something to spy on."

Vivian throws the photos on the ground. They scatter around us. Ridge puts a photo in his pocket. I'm tempted to grab one too. My parents don't need to get back together, but it's nice to see them getting along.

"Why isn't this working?" Vivian clenches her fists. "What about Supernova Quest?"

"Is that a video game?" Ridge asks.

"Stella and I have been trying all summer to break you up," Vivian continues. "The horoscopes, the crystals, the psychic . . ."

"What are you talking about?" Whitney's voice is ice. Spiky, deathly cold ice.

"Tell them, Stella," Vivian says. "About our deal."

No one talks. No one breathes. If they were all superheroes

with laser-beam vision, I'd burn right to the ground under the intensity of their stares.

My stomach instantly cramps. I can't look anyone in the eye. "Whitney, I mean . . . that was weeks ago."

"We lit manifestation candles *yesterday!*" Vivian says.

"You were manifesting our family!" I shout.

"But you put that light out, didn't you?" Vivian shouts back. "You don't want us."

"This?" I wave my arms around in huge circles. "War? Anxiety? Yeah, genius. I don't want this."

Ridge shoulders next to me. "Leave my sister alone."

"You can *keep* your sister," Vivian says.

"You're a spoiled brat who always gets her way." Ridge crosses his arms over his chest. I have never loved him more. "No one even likes pepper and sausage, okay?"

As if on cue, the doorbell rings.

Dad and Whitney exchange a tired look.

"Okay. Okay." Whitney takes Vivian by the hand.

Dad puts his arms around me and Ridge, squeezing our very tense shoulders.

"Micah and I are going to have a talk," Whitney says.

"That's a good idea." Dad's voice breaks. "You guys . . . eat your pizza."

"I'm not eating with *her*," Ridge says.

"Then eat in the living room." Whitney throws up her hands. "In the garage. I don't care anymore."

Dad slides a hand on Whitney's waist and gently leads her to the bedroom.

We don't talk to each other or the pizza lady as we pay.

Vivian props her box on her hip. "I can't be around you right now."

"That's fine." Ridge shrugs. "We don't have anywhere to go because our house is in another state. So I guess *you* can leave."

I try my best not to smile at Ridge's don't-mess-with-us attitude. Vivian grabs a Diet Coke out of the fridge and slams the front door behind her.

Ridge and I eat in total silence. With anyone else, it would be awkward, but with Ridge the silence is comforting. We don't have to talk about not talking.

"I need to slay some orcs," Ridge says, wandering into the living room to play his video game.

"Okay. Um . . . thanks for helping."

"I'm sorry your plan was a mess," Ridge says.

"The funny thing is, I switched to your plan."

"Maybe we make a new plan now," Ridge says.

"Can we please stop saying the word *plan*?" I ask.

I grab another slice and wander into my room. Vivian's room. Whoever's room. I'm about to put on some meditative music when I hear Dad and Whitney's murmured conversation. Didn't Whitney say she can overhear conversations from the air vents?

I stick my head close.

"You're right, Whit," Dad says. "You're absolutely right."

I pull my head back. I shouldn't. I really, really shouldn't. Like Whitney said, these are adult issues. But, in my experience, adult issues create equally large kid issues. Kid issues that the kids don't have the power to do anything about.

Pog scratches at the door. His breathing might block the sound, so I don't let him in.

I lie belly down to listen.

"I don't know what else we can do," Whitney says.

"Therapy," Dad says. "We can do family therapy."

"That . . . yes. We should. We should have done that from the start."

"And we can talk this out," Dad says. "These emotions are normal, I'm sure."

"But, Micah." Whitney sighs a sigh so big I can feel it through the vent. "They tried to *sabotage* us all summer. They've been trying to tell us something for months and we didn't want to hear it."

Dad stays quiet. Then I hear . . . sniffling. Oh my gosh, he's crying. I've only seen my dad cry one other time—when he told Ridge and me about the divorce. "There has to be another answer."

"This isn't like Viv," Whitney says. "And from what I know about your kids, it's not like them either."

"I know but . . ." Dad swallows. He's still crying. "I screwed up in college. I wasn't ready and I let you go. And then to go through everything we went through in our previous relationships and find each other again? That's a miracle. *You're* my miracle."

Pog barks. I kick open the door and motion to him to come over. He waddles across the room, all proud that he got his way.

There's more quiet and, ick, kissing sounds. Now I should definitely stop listening. But then Dad starts talking.

"I love you, but . . . I love my kids too," Dad says. "This was selfish of me. I should have . . . I don't know what I should have done. We knew this was coming."

"Well, I didn't know my daughter was trying to turn the universe against me, but yeah." Whitney laughs softly. "We did things backward. We owe them. They deserve choice."

They go quiet. Pog barks again so I pull back. It's fine. I've heard enough.

Pog curls into me. I pet him for a few minutes, but I need a strategy that will turn off my brain.

I look around the room. I need distraction. I need consistency. I need *Tetris*.

Pog lies down next to my feet. I lay there on the ground and play a speed game. The cubes stack against me in record time.

I text Cooper. **Want to play another Tetris match?**

He shoots back. **Can't. With my family. Later?**

I send him a smiley face emoji.

Ugh, there are still too many thoughts in my brain. Pog snorts at me, his eyes wide and willing. I don't want comfort. I want answers.

My Magic 8 Ball is on my new nightstand. I try to settle on a question, but my whole existence is a question right now. My head hurts and my stomach aches. My chest is tight, and I keep swallowing, trying to push down the familiar panic.

I give the ball one long shake. Then I can't stop myself. I do two quick shakes. One more long. Then ask . . .

Are Dad and Whitney breaking up?

BETTER NOT TELL YOU NOW.

Are we moving home?

CANNOT PREDICT NOW.

I need a new shaking strategy to make it work. I do three hard jiggles, blow on the ball, rub it on Pog's fur, and ask again.

Is everything going to be okay?

MOST LIKELY.

Which is a good answer.

I just don't believe it.

Chapter 30

Half an hour later, Dad knocks on my door.

"Do you want to go on a drive with Ridge and me?"

"Where's Whitney?" I ask.

"She borrowed a friend's car. She took Vivian . . ." He shrugs. "Somewhere."

Ridge and I sit in the back like Dad is our driver. He inputs Luv-it Frozen Custard on the GPS, some local's favorite on the far side of the Strip. We listen to our family playlist as Dad eases through the suburban neighborhood. Mom made this playlist years ago for long car trips. We each got to pick one fourth of the music. There's a mix of Grateful Dead, Pearl Jam, Beyoncé, Broadway musicals. I wondered if Dad would make a new playlist after the divorce, but he never did. We own the songs equally now.

Dad turns down the music and sniffs loudly, which reminds me of Aunt Maggie and her excessive throat clearing back when she tried to tell me about Mom's letter. She chickened out then, but Dad doesn't have that option.

"First off . . . I'm sorry, kids." Dad sniffs again. I wish I had a tissue. "Whitney and I botched this. We should have talked to you more. From the beginning."

"I forgive you." Ridge doesn't look at Dad, just out the window.

"Me too," I say.

"Good. Good." Dad turns onto the freeway. "I'm glad."

When he doesn't add a follow-up, I ask, "Are you breaking up?"

"I would like to marry Whitney." Dad hesitates. "But I want to hear what you think."

All of this would have been avoided if he'd asked us that question *in the first place*. Or maybe introduced us to Whitney as a friend, then dated for a year or two, figured out the whole living situation before a proposal. You know, had a *relationship*. Call me old-fashioned.

But my Whitney feelings have shifted so much this summer. I think of the way Dad looks at her. The sub sandwiches she bought for our first Vegas meal. Teaching me how to shave my legs. Reading her horoscope at Cowabunga Canyon. The wedding planning. The cafeteria tray. I wouldn't have experienced any of that if Dad asked us to weigh in from the beginning. Things worked out the way they worked out.

"I really like Whitney," I say.

"Same," Ridge says. "Go ahead and marry her."

"Whew." Dad's shoulders relax. "That's great."

"Why didn't you ask us that to begin with?" Ridge asks.

"Exactly!" I say.

"Guys, I don't know if you know this about me, but I am not, what you might call, *smooth*." Dad lets out a thin laugh. "I freeze when there's conflict. Sometimes I freeze when there's calm. I blurt out the wrong things. I jump into hornet's nests. I have a lot of anxiety so—"

 224

"Wait, since when do *you* have anxiety?" I ask.

"I remember throwing up on the rug in kindergarten when my teacher asked me to read the sentence of the day," Dad says. "So . . . then?"

"Why haven't you told me this?" I ask.

"Clearly, on top of everything else, I have bad communication skills," Dad says. "Maybe I was trying to be strong. Or I didn't want you to feel like I was overshadowing your anxiety."

"You can have anxiety and be strong," Ridge says.

"Yeah, I'm learning that." A car honks at Dad. He puts on his blinker and eases off the freeway. "I do take medication for it. And Whitney and I agreed we're both going to therapy. Together and separate."

"Can I go back to therapy?" I ask.

"Of course," he says. "Therapy for all."

I know therapy is not as easy as saying Go to Therapy. We'll have to find someone—hopefully Dr. Matt does video calls. We'll have to pay. And the sessions are sometimes exhausting. But Dad gets it. He gets it way more than I ever imagined.

Dad pulls the car into an In-N-Out parking lot. He parks and shifts in his seat.

"Sorry, switching destinations. I need to get this part out."

Good. My stomach would not appreciate thick ice cream right now.

"So here it is," he says. "If all of the kids, including Vivian, are okay with the wedding, then we need to talk about where you want to live."

"Tacoma." I'm proud of my answer. No apologies or excuses. I simply state my need without changing it to make Dad happy. Add in Ridge's vote, and we outweigh Vivian.

225

"Las Vegas," Ridge says.

"What?" I jerk back, almost hitting my head on the window. "Is this reverse psychology? You were the one with the Washington Plan."

"Do I want to know about this Washington Plan?" Dad asks.

"I have a lot of friends here," Ridge says. "It never rains. The pool is awesome. Whitney is a good cook. And the gaming club is my destiny."

"What about Mom?" Ridge never forced Mom on me so I shouldn't bring her up but . . . *what*? If Ridge votes Vegas and Vivian votes Vegas, then I've lost all control once again.

"Dad asked my opinion," Ridge says. "I still love Mom."

"But Mom wants us to move back there. You're switching things."

"There's no switching something that was never set in the first place."

"Kids!" Dad honks his horn, startling a couple walking into the restaurant. One of the ladies flashes Dad a rude gesture.

"Sorry!" He waves. "I think I scared them. Let's . . . we'll drive away. Right now."

Dad speeds out of the parking lot, headed toward the Strip. His leg jitters under the steering wheel.

Has he always been so me-ish?

"Sorry, Dad," Ridge says. "I can live wherever."

"It's all right," Dad says. "I already talked to your mom about this. And we weren't kissing, by the way."

"Gross," I say.

"Whitney and I knew there'd be different thoughts on location," Dad continues. "I think we have a solution that will make all of the kids happy."

"Teleportation?" Ridge asks.

"We get married, like we planned," Dad says. "Then we live in two different places. In fact, you guys can go back to Washington right after the wedding. I'm sure Whitney will have a schedule spreadsheet in no time."

"Where does Vivian live?" I ask.

"Here," Dad says. "Whitney and I will fly out on available weekends. You can stay with your mom sometimes, when she's ready. My company has offices in both places so . . . I'm not worried about work. We have three years until Vivian graduates high school. Then we'll reevaluate."

"So when are we in Vegas?" Ridge asks.

"I'm sure Whitney will let you stay here during the summers, Ridge. More than that, if you want."

"Cool," Ridge says. "'Cause there's a *Cosmo Kingdom* convention in November."

Dad turns the car right at Excalibur, a castle-themed casino on the Strip. There's an advertisement for the Tournament of Kings, a dinner show with dueling knights. I bet the winner picks a princess at the end. I bet they ride off on a noble steed into a happy ending without any stepfamilies or mystical paths or multiple households.

Actually, the show probably ends with the audience playing slots.

"Don't worry, Stella." Dad's voice is more confident now. "I know you need a break from Vivian. You don't need to see each other. You'll be in your school. Vivian will be in hers. We'll switch off a few holidays, but otherwise . . . you can go back to life as usual."

I should be full of relief. Dad and Whitney are getting married.

I get to keep my home, school, friends. So does Vivian. Ridge can do his masterful jump in and out of all different situations and make friends along the way. No one has to compromise.

Everyone wins.

We pass Luxor's pyramid. Beyond that is the gold facade of Mandalay Bay. Cooper said there's a huge wave pool. I won't see it unless we go next time I'm in Vegas, which could be two or three Christmases from now.

There's a souvenir shop across the street and next to that a familiar billboard.

A destined billboard. Two eyes. Red hand in the middle. PSYCHIC READERS.

"Mystic Shonda," I whisper.

Mystic Shonda told Whitney, well me, that there would be a large gathering and a dark storm. But she never said the storm was *during* the large gathering. And sometimes the predictions are metaphors. So what if . . . this fight *is* our dark storm?

And if it is, then . . . I want it to end? Or get fixed? The large gathering—wedding—is definitely on, but Vivian and I aren't. I knew pushing for the Washington Plan would make things hard but . . . I *hate* this dark storm. I want her back. I want us to text. To hike through forests or shop at outdoor malls. To buy sister crystal bracelets.

I just need to call the one person who can foresee if any of that, any of *us*, is still possible.

I wait until Dad's asleep to find his wallet. I take his credit card and leave eighteen dollars and a note letting him know this isn't stealing, it's switching a form of payment. Besides, this phone call is going to end the dark storm. Dad will totally . . . *most likely* . . . understand.

I place my amethyst on the couch cushion before dialing the number.

A recorded voice picks up on the second ring. "Welcome to Psychic Readers! Our services are twenty dollars for fifteen minutes, forty dollars for a half hour, seventy per hour with no required limit on sessions. We accept all major credit cards up front. Press pound to speak to a—"

I hit pound and breathe out. It might be the first time I've breathed today.

"This is Medium April," the real live voice answers. "Are you calling to book a session?"

Of course they have multiple employees. I wonder why some are called mystics and some mediums? Should I add a name before my name too? "Hi, yeah I am."

"Great!" she says. "Let's look at some openings in our schedule."

Relief, relief, relief. Knowing that I'm about to find clarity with Mystic Shonda makes the storm lighter already. And while we're at it, I might ask about long-distance middle school relationships.

"When is Mystic Shonda's next session?" I ask. "The sooner the better. And I have my credit card number to prepay."

"Mystic Shonda is no longer available."

"Oh yeah, it's late?" I glance at the clock: 11:24. It didn't occur to me that psychics have work schedules. We called earlier at night last time. Although, Mystic Shonda *is* psychic, so she should already know when I'm calling, right? "I can wait until tomorrow. Or her next shift."

"Mystic Shonda no longer works for our company," Medium April says. "We have a session available with Angel Dominic on Thursday at ten A.M."

I can't see anything. There's a light on down the hall but everything is dark. Like I'm looking down a tunnel. A dark, stormy tunnel.

"I don't want to talk to Angel Dominic!" I shout. "Dominic doesn't know how to fix the mess that Shonda started!"

"All of our psychics are highly trained in metaphysical arts and use the third eye to—"

I hang up.

My body breaks into an instant sweat. I'm shaking. I feel like I'm going to pass out. Like I'm going to die.

I know I know I know I'm not going to die. I know what this is. I know what is happening. Dr. Matt and I discussed what to do when my anxiety was astronomical. But this is different. Bigger. What's another star pun?

Supernova.

I'm going supernova.

I exhale.

Count to four.

Hold it.

Inhale.

One, two, three, four.

Close my eyes.

Open.

Wrap my arms around myself. Clutch my crystal. Take in every detail, the jagged, purple lumps.

Vivian is over me. Gone.

Breathe more. Breathe more. I . . . breathe.

Pull Pog out of his kennel. Listen to his snorts and snores as he falls back asleep. Hold him, pet him, love him.

Heart beats slower.

Pull blanket tight tight tight until I'm safe. Safe-ish.

Wait.

    Wait.

        Wait.

Dark storm, dark storm.

I flop back on the couch, trying to imagine what Mystic Shonda might say. Or Dr. Matt. Or someone I love. Or . . . anybody.

"It's going to be okay," I hear a voice say. Who is that? I look around the room.

"It's going to be okay." I realize it is *my* voice. This is me. That's who I have to talk to. Myself.

"Stella Blue North. You will be okay."

I repeat it over and over, cocooning in the blanket with Pog until finally finally finally the panic attack subsides and I slip into sleep.

Chapter 31

M om stops by the next day to say goodbye.

She stands awkwardly on Whitney's front porch. I think about inviting her inside but maybe that's against divorce rules. Dad and Mom really need to tell us the divorce rules.

"When is Aunt Maggie coming back?" I ask.

"Three or four. Want to go on a walk?"

"It's two P.M.," I say.

"Did you have something planned?" Mom asks.

"No, but it's July? In Vegas?"

"Oh, because it's hot?" Mom asks.

"Hold on," I say. "I'll grab Pog."

We don't talk for the first few blocks. Pog barks at every dog, big or small. He usually has two settings—happy and happier—but he's been agitated since the fight. Vivian won't play with him and all I seem to do is squeeze him too tight. He likes Mom, though. She squats down to pet him.

"I had a good talk with Dad," Mom says.

"Yeah, I saw the evidence."

"What does that mean?"

I don't explain Vivian's photos. I'm working on a new plan: Operation End Dark Storm.

"I gave Dad my blessing on Whitney." Mom laughs. "Which they don't need, but . . . you like her?"

"Honestly? She's fantastic."

"Oh. Fantastic." Mom stops at a crosswalk. She holds her arm out to stop me from stepping into traffic. I've followed pedestrian laws since I was oh, four, but maybe it's instinct. "I might have some jealousy, but . . . I want you to have a great stepmom."

"Did you and Dad talk about living situations?" I ask.

"I shouldn't have discussed that with you," Mom says. "It's getting . . . sorted."

The green walk light blinks. We cross the street. I realize I already know where I'm taking Mom. Or *who* I am taking Mom *to*.

"It doesn't matter anymore," I say. "We're moving back to Washington. Dad and Whitney are doing a long-distance relationship. Like celebrities."

"What?" Mom stops abruptly. "That's not what we . . . living like celebrities? What happened?"

"Plans changed," I say, putting it as mildly as possible. Although I'm curious what they talked about. Mom and I had a plan going into that conversation. So why were they hugging in those photos?

Finally, we make it to my 7-Eleven.

"Oh, thank goodness," Mom says. "It's like living on the sun here."

"Want a Gatorade?" I ask.

"Yeah, yellow," she says.

"Green," I say.

"Lemon-lime," we agree at the same time.

I take Mom to the back for our Gatorades. We get the big ones. More electrolytes.

I haven't seen Zara since she foretold Mom's arrival. Part of me wants to point to my mom and shout *Look! You called it!* But my other part is shy. Because introducing Zara to Mom reveals a new side of me, a side I've tried to hide for a long time.

"How's it going?" Mom sticks her Gatorade on the counter and smiles at Zara. "Ooh, I love that purple flower on your arm."

"Hyacinth." Zara rubs her bright tattoo. "They're believed to attract our soul angels."

"Mom." I put my Gatorade next to hers. "This is Zara."

"Oh, so you know each other?" Mom cocks her head to the side.

"Zara was the first person I met in Vegas," I say.

"Yep." Zara scans our Gatorades. "You and that drooling dog."

"Zara is a spiritual guide," I say. "She has her own business— reading palms and tarot cards."

"I'm also great in the kitchen." Zara smiles at Mom.

"Hmm. How do you attract your clientele?" Mom asks.

"Excuse me?" Zara asks.

"I mean, do you have an online presence?"

"Um, I'm working on that," Zara says. "I started charging a few months ago. I'm in school and I work here so . . ."

"Mom, it's rude to grill people on their jobs," I say. Especially when I'm hoping to use their services.

Mom unscrews her Gatorade and takes a big chug. Once she's full of electrolytes, she whips out her phone. "My sister runs this website that creates micro sites for women-run businesses within a shared community. She's looking to branch out in Vegas."

"Really?" Zara looks at Aunt Maggie's site on Mom's screen. "That would be . . . prime. Your daughter's already brought in business for me."

"That's because you're so gifted!" I say. "Here, you can show my mom your skills—"

"Stella will send my sister Maggie's number. We'll get you linked up." Mom sticks her phone in her purse. "And thanks for being there for my daughter."

"She's cool, for a Virgo."

Mom turns to leave but I stay planted in place. We aren't here for Gatorade. I need Zara to work her magic. I need to see how Mom is going to handle Dad's marriage and our move back to Washington and a new job and sobriety.

It's a lot to cover. Hopefully, there are plenty of lines on her hand.

"Mom, wait," I say. "I want Zara to read your palm. She already looked at Ridge and me."

Mom waves me away. "Oh, I'm okay."

"Just real fast," I say.

"Or you can book an appointment," Zara says. "Then we can add some tarot, maybe a natal chart."

The sliding doors chime. A group of loud, grungy rocker types walk in. A few shuffle to the back refrigerator while three guys head right to the potato chips. I smell them before they get close, a heavy mix of pot and alcohol.

Mom fumbles in her purse until she finds a gold circle that resembles a poker chip, except there's a triangle in the middle with words inscribed. She stares straight down, rubbing the plastic between her fingers.

A thirty- or fortysomething white guy with bleached tips and tight pants stands next to us. He tosses his barbecue Corn Nuts on the counter. "Clara North?"

Mom looks up. Her expression shifts thirty moods in thirty milliseconds. *Confused, shocked, happy, worried, excited, guarded, blank.* "Hank?"

"Of all the 7-Elevens in all the world." Hank grabs Mom into a hug. She pats his back three times, real quick.

Mom moves away, readjusts her shirt. "Stella, this is—"

"Hank," I say. "I heard."

Hanks leans on the counter. "Is this your little sister?"

This Hank guy. Is flirting. With my mom. It's so foul, but also why wouldn't he because Mom is gorgeous, but yikes, he's obviously high right now. They all are.

"This is my daughter, Stella." Mom puts a stiff arm around my shoulder. The chip is still between her fingers. "We're on vacation, just taking the dog on a walk."

Hank notices Pog. His eyes widen. "Yo, that's a dope doggy."

"Thanks." Either Hank needs to leave or we do. I smell danger. Danger and marijuana.

"You living here now?" Mom's eyes dart back to Hank's friends in the beer section.

"Nah, we're opening for this teen punk band." Hank nods at Zara. "Mojo vape, if you have it."

"Sure thing," Zara says.

"Well, weird running into you!" Mom's voice is overly bright.

Her left leg jiggles while my right leg wobbles. We are a jiggling jumble.

The group buys their cases of beer and Slim Jims. Everyone is super nice to Pog. One guy offers to buy us a doggy treat.

Hank hasn't stopped staring at Mom. "You're as illuminous as ever, Clara Bear-a."

He might mean *luminous*. And he might know my mom well enough to give her a nickname. A dumb nickname. "Oh, stop it." Mom's pink skin is crimson red. I can't tell if she likes this attention or not. "Let's catch up next time you're playing Seattle."

"I actually have backstage passes to the show tonight," Hank says. "We're at the Cosmopolitan. After-party should be high-end."

"She's busy," I say, very stern, like I'm the mom and she's my kid. "Nice to meet you, Hank."

"Yeah." Hank chuckles. "This one is definitely your daughter."

They leave, taking all the oxygen with them. Mom closes her eyes. She takes deep, purposeful breaths. Zara wipes down the counter even though she just wiped it.

I count to ten before I tap Mom's arm. "You good?"

"Yeah." Mom shakes her head. "Yeah. Let's go."

"But what about your palm reading—"

"I don't *need* it, Stella." Mom's voice comes out sharp. "Come on. Now."

"Sorry." I shrug at Zara as Mom rushes outside. "Her electrolytes haven't kicked in yet."

"Call me later." Zara sticks her hands in her pockets, like she's trying to stop herself from doing something else. "I'll meet with her when she's ready."

"Yeah, she just found God and sobriety, so it should be soon."

I hurry out of the store. Mom sits cross-legged on the grass next to the building. She spins her empty Gatorade bottle around in circles on the sidewalk.

"Why did you run out of there?" I ask. "Zara can totally help you."

"I already know my mistakes." Mom spins the bottle. It points toward the gas pumps. "I don't need my hand to tell me more."

"Yeah, but if you see your future, you'll see that everything is cool. You'll be sober and loving your job and going to concerts again with Aunt Maggie."

I regret it as soon as I mention *concerts*.

Mom scoffs. "Yeah, that's where I met Hank."

"Did you date him?" I ask.

"Date?" Mom tosses the bottle next to her on the grass. "Not really. I can't remember."

So . . . yes.

The concept of dating other people is already sticky. It's still an adjustment seeing Dad and Whitney hold hands. Difficult to imagine Mom putting on a nice top to meet a guy she met on a dating app for dinner. But Hank? Not a let's-get-engaged-and-blend-our-family kind of guy. More like a let's-hop-into-my-van-and-drink-a-six-pack bro.

Mom's phone buzzes with a text. Hank. Big shocker.

"Just block him," I say.

"I don't want to block him." Mom reads the text. Her face is doing that expression metamorphosis again. "I mean, he *has* two tickets. Aunt Maggie could come with me."

My mouth hangs open. Is she seriously considering this? Hank said there's an after-party. Mom shouldn't be at any party—past, present, or future. What happened to that I-just-want-to-be-your-mom-again lady from five days ago?

Mom flops dramatically onto the grass, letting out a big exhale. I couldn't imagine Whitney doing something so child-like in a million years. She wouldn't lie on this grass. It might stain her white shorts.

I lie down next to my mom. The grass is hot but what is new.

Mom pulls out that gold chip again and flips it through her fingers. "This is my four-month sobriety chip from AA. I'm a hundred and thirty-four days sober. Next chip is five months. I think that one's red."

"Mom, are you okay?" I ask.

"No." She covers her face with her hands. "One day at a time, Clara. Easy does it."

I wouldn't want someone talking to me while I was talking to myself. So I watch the sky and give Mom space to Mom. There's more clouds than usual today, gray and fluffy. I try to find a shape or meaning, but all I see is Hank's sketchy face.

"This is why I had to talk to your dad," Mom says. "I told him . . . I told him I'm okay if you move here."

"You what?" I roll onto my stomach and stare down at her. "So you don't want us?"

"You are my *everything*. I always want you." Mom reaches up and cups my face with her hands. "But I also want pills. Right now, smelling that pot when I hugged Hank . . . I want to use so bad. One text to Hank and in ten minutes he'd deliver a personal pharmacy."

"This isn't fair." I brush her hands away from my face. "You're sober. That's why you came to see us in Las Vegas. That's why we can see you now in Tacoma."

"Yeah. Look . . . I won't go to the concert," Mom says. "I'll drop you off and get to an AA meeting right away."

"You said you were better," I say.

"*Better* never happens," Mom says. "Progress, not perfection. I need to be realistic about my limits. Dad and I agreed that a few more months of sobriety would be smart before we do long visits. I'll save money, get my own place. That would be the situation wherever you live."

"Then that's what we'll do," I say stubbornly. "Back home. In Tacoma."

"But you're thriving here! You're on this remarkable path with incredible people in your life. Look at what you have!" She waves her arm wide. She doesn't sense the irony that she is motioning toward a sticky 7-Eleven parking lot.

"What exactly do I have?" I ask.

"Safety. Security."

The hairs on my arms stand straight up. *The tea leaves.* "What did you say?"

"Safety and security." Mom sits up. She has grass in her wild hair and Gatorade on her shirt. She is messy. She is ethereal. "If your dad moves back to Tacoma, that's fine too. Whatever works for our family. Our relationship dynamic got so out of whack. I'm the adult. You're the kid. My goal is to get stable and solid so I can be there for you. Wherever you are."

"And what would happen if we actually did move to Vegas?"

"Then I'd move here too," Mom says simply.

I flash back to our Springs Preserve conversation. I was so consumed with getting back to Washington, I probably didn't recognize that I was asking for leaps when Mom was just starting to take steps.

But this offer isn't nothing.

Mom is trying. She's trying so hard.

"You would . . ." I swallow. The world's biggest lump has formed in my throat. All the electrolytes in the world couldn't wash it away. "You would move to sweaty Vegas to be with us?"

"Absolutely," Mom says. "Just as long as I have central air."

This Vegas hypothetical doesn't matter. We're moving home. That's set. But Mom's . . . I don't know what to call it . . . proposal/offering/gift shows there's hope for hope. Maybe we can talk more often. Have some sort of relationship. Not a mother/daughter relationship that girls like the Dippers have, but something consistent. A new kind of safe and secure.

We walk Pog back to Whitney's house. Aunt Maggie's car is outside. Mom stops on the sidewalk and takes my hand.

"Hey, I know this is different, but do you mind saying a prayer before I leave? We do this sort of thing in AA."

"You're right," I say. "That is different. And strange."

"I'll make you a deal." Mom folds her arms across her chest. "I'll call Zara and schedule a palm reading if you talk to God with me."

We're sweating in front of the house. I need to set Pog in front of a fan before he overheats. I don't want Whitney, or worse, Vivian, to look through the window and see my mother and I joined in prayer.

"Okay, fine," I say. "But make it fast."

Mom spreads her legs shoulder-width apart and takes both of my hands. "Is this okay?"

"Sure."

She bows her head. Standing close like this, I can smell her pineapple shampoo. I bow my head. When she speaks, her voice is velvety soft. Earnest. Honest.

"Dear Lord," she starts. "Thank you for this beautiful life."

She's only said one sentence, but suddenly I am bawling.

"We are grateful for your eternal love. Thank you for the sun, moon, and stars. For connection. For light. For daughters. For Gatorade."

A tear drips down the tip of my nose. I forgot that Mom was funny. I forgot that she was human. I forgot how her love shines.

"We see your hand in everything. Please grant Stella comfort. Bless her to listen to her gut. To find her true path. To keep doing what she's doing. And to recognize that she's a totally awesome kid who is cute, of course, but also strong, brilliant, and loved."

I hug her. She hugs me back. I let myself melt into her—shoulders, arms, heart. Lawn mowers whir, birds chirp, cars drive past. And we breathe our peaceful pulse.

"Can you pray for my friend Talia's sick grandma?" I mumble into her hair.

"And bless Talia's sick grandma that she can have healing, and if not healing, peace. And grant clarity and connection to the rest of Stella's family—Ridge, Micah, and me. And now Whitney and Vivian." Mom pulls back and takes my hands. "Let's end with the Serenity Prayer. God, grant us the serenity to accept the things we cannot change, courage to change the things we can, and wisdom to know the difference. Amen."

I don't know if I believe in vibrations or prayer. I'm not sure what I know about God or the universe. But I believe in believing *something*. Because here, in a sweltering Las Vegas cul-de-sac, I'm finally starting to believe in myself.

Chapter 32

Talia,
I hope you had a chance to make some happy memories with your grandma. I'm so sorry for her health issues. Thank you for sharing with me.
 My dad is getting married next week. We are coming to Tacoma two days after that. We will have homes in two states. So I get the best of both worlds—to come back, but also to get a new stepsister. Although that stepsister isn't talking to me. Maybe by Christmas she will be. That's the next time I'll be in Vegas. I think. I'll have to check Whitney's Google Calendar.
 So I get to see you end of next week! Can't wait. Let's go to the pool with the Dippers. I'll have plenty of stories to tell ☺
Lots of love,
Stella

Vivian stays at her dad's house for the next two weeks. Whitney said she needs time. I get it and I don't. Vivian wasn't the only one hurt. She took those photos and said mean things about my mom. But holding on to those feelings just makes the storm worse. So I try to release those negative thoughts whenever they come, either through prayer or through meditation.

Although one time, I was squeezing a crystal trying real hard to Let Go and Let God, which is one of Mom's AA slogans, when I thought, did Mystic Shonda ever say *when* the dark storm ends? And of course she didn't, only BEWARE! Which means the storm could essentially go on forever, crystals and slogans aside, and I don't want to start seventh grade without Vivian's guidance and wisdom, specifically what kind of shoes I should wear on the first day, so I either need to double up on putting positive energy into the universe OR go sit outside Travis's house until she finally forgives me, but everyone is so busy with the wedding that I don't have a ride over there and . . . anyway. I'm fine.

The day before the wedding, Cooper asks me to his country club to play tennis.

"I don't think I'm fancy enough for that," I say.

"Then we'll pay extra," he says.

"Really?"

"Stella."

I borrow a tennis skirt from Vivian's closet. It's not even a real tennis skirt, it's a *skirt* skirt. Apparently, she went through a preppy phase so I am full country club cool.

Whitney drops me off on the way to her hair appointment.

"So you'll be home by two," Whitney says.

"Promise."

"Because we have nail appointments with my sisters and Mom at three."

"I know."

"And then prerehearsal family photos at five."

"Uh-huh."

"Dinner's at six."

I reach across the seat and put my hand on Whitney's arm. "I read the itinerary. All three pages. I'll be there."

"Can you believe I'm getting married tomorrow?" She smiles. "Doesn't it feel like it happened so fast?"

"That's because you had a two-month engagement," I say. "It *was* fast."

"See you at two," she says.

I turn to get out of the car but stop. I was going to do this whole thing tonight, after the dinner, but I have no idea when I'll be alone with Whitney again.

I reach into my tote bag and come out with a silver box. "So, no big deal, but I got you something."

"You did?" Whitney's hand flies to her chest. "That's a very big deal."

"Open it first."

She unwraps a blue beaded bracelet.

"It's lapis lazuli," I say. "You work at Caesars Palace, and this stone was valued in ancient Rome. The Egyptians thought it opened the heart for love? And Janice . . . that's the lady at the crystal store . . . told me that it enhances empathy and compassion when dealing with others. Especially teenagers. It can be your something blue."

Whitney slides the bracelet onto her wrist.

"I figured I should set, like, a good intention for a stone?" I fiddle with the hem of Vivian's skirt. "To make up for the Supernova Quest. You're . . . I'm glad you're marrying my dad."

"I'm glad I'm marrying your dad too. And I'm glad I get to

be your stepmom." She takes off her sunglasses and waves her hand in front of her face. "This is such a special moment."

"Whitney?" I say. "Special moments are more special if you don't mention the specialness."

"Just one more." She smiles. "As much as I love this bracelet, I already have my something blue. *You.*"

"Huh . . . oh, like Stella Blue?" I roll my eyes. "Did you think of that beforehand?"

"Of course I did." She shifts the car gear. "Now get out of here before I start crying and ruin this makeup."

I run into the entrance of the club. Cooper waits in the front lobby with his tennis racket against his knees. He shoots up when he sees me. "Oh, hey. You ready?"

"Yeah."

"Do you want to see the bathroom first?" he asks.

"Why, is it *fancy*?" I ask.

"I'll play some *Tetris*," he says. "You're going to be a while."

Woo boy. Fancy city. I am really, really tempted to use the shower, but Cooper is out there waiting. I bet I can shower after we play, which is the more normal time to shower anyway.

I push out of the bathroom stall just as two girls walk in.

"So your moon is in Leo," a familiar voice says. "Which is a fire sign."

It's Gemma.

And Vivian.

Vivian sees me and promptly turns around. "Nuh-uh."

"Vivian." Gemma grabs her by the shoulders. "This is for your own good."

"Wait, you guys are obsessed with fancy country club bathrooms too?" I ask.

"No, dummy," Vivian says. "Cooper and Gemma obviously arranged this so we would talk."

"Oh." This could have been avoided if I'd followed my showering instincts.

"This is a sistervention," Gemma says. "Cooper and I have been trying to stage this for a whole week. Trust me, I get how annoying siblings can be."

"I don't have any siblings," Vivian says.

"Tomorrow you will." Gemma nudges us to the ladies' lounge. This one is more lavish than that other country club, with a large crystal chandelier illuminating the space. "Come on, you're a Scorpio and a Virgo. You like consistency and dependability. Stella, you're a mutable sign, so you can adapt with a fixed, stubborn Scorpio."

"Thanks a lot," Vivian says.

"Scorpios are also intuitive," Gemma says gently. "Virgos have a hard time tapping into their emotions. So lean on each other. Besides, I checked your charts and you both have Venus in Cancer. You can be nurturing and loyal if you let go of your rejection fears."

"You both have Venus in Cancer," Vivian mimics, but she eases onto the brocade couch all the same.

Vivian avoids looking at me, so I take the time to get a glass of cucumber water and handful of trail mix. Freshly made trail mix, with cranberries and dark chocolate. Highest fancy level unlocked!

I sit across from Vivian on a plush chair. "How've you been?"

"Is that my skirt?"

"You don't talk to me for weeks and that's the first thing you ask me?"

"Is it?"

"Yeah." I brush off some lint. "Thank you for loaning it to me."

"I didn't." She picks at her nails. "Give it back to me before you leave."

"Done."

I look at the ceiling, the floor, the wallpaper, the chandelier. Gemma is right. I am not so great at emotions. I already had a whole moment with Whitney in the car. Plus there was that goodbye with my mom, followed by multiple phone calls. Which isn't all emotion—I'm helping Zara set up her section on Aunt Maggie's website. And tomorrow, Mom wants me to mention the website to vendors. You know, at her ex-husband's wedding. Not confusing at all.

"So are you going to talk or what?" Vivian asks.

"Did you see the mouthwash?"

"Do they have mints?"

We rush over to the sinks and examine the spread of freebies. Vivian sprays hairspray. I stuff Q-tips into my pocket. We glance up at the same time, making eye contact in the mirror.

"That skirt actually looks cute on you," Vivian says. "Keep it to remember me by."

"I'll be back at Christmas," I say. "I can give it to you then."

"Whatever." She breaks eye contact and squirts out globs of soap.

"Do you remember when Zara read my cards?" I ask. "She talked about my second path?"

"Your get-back-to-Washington path?" She dries her hands. "Yeah, I picked up on that."

"I think you're my Page of Wands."

"The quest is over now," she says. "We don't have to do all this zodiac talk."

"She said I could trust the Page of Wands. That they're a true friend." I turn to face her. "I would love being that for each other. You mean a lot to me. We said some nasty things, but I think we can move past the dark storm."

"Wait, you think our *fight* was the dark storm?" Vivian seems to mull this over. "Huh. Mystic Shonda never said the dark storm happened *at* the gathering. Maybe it's a metaphor?"

I grin. "The quest is over now. We don't have to do all this zodiac talk."

"Fine, I guess we're doing this." Vivian finally looks at me. Like square on. Face to face. Friend to friend.

Sister to sister.

"I'm sorry," she says.

"I'm sorry too." Those three words release all the tension in my body.

I stand straighter. Steadier.

Breathe. Swallow. Smile.

"Glad *that's* over." Vivian shoulders past me. "Is your whole supernova thing over too?"

My skin prickles. How did she know about my panic attack? "What's that supposed to mean?"

"Exploding? Transforming? Shining all bright?" Vivian opens the lounge door. Music from the lobby echoes down the hallway. "Your name means star, blah, blah, blah. Why am I explaining this? You're the mystic here, Stella Blue."

"In that case, no." My voice rings strong. Proud. This is a

compliment. Or as close to a compliment as Vivian ever gets. "I might even be above supernova."

"North of Supernova?" Vivian chews on her lip. "Gosh, that's a good band name."

Cooper and Gemma sit in the front lobby. Gemma's talking animatedly on her phone while Cooper plays *Tetris*. They look up at the same time.

"You fixed now?" Cooper asks.

He's so adorable, sitting there in an uncomfortable high-back chair. So adorable—helping me like this. Especially with his sister, who probably matched our star charts against his will.

"Can I beat you in tennis now?" I ask.

Gemma and Vivian beeline to the pool. Gemma's new crush is a lifeguard. And a Pisces.

The tennis courts are, no surprise, fancy. We hit for a while. I remember how to swing. My serve comes back to me. My backhand's improved.

Cooper asks if we want to play a full match. He spins his racket. The bottom tip of the racket has a letter *W*, which can also be an *M*. I'm supposed to call out *M* or *W* while the racket spins. Winner gets to pick serve or choose a side.

"W," I call.

"Dang," he says. "Okay, serve or side."

"Serve."

He hands me a bottle of fresh tennis balls. I pull back the lid and listen to the air escape. I missed this so much. Every bit of it. Who'd have thought I'd find myself rediscovering the thing I love in a place so far away.

"Oh, I got you one more thing." Cooper rifles in his tennis bag and pulls out a Gatorade. "You like green, right?"

"How did you know that?" My whole body is on hyperalert.

He shrugs. "Because you told me."

My head feels light and my heart full. I've never met anyone who pays attention to details like Cooper. He staged a sistervention for me. He is halfway decent at *Tetris*. We are both earth signs. He has cold hands, kind eyes, and a Gatorade smile.

The dark storm might be over but there is still room for destiny fulfillment. Mystic Shonda tasted lime, with romance tied to it. And it wasn't for Whitney. The predictions were never for her.

This future is mine.

I lean over and give Cooper a kiss on the cheek.

He freezes. "Whoa."

I hop onto the court and take my place.

Cooper stays on the bench.

"You going to play or what?" I call.

He grabs his racket and sprints to the other side of the net. I'm about to serve when he calls out. "Hey, you have to say the score."

I bounce the ball three times quick. Maybe next time I'll bounce the ball two times slow. No big deal. "Zero, zero. Love, love."

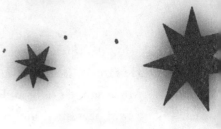

Chapter 33

I t is 105 degrees at 9:00 A.M. the morning of the wedding.

Whitney doesn't notice.

The flowers wilt in the heat.

Whitney doesn't notice.

The photographer gets in a car accident on the way to the ceremony and has to send their assistant instead.

Whitney doesn't notice.

They keep Grandma North in the museum until right before the ceremony to avoid heat exhaustion.

Okay, maybe Whitney notices that one.

But everything magically falls into place ten minutes before the ceremony begins.

Ridge and I are fourth to walk down the aisle—after the other bridesmaids and groomsmen but before the flower girl, Whitney's niece (who I guess will be, what, my stepcousin now? Whitney said she'll make me a flowchart).

Ridge keeps adjusting and readjusting his bow tie.

"It looks fine," I say. "Stop messing with it."

"You try having something squeezing your neck."

"Um, I'm being squeezed from the waist up." I motion

toward my lavender bridesmaid dress, which is corseted with a flowy skirt. I look at least fourteen.

Ridge peeks around the taller groomsmen. "I think they're going to start walking in a minute."

"Okay." I take a breath. "Okay."

"Are you?" Ridge looks at me with earnest eyes. "Okay, I mean? You anxious at all?"

I check myself. My body, my breath. "I'm more excited than nervous. No one is thinking about us, you know. Just the bride."

"Yeah." Ridge fiddles with his bow tie again. "I wish we didn't have to say goodbye to everyone right after we meet them."

"Seriously?" I ask. "Most of these people are strangers."

"Now they're our family," Ridge says.

"I mean, technically."

Two couples walk outside.

"Did you read your horoscope today?" Ridge reaches into his pocket for a curl of paper. "I printed ours out. I figured it would help you feel better before we walked."

"You brought *both* of our horoscopes?" I ask, touched.

"Yeah, mine says, *Home isn't a place.* That's yuck." He looks more closely at the paper. "Wait, Virgo. That's you. Mine is, *Your imagination is wild. Dream big.* Never mind. They're all yuck."

"Can I have that?" I ask.

Ridge hands me the crinkled slip of paper. I don't have a pocket, so I wrap the words around my bouquet, hidden by my hands.

"You're next," the wedding planner says.

Ridge holds out his elbow and I tuck my arm into his.

The wedding planner smooths out my dress, rearranges a flower in my bouquet, and sends us into the aisle.

I pick up the hem of my skirt so I don't trip. That is my big goal for the next torturous minute with eighty pairs of eyes on me. No tripping.

Two violinists seated to the side of the wedding chairs set our musical pace. Ridge smiles and points his finger at our cousin. The crowd laughs. We make it to the three sets of stairs that lead to a small stage. Dad gives us a dorky thumbs-up. We turn around in time to see the flower girl dump out the remains of her basket and stomp up the stairs.

A breeze puffs my sleeves. A wisp of hair lands in my lip gloss. I try not to fidget. Try.

The violin music shifts to the Grateful Dead song "They Love Each Other." The guests rise.

Whitney and Vivian stand together at the end of the aisle. Vivian's dress is sage green, strappy. Her hair is braided and flowy. She has on fake eyelashes, which Whitney fought and apparently lost. Vivian isn't frowning, which for her is practically a smile.

Whitney is lovely—she's a bride, of course she's lovely—but more than that she is *radiant*. Synonyms: brilliant, luminous, aglow. She grins at Dad and he grins at her, and the two never break eye contact the whole time Vivian walks her mom down the aisle. They stop at the bottom of the stairs. Vivian gives Whitney a hug, a total body clutch that makes the wedding planner wince.

Vivian slips to the side, next to me. "Hey, Twinkle."

"Who told you that nickname?" I ask.

Ridge snorts, as if to answer my question. Traitor.

The breeze gets breezier, enough that they have to turn up the volume on the mic. The officiant, Whitney's mom, doesn't

254

need the microphone. She does a decent job, except when she mentions that they wouldn't have to worry about the weather if they got married in a church. I guess moms can be prickly even when you're an adult?

Whitney ended up adding the next part for her mom. Her sister, who flew in from Florida, reads a Bible verse. Ridge is next. The paper in his hand shakes, and not from the wind.

"Psalm 33: The earth is full of the goodness of the Lord."

I don't listen to the rest. I'm thinking about those first words as I take in our surroundings. *The earth is full of the goodness of the Lord.*

The dresses, flowers, and archway are stunning. But there's more beyond that. Like the cacti straight out of a western cartoon, with long arms and thick spikes. Aloe plants and succulents. Joshua trees and blossoming bushes. Yellow wispy grass that towers over the chairs. Even the Strip view is breathtaking, with the Stratosphere grasping for the clouds.

Vegas is full of goodness. And beauty. You just have to open your eyes and heart to notice.

Dad weeps during his vows. I wish there was a stopper I could stick in his eyeballs. Public emotion is so uncomfortable. Whitney starts off fine, bubbly and intent. But then her vows go straight syrup.

"When I saw you in that lobby," Whitney says. "It was like spotting a unicorn. You are rare and wonderful, and I promise to never let you go again."

"Did she just call Dad a *unicorn*?" Ridge mumbles.

"Most of all, I love how you love your kids." Whitney turns her body away from Dad. Toward Ridge and me. This was not a part of the rehearsal dinner. "Stella, I know you hate surprises, but I want to say to you and Ridge . . ." And then she starts crying. Really crying. Bride-makeup-in-danger crying.

The wind blows into the microphone. All eyes are on us.

But I don't look at them. I'm watching Ridge, who is also crying. And so is Vivian. And Dad.

"It is a privilege to stand by your side and commit to you all," Whitney says. "I am so blessed to be a mother to Vivian, my world. Now marrying your dad . . . I get to be a stepmom too. And I thank my lucky stars . . . that I do."

I don't cry. It's not that I don't want to or don't feel anything, but I'm sort of frozen with all these eyes bearing into my skull. Vivian flings her arm around me.

"You are such a Virgo," she whispers in my ear.

I smooth my hair. The ribbon from Whitney's bouquet flaps in the wind. Ridge's bow tie is once again crooked.

They do the whole marriage part, where they slide on the rings and say "I do." It is beautiful and sweet. I can't wait until it's over.

Except that's when things go terribly wrong.

"Friends and family." Whitney's mom extends her arms. "For the first time as a married couple, Micah North and Whitney Lionetti!"

Dad and Whitney kiss. The wind is . . . wow. Windy. It rips at Whitney's veil—she barely catches it in time. They turn to the crowd and hold up their hands.

There are cheers and whistles.

Until the wind roars.

Roars isn't a strong enough term. Billows. Blasts. Gales.

Gusts of wind practically pick *us* up as it surges around, mini dust devils swirling in the desert landscape. Whitney's dress flies up to her knees. My hair slaps my face and dust stings my eyes. The violinists try to play interlude music, but it comes out as screeches.

Chair by chair, everyone stands. Grandma North coughs, like gasping coughing. There's surprised sounds, like "Whew!" and "Argh!" but even those are hard to hear beneath the shrieking wind.

"Inside!" Dad shouts at the guests. "Go!"

If we were following etiquette, the bridal party would leave first. But the etiquette blew away. A rush of guests pushes toward the banquet hall. My family stays immobile on the stage. Then Dad holds out his arms, like his body is a tent. We squeeze together in a sandy huddle of five.

"Close your eyes," Dad says. "Stick together."

And we do. Clustered like that, with Vivian's bouquet poking my ribs and Whitney's hair in my mouth, I am crushed with a surge of love for these people. Who are now my family.

"Stella." Vivian giggles. "Dark storm."

"Not a metaphor," I say.

We laugh so hard. Dirt sticks in my teeth. I try to cover my mouth. When I move my hand, Ridge's horoscope flutters out of the bouquet and whips me in the forehead.

Home isn't a place.

Vivian told me there are different versions of herself. Maybe I'm the same way—maybe everyone is. There's Washington-Stella, who loves walking through the forest, hanging with the Dippers, petting Pog inside her panic room. Someday she'll go to sober concerts with her mom, parties with Talia, and intern for her aunt.

But then there's Vegas-Stella. She loves tennis (again), shares a room with her Scorpio stepsister, collects crystals, and will love the weather come November. She wants to know this place better, to swim in new pools and blaze desert trails. She wants to know herself better, this girl who would kiss her crush and sabotage a wedding.

Like another horoscope told me: *Choose wisely — this will set your course for years to come.*

Dad's arms loosen. "It's dying down."

We rise up and take stock of the space. Half the chairs fell over, the flowers are trashed, and the sign that says MICAH + WHITNEY FOREVER snapped in half.

"Did you guys do some spell?" Whitney laughs, but she's only partway joking.

"I'm sorry, Whitney," Ridge says. "You looked pretty."

When Zara laid out those paths, the cards didn't set a destination. I don't think any part of the Supernova Quest did. Because of all the things Mystic Shonda told me, the most essential thing is this: *Your future changes with you.*

I grab Dad's hand. "What do you think about living here?"

"Here?" Dad shakes sand out of his hair. "I told you I'm going to Tacoma with you guys."

"No, I mean, *all of us*," I say. "In Vegas. For a while. Go to school. Try it out."

"Yes." Ridge pumps his fist. "I am going to *destroy* gaming club."

"Wait, are you serious?" Dad bends low so we are eye-to-eye. "It's not a decision we need to make right this second. I only got married ten minutes ago — let's wait until we cut the cake?"

"Okay, we'll talk later," I say. "As a family."

"I can get them registered for classes tomorrow!" Whitney says. "Actually, give me two days. You'll probably want an instructional PowerPoint."

And then Dad pulls us into a messy, beautiful lump. Vegas-Stella couldn't be happier. Washington-Stella too.

My future was eerily foreseen and an absolute shock. The lime kiss, the red rocks. Backpack letters and country club bathrooms. The clarity of crystals, the power of prayer. Because after the storm, we are still standing.

Safe and secure.

Epilogue

Talia,
I bought a pack of postcards at a souvenir shop in the mall. The next one you're getting is the "Welcome to Las Vegas" sign. Sorry to ruin the surprise. P. S.—we went there and had to wait in line for thirty minutes to take a picture. Ugh, tourist traps.

Thanks for talking the other day. I'm so glad we're friends. I'm so glad your grandma is doing better. I know we set up Sunday nights to call, but I still want to send postcards. I like to picture you walking down our street to the mailbox. I like to think that sometimes the postcards get wet in the rain. Besides, the nosy mail carrier would miss reading our exciting correspondence.

Enjoy the rest of your summer! Mine was way too short. Can't wait to see you this Thanksgiving and introduce you to my mom.
Viva Las Vegas,
Stella

It's hard to pinpoint the exact moment a journey ends. Not everyone clicks their red slippers like Dorothy or grows up like Peter Pan. Instead, it's just wild, wacky days that somehow smooth back into regular without any planning or warning. At least that's what happened to me.

This story ends in a sticky booth at a Las Vegas, Nevada, Panda Express. It's my first day at Teri Dean Middle School. I can't begin to list all the different things here—outdoor hallways, open-toed shoes, and huge class sizes. And *apparently* my biology teacher's mom once dated Elvis Presley. Or maybe it was an Elvis impersonator?

"You know this isn't healthy, right?" Whitney asks. "I'm giving up deep-fried food. Less preservatives and junk."

I give Vivian a meaningful look. Maybe some of the predictions *were* meant for Whitney. "Oh, so you're changing your diet?"

"I'll eat yours." Vivian shoves a forkful of food into her mouth. "I'm starving. I didn't eat lunch."

"But Whitney packs the best lunches," Ridge says.

"I was so nervous," Vivian says. "There was this junior I met at Gemma's party who totally nodded at me in the hallway. But I didn't realize that until after he'd walked past me, so now I have to make sure I pass him again tomorrow and nod so he doesn't think I'm a brat."

"What crystal did you bring?" I ask.

Vivian pats her pocket. "Citrine. Happiness. Positivity. My birthstone. You?"

"Tiger's-eye and rose quartz." I pull my necklace out from under my shirt. "And my moonstone necklace. It's for new beginnings and accepting change."

"Did it work?"

"I met two girls in English class." I take a bite of fried rice. "I signed up for the tennis clinic. And Cooper saved me a spot at lunch."

"Coooooo-ooooo-ppppperrrr," Ridge says, all singsong.

Dad immediately changes the topic. "Make sure you two call your mom and tell her about your first day."

"I called her this morning to pray," I say. "I'll call her before bed."

"She doesn't like Panda Express either, Whitney," Ridge says.

"Your mother has great taste," Whitney says.

"Oh, I almost forgot these." Dad reaches his hand into his pocket for a fistful of fortune cookies. He tosses them onto my tray. "You girls want one or are your fortune-telling days over?"

"Their days are over." Ridge reaches across the table and grabs all of the cookies. "Mine are not."

"At least let me break one open," I say.

Ridge pushes me away. "I'll give you the one I don't like."

He cracks open the first one.

"'Your sensitivity is an asset'?" He crumples up the paper. "What is that junk supposed to mean?"

"Panda Express appreciates irony," Dad says.

"Next one." Ridge snaps another cookie. "'Your career plans look bright.'"

"Ooh, I like it." Whitney snatches it from Ridge. "I'm keeping that one."

"Last one for Stella." Ridge stands up and clears his throat. The couple in the next booth watches him. He can be such a Sagittarius. "Your fortune says . . . 'You are exactly where you're supposed to be.'"

No one makes any commentary. It's too special. Ridge drops the fortune in my hand. I'll hang it on my side of the bathroom mirror tonight.

A group of kids my age, maybe a little older, walk into the restaurant and commandeer a booth. Two moms follow behind them, keeping a cool distance. The kids are giggling, bright.

"Ugh. I'm so glad I'm done with middle school," Vivian says. "Let's go, I want to pick out my outfit for tomorrow."

One of the girls catches my eye and waves. I almost look behind me to see if she's waving at someone else, but then she walks over to our booth. "Hey, aren't you in my algebra class?"

"Me?" I point to myself when I say it, just to make it extra awkward.

"Yeah. Stella, right?" She smiles. "I'm Emma. You probably met a hundred new people today; I don't expect you to remember."

"I love your necklace," Vivian says. "Is that jade?"

"It's green aventurine." Emma plays with her necklace. "Do you know crystals?"

"Not like my sister does." Vivian slaps my back. "She's got a rose quartz and tiger's-eye in her pocket."

"Oh my gosh, I love rose quartz." Emma lowers her voice. "Sometimes I put one in my bra so it's close to my heart. Do you want to come sit with us?"

"Absolutely!" Whitney gives an encouraging smile. And a vigorous nod. "Stella is dying to make new friends."

"Whitney," I say at the exact same time Vivian hisses, "Mom."

Emma leads me to the booth. We aren't the only ones carrying crystals on the first day of school. Jordan shows me their smoky quartz before mentioning a back-to-school party this weekend.

"Can you come?" Jordan asks.

Another large gathering in my future? "I would absolutely love to!"

This isn't the group of friends I was planning on. Nothing in my life is what I planned. I can see why Mom didn't want to see into forever, to know the details of her future.

It's not very Virgo of me to say this, but maybe there *is* such a thing as good surprises.

The End

Acknowledgments

This book is in your hands thanks to a galaxy of extraordinary constellations.

My Editors: Rachel Murray, Kortney Nash, Laura Godwin, and Julia Sooy.

Julia: My Scorpio birth parent! Thank you for that forced run to a Utah soda bar that led to a magical idea and sample. Rachel: My Sagittarius queen! You raised this book from infancy all through childhood. Thank you for teaching Stella how to walk, talk, feel, and love. Kortney and Laura: The Aquarius and Virgo stepparents who stepped up during the teenage years. Thank you for guiding Stella into the world with savvy and grace.

My Agent: Jenn Laughran, for getting this book (and me) from the get-go. I adore your Aquarian vision, creativity, and quirk. And thanks to Sarah Davies for a lovely, Leo-aligned career pre-Stella/retirement.

My Mentors: Deborah Noyes and Loree Griffin Burns. Lorce, your workshop read on the first pages helped me take this book in a strong direction right from the start. Deb! I want to write every book with you. You are so savvy and talented and wise and wonderful. Thank you for the star treatment.

My Beta Readers: Katie Nelson, Matthew Kirby, and Veeda Bybee. If you read this book again, I bet you can figure out the scenes I changed based on your notes. I bet you'll also figure out that these are the best scenes in the whole book.

My Pub Team: Macmillan Publishers started when brothers Alexander (Libra) and Daniel (Virgo) opened their first bookshop in 1843. And here we are, 180 years of literary tradition later, publishing this book together. Are you amazed? Me too. Thank you to the team of artists and visionaries for making *North of Supernova* shine. Veronica Mang and L. Whitt for sparkly design; Ericka Lugo for a JAW-DROPPING cover that made me weep, I said *weep*, tears of joy; Kristen Stedman for production edits and Kelley Frodel for copy edits and a style guide to rival all style guides; Jie Yang for production management; and my school and library, publicity, and marketing teams for your astronomical efforts.

My Experts: I didn't know what I didn't know and now I know what I know (and these readers are in the know) because of you. Thanks to: Jody Miller, childhood bestie and present-day astrologer. Not only did you educate me on the mysteries of the zodiac overall, but my personal readings opened my awareness of writing and humanity. Brook Andreoli: You're cool. Thanks for the lengthy tarot reading and discussion, as well as insight on Stella's reading. Psychics Judith and Zarin. I went to you for research and I got so much more from the experience. Thank you for sharing your gifts. Fingers crossed all the predicted Good Stuff happens fast, because I am a decidedly unchill fire sign. Employees at Aspen Grove Rustics, Sacred Energy, and Silver Post for your help with all things crystals. I went to many, many other stores but I can't name them all. Besides, I spent half my book advance there anyway. My dear friend and member of Alcoholics Anonymous—you are my secret favorite. Finally, to every teen and preteen I pitched this book to: I hope I got close to what you hoped this book would be.

My Writing Retreaters: I wrote a significant portion of this book at writing retreats, wherein we discussed astrology and psychology and relationships and tea. Thanks to Ally Condie, Ann Dee Ellis, Shannon Hale, Yamile Saied Méndez—moon goddesses, all. Thanks to Nicole Crail, Natasha Fischer, Jen Adams, Sadie West, and Bree Despain, for a few days of plotting and not plotting that pushed me through the middle-of-book blues. Thanks Alycia Kelly for movie misadventures in Nowhere, MA. And Ally Carter and Rachel Hawkins for my first tarot reading in Orlando. You might have predicted this all but that was pre-Covid, so who can remember.

My Family: I LOVE YOU. Thanks to Mom and Dad for providing me a magical Vegas childhood to use as complete juxtaposition. My siblings Brett, Zach, Morgan, and Rachel for being the best siblings I've ever had. And the Browns/Leavitts for two patient years listening to, "I need you to get this room Capricorn clean," or "Hi, I'm Talin's Mom. What's your birthday?" This book demanded a lot during a demanding time for everyone. I don't know if any of us knew what we were getting into when James and I got married, but this family is the greatest blessing of my life. I thank my lucky stars for the mess, milestones, and memories. Well, maybe not all of the mess. Please put your shoes in the basket.

My Readers: I don't know all of you yet, but the best part of this job is always you. This might be the first book of mine you've read or the tenth. However you got here, to the back of this little book in this big universe, thank you. Keep reading, exploring, loving, trying. And drink a green Gatorade every now and then. Electrolytes. (No, I am not a sponsor. YET.)

Further Zodiac Info

Aries (March 21–April 19)

Taurus (April 20–May 20)

Gemini (May 21–June 20)

Cancer (June 21–July 22)

Leo (July 23–August 22)

Virgo (August 23–September 22)

Libra (September 23–October 22)

Scorpio (October 23–November 21)

Sagittarius (November 22–December 21)

Capricorn (December 22–January 19)

Aquarius (January 20–February 18)

Pisces (February 19–March 20)

ARIES: RAM. FIRE SIGN. RULED BY MARS.

As the first sign, Aries is the baby of the zodiac, making them raw, impulsive, and trusting. Young Aries gets bored quickly but loves holding everyone else's complete attention and loyalty. They are, in turn, loyal themselves, as well as warm and caring. Aries are born problem solvers and natural leaders. The ram is a social creature with a boundless source of energy. Sometimes their honesty is thoughtless, but their intention isn't to hurt. (Something this author reminds herself when her Aries daughter asks, "Why are you wearing that ugly shirt?") Their Mars ruling makes Aries competitive and driven. If you're on their team, great! If not, welp. Good luck.

TAURUS: BULL. EARTH SIGN. RULED BY VENUS.

Don't let the bull fool you. Taurus is an extra sensitive sign. At best, they're hyper-attuned to their five senses and the needs of those they love. But a Taurus also doesn't love change. Like, at all. No, seriously, don't ask a Taurus to jump into that lake—they're going to wrap themselves in a thick towel and watch from the side. This fixed earth sign likes routine and predictability and will stubbornly dig in their heels when life requires compromise. The ruler of Taurus is Venus, the planet of love and beauty, so regal Taurus seeks quality and luxury, especially in their home environment. Finally, the steady and practical Taurus makes for a reliable, lifelong friend.

GEMINI: TWINS. AIR SIGN. RULED BY MERCURY.

Oh, Gemini, Gemini. Such a curious, charming chatterbox. These social butterflies juggle a variety of interests, jobs, and hobbies. Represented by twins, Geminis are known for double trouble, double fun. Their moods and minds can switch by the day or even hour. This duality can make Geminis indecisive and inconsistent. They may switch activities and even personalities, fully expecting others to keep right up. But their Mercury ruling makes the twins open, intrigued, and adaptable. Geminis attract a wide range of friends because they're so fascinated by people. And experiences. And, really, the universe.

CANCER: CRAB. WATER SIGN. RULED BY THE MOON.

It's a good thing crabs have that nice protective shell to hide in because Cancerians are a sensitive lot. They can be hyper-emotional and moody, but also imaginative and loyal. It's no wonder these dreamers are ruled by the moon, which intensifies intuition and psychic ability. Home is a Cancer's happy place, especially when surrounded by loved ones and friends. They won't give up on relationships and work hard to achieve their life goals. For the most part, this water sign is calm and caring, but can easily take offense and hold a grudge. Cancers do best when they lower their pincers and open their hearts.

LEO: LION. FIRE SIGN. RULED BY THE SUN.

Leo is the greatest sign of all the zodiac (but that may be the author's bias). The lion is the king of the jungle and Leo is ruler of the zodiac—destined for a life of luxury and glamour. Joyful and generous, this fire sign shines bright like the sun. Sometimes their powerful, take-charge attitude can feel controlling or aggressive. Pride might stop Leos from noticing when they've hurt feelings or cut someone off. A devoted heart and fun spirit makes up for the occasional roar. Final word of advice: Don't lie to a Leo. Honesty is the most important relationship quality to this warm sign, and you don't want their shade. You really don't.

VIRGO: GODDESS OF WHEAT. EARTH SIGN. RULED BY MERCURY.

Virgo is the greatest sign of all the zodiac (but that may be our protagonist's bias). The earth-loving Virgo is a healer with an intuitive connection to nature. Like Gemini, Virgo is ruled by Mercury, which promotes logic, curiosity, and research. This is perfect for brainy Virgo, who has an eternal quest for knowledge and pays strong attention to detail. Sometimes they can be *too* focused on details, obsessively picking at the smallest thing. Virgos are their own worst critic with a perfectionism that sparks worry and anxiety. Take a breath. Dependable and gentle Virgos thrive on stability and security. They are happy to help create a world of order and goodness, making this one of the most loving and selfless signs.

LIBRA: SCALES. AIR SIGN. RULED BY VENUS.

Peacemaker Libras are all about harmony and equality. As such, they're able to look at a situation and see every angle. Extroverted Libras love to bring people together for lavish events and social causes. They have a strong sense of justice and are able to direct and persuade using their natural charm and intellect. When there's conflict or disarray, people-pleasing Libras might sacrifice their own wants or needs to stabilize the overall group. Their desire for balance can also lead to indecisiveness or unreliability as they spend time weighing the scales. Ruled by Venus, the planet of beauty and love, this air sign appreciates sophisticated aesthetics and stunning environments. Count on Libras to share their inherent beauty with everyone they meet.

SCORPIO: SCORPION. WATER SIGN. RULED BY MARS.

Scorpios are the most clairvoyant of all twelve zodiac signs. If it seems like they're reading your thoughts, they probably are. Good luck knowing what is going on inside their mysterious minds. Scorpios are not ones to reveal their secrets or even their emotions, but there is a lot happening inside. This water sign is deep, dynamic, and brilliant—sometimes even genius. Those born under this star sign are incredibly dedicated to their goals and know how to work a crowd. Honest, brave, and loyal—this is a sign that does not hold back. Ruling Mars is the planet of passion and war, making the scorpion's sting especially sharp. Although it takes a while for Scorpio to trust, the friendships they make are for life.

SAGITTARIUS: ARCHER. FIRE SIGN. RULED BY JUPITER.

Life is one big adventure, and Sagittarius is here for it. Playful and spontaneous, the archer easily (and often eagerly) adapts to change. They love to travel and learn. As the planet of vision, expansion, and luck, Jupiter inspires Sagittarius's endless energy and optimism. It's hard to keep a Sagittarius down (or to keep them around at all. Where did they go this time?). A Sagittarius highly values their independence and may jump from project to project without following through. This fire sign is honest, sometimes brutally so, but also compassionate and empathetic. This is the rarest zodiac sign, making extroverted Sagittarius one of a kind.

CAPRICORN: SEA GOAT. EARTH SIGN. RULED BY SATURN.

Practical and organized, Capricorns are the old souls of the zodiac. They love to plan, and plan to succeed. Capricorn's ruling planet is Saturn, which represents hard work and responsibility—the planet that keeps everything in line. The sea goat is willing to patiently work hard to achieve their goals, making the enterprising Capricorn an ideal addition to any team. They may hold others to their own high standards and act stubborn when their carefully laid plans change. Yes, they're serious, but this earth sign is also sensitive and sweet. Little can stop a Cap when they channel their massive energy and thirst for life into any pursuit.

AQUARIUS: WATER BEARER. AIR SIGN. RULED BY URANUS.

As the water bearer, you might assume Aquarius is a water sign. But Aquarians keep you on your toes. Like its element—air—this sign doesn't have a defined shape. Aquarians flow and expand into different activities and personality traits. They're original, quirky, and creative, spouting off fresh ideas and starting trends on a whim. But they're also analytical and logical—they aren't going to believe you without cold hard facts. They may feel detached and in their own head, but that's just because they're detached and in their own head. Ruled by Uranus, the planet of revolution and innovation, Aquarians are natural humanitarians, here to ignite a world of change.

PISCES: TWO FISH. WATER SIGN. RULED BY NEPTUNE.

The final sign in the zodiac, Pisces views the world with the empathy and experience of all of the zodiac combined. These fish swim through a mix of emotion, fantasy, and creativity. It can be hard for them to keep their feet on the ground, especially with their Neptune ruling—the planet of dreams, imagination, and illusion. Pisces may see the world through rose-colored glasses, often as a protection from facing the harsher reality, because Pisces feel emotions so strongly. When they're really focused (sometimes a struggle), they're a great person to talk to because they're so in tune with others' needs. Mystical and romantic, Pisces pursue love, in relationships and life.

Crystals

ARIES
Carnelian: creativity & courage
Bloodstone: balance & nurture

TAURUS
Rhodonite: safety & patience
Malachite: transformation & prosperity

GEMINI
Amazonite: comfort & protection
Celestite: communication & focus

CANCER
Moonstone: grounding & intuition
Hematite: concentration & harmony

LEO
Tiger's-Eye: self-empowerment & vitality
Sunstone: joy & regeneration

VIRGO
Amethyst: power & tranquility
Lepidolite: unity & stabilization

LIBRA

Rose Quartz: love & empathy

Lapis Lazuli: creativity & enlightenment

SCORPIO

Smoky Quartz: release & stability

Citrine: happiness & cleansing

SAGITTARIUS

Obsidian: self-control & truth

Jade: optimism & good fortune

CAPRICORN

Garnet: manifestation & strength

Blue Lace Agate: serenity & confidence

AQUARIUS

Aquamarine: clarity & courage

Pyrite: justice & wealth

PISCES

Black Tourmaline: equality & awareness

Green Aventurine: luck & renewal

Palmistry for Beginners

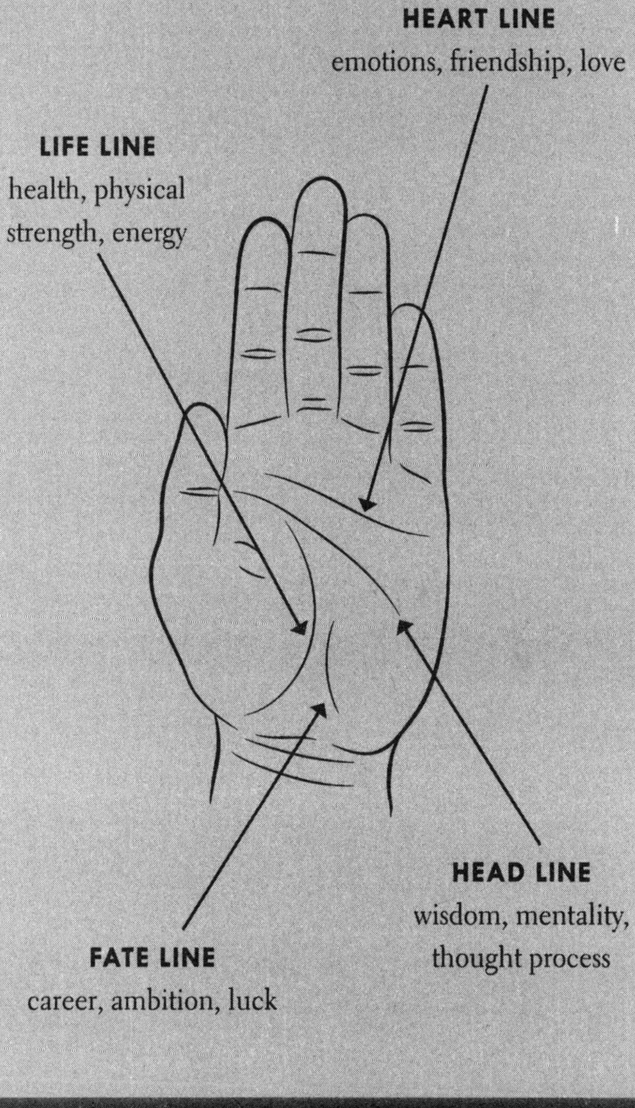

HEART LINE
emotions, friendship, love

LIFE LINE
health, physical
strength, energy

HEAD LINE
wisdom, mentality,
thought process

FATE LINE
career, ambition, luck

Chinese Zodiac

The story of the Chinese Zodiac: Many, many years ago, the Jade Emperor decided that there should be a way to measure time. For his birthday, he told the animals they were to compete in a swimming race. The first twelve animals would be rewarded by having a zodiac year named after them. The animals are listed in the order in which they completed the race.

RAT
inquisitive, quick-witted, nimble, forthright, persuasive

OX
diligent, patient, stubborn, faithful, prosperous

TIGER
emotional, courageous, restless, passionate, impulsive

RABBIT
elegant, compassionate, tender, popular, levelheaded

DRAGON
charismatic, fearless, warmhearted, demanding, strong

SNAKE
thoughtful, graceful, generous, mysterious, wise

HORSE

energetic, independent, headstrong, cheerful, extravagant

SHEEP/GOAT

gentle, fashionable, moody, sincere, creative

MONKEY

brilliant, honest, mischievous, flexible, innovative

ROOSTER

ambitious, practical, bright, critical, observant

DOG

playful, loyal, anxious, straightforward, caring

PIG

loving, tolerant, naive, gallant, sturdy

CHINESE ZODIAC SIGN	YEARS
RAT	. . . 1948, 1960, 1972, 1984, 1996, 2008, 2020 . . .
OX	. . . 1949, 1961, 1973, 1985, 1997, 2009, 2021 . . .
TIGER	. . . 1950, 1962, 1974, 1986, 1998, 2010, 2022 . . .
RABBIT	. . . 1951, 1963, 1975, 1987, 1999, 2011, 2023 . . .
DRAGON	. . . 1952, 1964, 1976, 1988, 2000, 2012, 2024 . . .
SNAKE	. . . 1953, 1965, 1977, 1989, 2001, 2013, 2025 . . .
HORSE	. . . 1954, 1966, 1978, 1990, 2002, 2014, 2026 . . .
SHEEP/GOAT	. . . 1955, 1967, 1979, 1991, 2003, 2015, 2027 . . .
MONKEY	. . . 1956, 1968, 1980, 1992, 2004, 2016, 2028 . . .
ROOSTER	. . . 1957, 1969, 1981, 1993, 2005, 2017, 2029 . . .
DOG	. . . 1958, 1970, 1982, 1994, 2006, 2018, 2030 . . .
PIG	. . . 1959, 1971, 1983, 1995, 2007, 2019, 2031 . . .